英語力 1

16堂流利英語聽說訓練課

Listening and Speaking in Everyday Life

作者 Owain Mckimm　譯者 丁宥榆

MP3
寂天雲 APP

如何下載 MP3 音檔

❶ 寂天雲 APP 聆聽：掃描書上 QR Code 下載「寂天雲－英日語學習隨身聽」APP。加入會員後，用 APP 內建掃描器再次掃描書上 QR Code，即可使用 APP 聆聽音檔。

❷ 官網下載音檔：請上「寂天閱讀網」（www.icosmos.com.tw），註冊會員／登入後，搜尋本書，進入本書頁面，點選「MP3 下載」下載音檔，存於電腦等其他播放器聆聽使用。

CONTENTS MAP

LISTENING	GRAMMAR	SPEAKING	PRONUNCIATION
◆ 在各種場合和人打招呼 ◆ 辨識會話中的關鍵語彙和主題	◆ be 動詞的現在簡單式 ◆ 代名詞：主格	◆ 用不同的方式和人打招呼 ◆ 詢問與回答關於人的姓名、工作和背景的問題	◆ 無聲子音： [p] [t] [k] [f]
◆ 透過介紹認識一些人 ◆ 記錄別人的聯絡方式	◆ 現在簡單式 ◆ 助動詞：do 和 does	◆ 將你的朋友介紹給其他人 ◆ 告訴別人你朋友的背景 ◆ 互相交換電子郵件和電話號碼	◆ 有聲子音： [b] [d] [g] [v]
◆ 辨識家庭成員和親戚關係	◆ There is 和 There are ◆ 冠詞：a、an、the ◆ 所有格形容詞	◆ 詢問和回答與家庭成員有關的問題 ◆ 詢問和回答關於你家的問題	◆ there is 和 there are 的簡寫念法
◆ 辨識和描述人的外貌 ◆ 辨識和描述人的個性	◆ 形容詞：位置 ◆ 使用 and 來分開形容詞	◆ 描述身高、體重和身體特徵	◆ 複習無聲和有聲子音： [p] [t] [k] [f] ; [b] [d] [g] [v]
◆ 辨識表達感謝、道別和祝賀的用語 ◆ 認識適當的回應用語	◆ 感嘆句 ◆ 代名詞：受格	◆ 在不同的場合中使用表示道別、感謝和祝賀的用語	◆ 無聲子音： [s] [θ]
◆ 傾聽他人的意見並做出回應 ◆ 辨識他人的情緒	◆ 情狀動詞與分詞形容詞	◆ 說明引發你某種感受的原因 ◆ 在會話中表達你的意見和情緒 ◆ 詢問他人對某件事的意見	◆ 有聲子音： [z] [ð]
◆ 辨識正確的時間 ◆ 辨識一些特定事件的時間 ◆ 在日曆上找出特定的星期和日期	◆ 時間介系詞 ◆ 詢問「現在幾點」、「今天星期幾」和「日期」	◆ 詢問和回答關於時間和日期的問題 ◆ 詢問某件事開始或結束的時間 ◆ 詢問人們的生日	◆ 複習無聲和有聲子音： [s] [θ]; [z] [ð] 複數名詞
◆ 聆聽別人描述天氣 ◆ 辨識四季之間的差異 ◆ 聆聽別人在不同的天氣下會做些什麼事	◆ 現在進行式	◆ 進行關於天氣的對話 ◆ 詢問和回答關於天氣或季節的問題	◆ 有聲子音： [ʃ] [tʃ] [h]

CONTENTS MAP

LISTENING	GRAMMAR	SPEAKING	PRONUNCIATION
◆ 聆聽某人每日的例行公事 ◆ 聆聽兩人安排會議行程 ◆ 辨識人們從事某些活動的頻率	◆ 詢問事情發生的頻率和持續時間 ◆ 頻率副詞	◆ 向練習的伙伴描述你的行程規畫 ◆ 詢問和回答關於你做某件事情的頻率	◆ 有聲子音： [ʒ] [dʒ] [l]
◆ 辨識人們所從事的運動 ◆ 辨識某人支持或效力於哪一支隊伍 ◆ 辨識誰擅長某一項運動	◆ 現在簡單式中的 Which 開頭問句 ◆ 情態助動詞：Can	◆ 談論你自己的運動能力 ◆ 談論你支持或效力的隊伍 ◆ 向練習伙伴描述運動員	◆ can 與 can't 的發音
◆ 從物品的描述來辨識物品 ◆ 辨識用來詢問物品的常用問句和用語	◆ 所有格代名詞 ◆ 形容詞的語序	◆ 詢問和回答關於物品的問題 ◆ 將你所擁有的物品和同學的做比較	◆ 複習無聲和有聲子音： [ʃ] [tʃ] [h] [ʒ] [dʒ] [l]
◆ 聆聽各種情境的道歉方式 ◆ 聆聽某人接受別人的道歉 ◆ 回應他人的道歉	◆ 介系詞：to 和 for	◆ 練習使用道歉用語來對話 ◆ 練習不同情境的道歉方式	◆ the 的各種發音
◆ 聆聽方向指示並依其找到目的地 ◆ 辨識到達某處的最佳路徑	◆ 祇使語氣 ◆ 表達「位置」的介系詞	◆ 詢問和指引方向 ◆ 告訴某人該搭何種交通工具	◆ 有聲子音： [m] [n] [ŋ] [j] [w] [r]
◆ 聆聽一組指示之後辨識主題 ◆ 將各項指示依正確順序排列	◆ must 和 have to	◆ 詢問和提供指示	◆ 表達指示時，音調的上揚和下降
◆ 辨識提議和建議的不同 ◆ 聆聽各種提議和建議的範例	◆ Wh 開頭的問句： how、what、who、where、when、why、which	◆ 針對不同事物詢問和提供提議 ◆ 針對不同的議題提供建議	◆ 表達提議和建議時，音調的上揚和下降
◆ 辨識兩種節慶的重要特色 ◆ 從描述中辨識節慶 ◆ 寫下常見美國習俗的相關知識	◆ 可數與不可數名詞 ◆ 計量用詞和片語	◆ 詢問和回答關於節慶或節日的問題 ◆ 用自己國家的習俗練習對話	◆ 不發音的字母和同音異義字

學習及教學導覽

《英語力》是一本什麼樣的書？

《英語力》是一本訓練英語聽力與口說能力的用書，旨在引領學生認識基礎英語會話。本書練習的編寫，皆是針對與母語人士對談時必備的英語會話，以期協助學生建立信心與理解力。

《英語力》如何協助您增進英文能力？

- 《英語力》提供了與**真實生活相符的情境和對話**，讓您與母語人士日常互動時能泰然自若。

- 本書運用生動而清楚的圖片，輔助您輕鬆學會大量的實用生字。

- 本書用清楚而簡潔的方式呈現文法要項，並提供豐富的範例。

- **大量的口語文法練習**，讓您在真實生活會話中能正確傳達訊息、避免誤解。

- 針對文意主旨、相關細節和其他具體資訊所設計的**聽力練習**，能訓練您不僅聽懂對話的梗概，也能理解更多前後文所蘊含的意義。

- 針對**關鍵片語和內文細節**所設計的聽力練習，能增進您對英文的了解，更進一步學習進階英語。

- 藉著與主題相關的各種口語練習，您將能熟練運用在本書單字、聽力、文法單元所學到的英文。

- 易懂易學的**會話範例**和輔助學習的**會話句型**，讓您能不費吹灰之力地自由運用在對話中。

- 透過本書大量的**兩人活動和小組練習**，您能獲得充分的口語實戰經驗。

- **豐富的圖片和建議主題**，讓您不再為了找話題而傷腦筋。

- 完善的**發音教學單元**能協助您熟悉英語的基礎發音，提供大量練習各種發音的機會，讓您的發音更像母語人士。

《英語力》是如何編排的？

- 《英語力》有 16 個單元。

- 每個單元分為六個部分。

單元結構：

I. Topic Preview 主題預覽
透過幾則簡短的會話範例，帶您進入主題。

II. Vocabulary and Phrases 字彙和片語
提供相關的字彙和片語，是您有效聽、說的重要工具。

III. Now, Time to Listen! 聽力時間！
透過各種對話、獨白和聽力練習，訓練您的聽力技巧。

IV. Now, Grammar Time! 文法時間！
正式介紹前三部分所應用的文法，並提供練習的機會。

V. Now, Time to Speak! 口語時間！
針對各單元主題，運用小組或兩人練習的方式，提供口說的練習活動。

VI. Now, Time to Pronounce! 發音時間！
每次介紹幾種發音，並提供練習讓您能認識並正確發音。

如何使用《英語力》進行教學？

- 請於每個單元的一開始，先進行 Topic Preview 的部分，依照**會話範例進行練習**，讓學生熟悉相關情境。同時利用這一小節來引導與主題相關的一些概念，並評估哪些概念可能較有難度。

- **介紹該單元的生字**，接著進行 Sentence Patterns 的教學。讓學生將學到的生字套用在句型裡，以期同時熟悉生字和句型。

- 在進行每一則聽力練習之前，先請學生**預測可能會聽到哪些生字和片語**，讓學生在練習聽力之前先有概念。

- 完成聽力練習之後，鼓勵學生挑選其中一段或數段，**再仔細聽一次，並盡量記住內容**，然後和同學一起練習會話。這是練習口語能力的好機會，也有助於他們記住常用的句型和會話模式。

- 在聽力的小節已經接觸到一些文法之後，學生對於如何使用該單元的文法結構應該已經有了粗略的概念，此時請他們**朗讀例句**，並且試著造出自己的句子。記得不時提問相關的問題，以確認學生是否完全理解。

- 本書的許多文法練習是必須兩兩分組進行的口語練習，為了鼓勵學生開口，在他們對話時先不要急著糾正，可以先將您所聽到的錯誤寫下來，在練習進行了幾分鐘之後才暫停，然後全班一起檢討剛才所犯的錯誤，逐一釐清學生不懂的地方。之後再練習一次，確認學生這次用對了文法。

- 本系列套書的口語練習部分，是希望藉由提供學生**大量的句型和輔助資訊**，讓他們盡量在無壓力的情況下開口說英文。如果您認為學生們已經可以自由練習了，就鼓勵他們以 Topic Preview 或者書裡任何一張圖片的情境為基礎，自由發揮對話。

- 在**發音練習**這一小節裡，讓學生先聽一次課本 MP3 朗讀發音，接著再聽一次，並且跟著播音員覆誦。當您認為學生們練習的差不多了，可以個別點幾個學生測試發音。

- 鼓勵學生盡量自然地**唸出單字的發音**，無須過度強調或加重某個特定的音。

ENJOY learning!
EMPLOY new language!
EMPOWER your English!

享受學習！
使用新語言！
活化英語能力！

Topic Preview

1 *Meeting someone for the first time / on a formal occasion*
初次見面／正式場合會面

How do you do? I'm Peter.
　Hello. I'm Peter. Nice to meet you.

It's a pleasure to meet you, Peter. I'm Jane.

Hi. I'm Betty. It's very nice to meet you, too.

2 *Greeting someone at different times of the day*
一日中各時段的招呼語

Good morning.
Good afternoon.
Good evening.

3 *Greeting someone you know well*
和熟識者的招呼語

Hi! How are you?
　It's so good to see you again.
　How's everything?

Not bad. How are you?
Everything's good.
Let's catch up over coffee.

4 *Asking about life, work, and other people*
詢問對方的生活與工作，以及問候其他人

How are you doing?
　How are things at work?
How's your father?
　How's Jane?

I'm doing well.
　Things are great.
Pretty good.
　Oh, so-so.

5 *Asking about someone's name, job, and where he/she is from* 詢問某人的姓名、工作與國籍

Hello, my name's Kenji. What's your name?
　Where are you from?
What do you do?

My name's Tina.
　I'm from Singapore.
I'm an editor.

II. Vocabulary & Phrases

taxi driver
計程車司機

veterinarian / vet
獸醫

server
侍者

farmer
農夫

dentist 牙醫

nurse
護士

police officer
警察

student
學生

flight attendant
空服員

businesswoman / businessman
女商人／商人

hairdresser
美髮師

construction worker / builder
建築工

teacher 老師

reporter
記者

Sentence Patterns

Greetings ▶
招呼語

Hello.
Hi!
It's so nice to see you again.
Good morning. / Good evening. /
Good afternoon.
How do you do?
It's a pleasure to meet you.
Nice to meet you.

◀General questions
一般問候

How are you?
How's everything?
How are you doing?
How are things?

Replying ▶
回答

Fine, thank you.
I'm good.
Everything's great/fine.
I'm doing well.
Pretty good. / Not too bad.
Oh, so-so.

◀Personal questions
個人問題

What is your name?
My name's <u>Brian</u>.

Where are you from?
I'm from <u>Canada</u>.

What do you do?
I'm a <u>doctor</u>.

III. Now, Time to Listen!

1 **(004)** Listen to the people greeting each other. Match each conversation with the best description of its speakers. The first one has been done for you.

1. _____e_____
2. _____
3. _____
4. _____
5. _____

a. They're colleagues, but not really friends.
b. They are meeting for the first time.
c. They are good friends.
d. They are in a hurry.
e. They are friends, but not close friends.

2 Listen and complete the conversations below.

(005) **1**

A | Hello, Susan.
B | Hi, Tom. It's nice to see you again. _____ ?
A | Oh, everything's fine. How are you?
B | _____, thanks.

2

A | _____. How are you today?
B | Great, thanks. How are you?
A | I'm doing _____ , thanks.

3

A | Hello, Jane.
B | Hi, Bob. It's good to see you again. How are you doing?
A | _____ good, thanks. How about you?
B | _____.

4

A | _____? My name's Jack.
B | It's a _____ to meet you, Jack. I'm Emily.
A | _____ to meet you, Emily.

3 Listen to the conversation between Tom and Jane. Check ☑ the things they talk about.

(006)
☐ They greet each other.
☐ They ask each other's names.
☐ They talk about someone they both know.

☐ They ask about each other's work.
☐ They ask where each other is from.

Circle the correct answer: Tom and Jane are old friends / meeting for the first time.

➤ **(007)** Listen again and check ☑ the phrases you hear.

☐ Hi!
☐ Good afternoon.
☐ Nice to see you!
☐ Let's catch up.
☐ How's everything?

☐ How are you doing?
☐ I'm doing well.
☐ Not too bad.
☐ Is Susan OK?
☐ How's Susan?

IV. Now, Grammar Time!

Subject pronouns and "be" 主格代名詞與 be 動詞

👤 Singular 單數		👥 Plural 複數	
I am ➡	I'm	we are ➡	we're
you are ➡	you're	you are ➡	you're
he is ➡	he's		
she is ➡	she's	they are ➡	they're
it is ➡	it's		

- Always write the pronoun "I" with a capital letter.
  代名詞 I 一定要用大寫。
- For other subject pronouns, use a capital letter only when they start a sentence.
  其他的主格代名詞只有在句首的時候要大寫。

The verb "be" be 動詞

Affirmative Sentences 肯定句	Negative Sentences 否定句	Yes/No Questions 是非問句
• I am a teacher.	• I am not a teacher.	• Are you a teacher?
• You are a nurse.	• You are not a nurse.	Yes, I am. / No, I'm not.
• My father is so-so.	• My father is not fine.	• Is your father OK?
• My name is Peter.	• My name is not Peter.	Yes, he is. / No, he isn't.
• We are good friends.	• We are not good friends.	• Is your name Peter?
• They are both from Singapore.	• They are not from Singapore.	Yes, it is. / No, it isn't.
		• Are they good friends?
		Yes, they are. / No, they aren't.

❹ **Complete the conversations using the correct form of the verb "be."**

Sarah Hello! I _____ Sarah. _____ you Jason?

Jason Yes, I _____. Nice to meet you.

Sarah Nice to meet you, too. How _____ you today?

Jason Not too bad. _____ you a student here, too?

Sarah Yes, I _____. I _____ here to study English.

_____ we in the same class?

Jason Yes, I think so. Where _____ you from?

Sarah I _____ from Japan. You?

Jason I _____ from Taiwan. This _____ my friend Sandy.

She _____ from Japan, too.

Sarah Hi, Sandy. It _____ so nice to meet you.

5 Look at the pictures and fill in the blanks in the conversations. The first one has been done for you.

a

What do you do?

I _am_ _a_ _police_ _officer_.

b

Where are you two from?

Paris

We _____ _____.

c

What's your name?

← Simon

_____.

d

_____ you ____ _____?

Yes, _____.

e

How is your father?

_____!

V. Now, Time to Speak!

6 Pair Work! Listen to the following conversations and then practice them. Replace the words in color with ones from the word bank.

WORD BANK

Jerry	pretty good	England	nurse
Annie	great	America	dentist
Alex	not too bad	China	taxi driver
Judy	fine	Japan	flight attendant

008 Conversation A

Bob : How do you do? I'm Bob.
Jane : It's a pleasure to meet you, Bob. I'm Jane.
Bob : How are you today?
Jane : I'm good, thanks. You?
Bob : I'm fine, thanks.

009 Conversation B

Andy : Hello. My name's Andy. What's your name?
Amy : I'm Amy.
Andy : Where are you from?
Amy : I'm from Taiwan. How about you?
Andy : I'm from Singapore.

010 Conversation C

Daisy : John! It's so good to see you again.
John : Daisy! You too! How are you doing?
Daisy : I'm doing well, thanks. Let's sit down and catch up.
John : Sure. What do you do now?
Daisy : I'm a doctor now. You?
John : I'm a teacher.

7 With a partner, discuss how you would greet people in the different situations below. Choose one and create a dialogue.

1	You meet one of your good friends in the street.
2	You meet your new boss for the first time.
3	At a party, you meet an old classmate from school.
4	You meet your professor outside the library at four p.m.
5	You meet your neighbor at the supermarket. You're in a hurry.

8 Group Work! Create a new identity for yourself.
Fill in the box below with your new information.

Name: ------------------------------------

From: ------------------------------------

Job: ------------------------------------

Now talk to your classmates and fill in the table below. Greet them using one of these expressions.

How do you do?

Hi! Nice to meet you.

Hello. It's a pleasure to meet you.

Hi. It's good to meet you.

👥 Name	🏠 From	👜 Job	😀 How is he/she?

VI Now, Time to Pronounce!

Voiceless Consonants 無聲子音 [p] ᶜ [t] ᶜ [k] ᶜ [f] ᶜ

9 **Listen and repeat the words you hear.**

(011)

[p] ᶜ	pick	please	part	happy	cheap

[t] ᶜ	tea	little	time	tale	net

(012) Listen and **circle** the words that you hear.

1 tin | pin **2** write | ripe **3** pack | tack **4** peach | teach **5** rope | rote

10 **Listen and repeat the words you hear.**

(013)

[k] ᶜ	can	key	kind	thank	cake

[f] ᶜ	food	life	fail	tough	fall

(014) Listen and **circle** the words that you hear.

1 kin | fin **2** kite | fight **3** leak | leaf **4** key | fee **5** lack | laugh

11 **Listen to the words. Do you hear [p], [t], [k], or [f]? Check ☑ the box that corresponds to the sound you hear.**

(015)

	[p]	[t]	[k]	[f]
1.			✓	
2.				
3.				
4.				
5.				
6.				
7.				
8.				
9.				
10.				

Meeting and Introducing People 互相介紹與認識

I Topic Preview 016

1 Introducing yourself 自我介紹

Formal

Good afternoon, ladies and gentlemen. Please let me introduce myself. My name is Tom Powell.

Informal

Hi, everyone. I'm Tom. Nice to meet you all.

2 Introducing someone to a third party 介紹某人給其他人認識

Formal

Mr. Wilson, this is my wife, Miranda. Miranda, this is my boss, Mr. Wilson.

It's a pleasure to meet you, Mr. Wilson.

Please call me John.

Informal

John, do you know my girlfriend, Mary? Mary, this is my friend John.

Hi, John.

Hi, Mary. It's good to finally meet you.

3 Telling people about yourself 描述自己

I'm a student. I'm from Taiwan, but now I live in New York.

4 Asking for someone's contact details 索取聯絡方式

Can I get your email address? What's your phone number?

Sure. My email address is linda1432@yahoo.com. My phone number is 0918-123-456.

II. Vocabulary & Phrases

housewife
家庭主婦

cashier
收銀員

mechanic
技工

tailor
裁縫師

beautician
美容師

salesperson
售貨員

judge
法官

friend
朋友

classmate
同學

colleague
同事

husband
丈夫

wife
太太

live
居住

work
工作

study
學習

Sentence Patterns

• Please let me introduce myself.
• I'm _Sally_.
• I'm _a judge_.
• I'm originally from _Japan_.
• I live/work/study in _France_.
• What's your _email address_?
  My _email address_ is _peter1432@yahoo.com_.

• I want you to meet my _wife_, _Mary_.
  This is my _friend Bob_.
  Do you know my _colleague James_?
• It's good to finally meet you.
• Please, call me _Peter_.

1 Listen to the CD. Then match each conversation with the picture that best illustrates it.

(019)

1. _____   2. _____   3. _____   4. _____

➡ (020) Now, listen again and complete the conversations below.

1

Sarah	Eric, _____ you _____ my friend Judy?
Eric	No, I don't.
Sarah	Judy, _____ my classmate Eric.
Judy	Hi, Eric. Nice to meet you.
Eric	Hi, Judy. Do you _____ here, too?
Judy	Yes, I study math.
Eric	Cool. Oh no! Sarah, we're late for class. Nice _____ you, Judy.
Judy	Bye, guys. See you later.

2

Mr. Morgan	Mary, this is my boss, Mr. Parker. Mr. Parker, this is my _____, Mary.
Mr. Parker	How do you do, Mary?
Mrs. Morgan	_____ nice to meet you, Mr. Parker.
Mr. Parker	Please, _____ Mike. Are you a _____ too, Mary?
Mrs. Morgan	No, I'm a teacher.

3

Bill	Nancy, I want you to meet Lucy and Harry. They're my _____.
Nancy	Hello, Lucy. Hello, Harry. It's nice to meet you both.
Lucy	It's _____ to _____ meet you, Nancy.
Harry	Hi, Nancy. It's great to meet you.

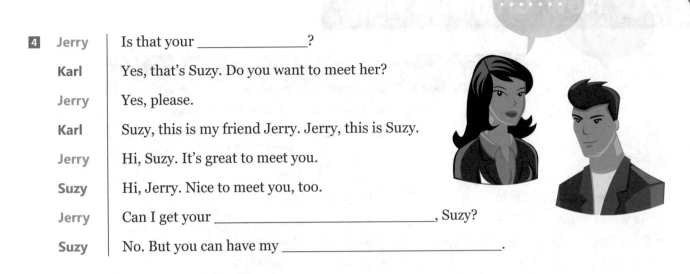

4	Jerry	Is that your _____?
	Karl	Yes, that's Suzy. Do you want to meet her?
	Jerry	Yes, please.
	Karl	Suzy, this is my friend Jerry. Jerry, this is Suzy.
	Jerry	Hi, Suzy. It's great to meet you.
	Suzy	Hi, Jerry. Nice to meet you, too.
	Jerry	Can I get your _____, Suzy?
	Suzy	No. But you can have my _____.

How do you say phone numbers and email addresses?

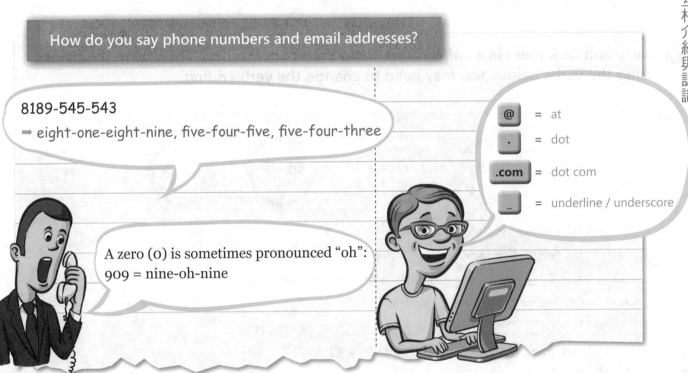

8189-545-543
➡ eight-one-eight-nine, five-four-five, five-four-three

A zero (0) is sometimes pronounced "oh":
909 = nine-oh-nine

@	=	at
.	=	dot
.com	=	dot com
_	=	underline / underscore

2 Listen to the following conversations. Fill in the table with the missing information.

021
_____ Jones
Businessman
✕

022
Mark Smith
_____
unimail_____
✕

023
_____ Lin
_____
gmail.com
_____

IV. Now, Grammar Time!

The Simple Present Tense 現在簡單式

Affirmative Statements 肯定句

Verb endings : he, she, it, Mary, John...

動詞字尾變化：當主詞是 he、she、it、Mary、John 等的時候

- I live in the United States.
- You know my friend Peter.
- He works in Japan.
- She plays soccer for the school team.
- We both study English.
- They come from France.

- live → lives
- know → knows
- work → works
- play → plays
- study → studies
- come → comes

❸ Garry and Jack meet in a coffee shop. Read their conversation. Then fill in the blanks using the verbs below. You may need to change the verb ending.

know study come speak work see

Garry Hi. I'm Garry. Nice to meet you.

Jack Hi, Garry. I'm Jack. I _____ you here every day.

Garry Yes, I _____ English in the school near here.

Jack Oh really? Do you know my friend Sally? She _____ English there, too.

Garry Yeah, I _____ her. She _____ from Russia, right?

Jack Yes. She _____ English really well now.

Garry So what do you do?

Jack I _____ at the bookstore next to the school. I _____ Sally there sometimes.

Auxiliary Verbs : do, does　助動詞 do 與 does

Negative Statements 否定句	Yes/No Questions 是非問句
• I do not live in the United States.	Do you live in the United States? Yes, I do. / No, I don't.
• You do not know my friend Peter.	Do you know my friend Peter? Yes, I do. / No, I don't.
• He does not work in Japan.	Does he work in Japan? Yes, he does. / No, he doesn't.
• She does not play soccer for the school team.	Does she play soccer for the school team? Yes, she does. / No, she doesn't.
• We do not study English.	Do we study English? Yes, we do. / No, we don't.
• They do not come from France.	Do they come from France? Yes, they do. / No, they don't.
• don't = do not doesn't = does not	

❹ Look at the pictures below. Then use the prompts to fill in the blanks.

_____ he _____ from Hong Kong?
　　　　　come

Yes, _____ _____.

He _____ _____ in Canada.
　　　not　　　live

_____ _____ in Greece.
　　live

_____ you _____ in a school?
　　　　　work

No, ____ _____. _____ _____
　　　　　　　　　　　work

in a shop.

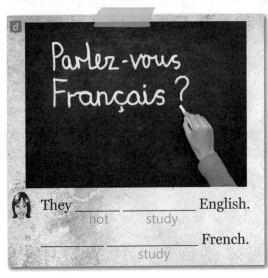

They _____ _____ English.
　　　not　　study

_____ _____ French.
　　study

V. Now, Time to Speak!

5 Pair Work! Introduce the following people to your partner. Use the model below to help you. Then tell the class about the people.

I want you to meet my <u>friend</u> <u>Amy</u>. <u>Amy</u> is a <u>teacher</u>. She's originally from <u>England</u>. But now she <u>lives</u> and <u>works</u> in <u>Taiwan</u>.

1 businessman 2 student 3 doctor 4 taxi driver

Here are some countries you can use in your introductions:

Russia   Japan   South Africa   Canada   Korea

6 Group Work! Find the phone numbers and email addresses of as many classmates as you can. Use the model to help you.

A	Hi, I'm John. Can I get your phone number?
B	Sure. It's 0913-621-602.
A	Do you have an email address?
B	Yes, it's <u>milly.white@gmail.com</u>.

Your phone number
_____

Your email address
_____

Names of classmates	Phone numbers	Email addresses

VI. Now, Time to Pronounce!

Voiced Consonants 有聲子音　[b]　[d]　[g]　[v]

7 Listen and repeat the words you hear.

(024)

[b]　book　　bus　　busy　　cab　　bulb

[d]　dark　　door　　desk　　deep　　add

(025) Listen and circle the words that you hear.

1 bad | dad　**2** bust | dust　**3** boat | dote　**4** cabby | caddy　**5** beam | deem

8 Listen and repeat the words you hear.

(026)

[g]　good　　god　　grip　　girl　　leg

[v]　van　　veil　　have　　voice　　very

(027) Listen and circle the words that you hear.

1 get | vet　**2** goat | vote　**3** goal | vole　**4** rogue | rove　**5** guile | vile

9 Listen to the following tongue twisters. Then try to say them as many times as

(028) you can and as fast as possible.

Does double bubble gum double bubble?
吃兩顆泡泡糖會吹出兩顆泡泡嗎？

Garry the vet gave his goat a green vest.
獸醫蓋瑞給他的羊穿了一件綠背心。

Talking About Families and Your Home
談論家庭與住家

Topic Preview (029)

1 Talking about family members 談論家人

How many people are there in your family?

There are four people in my family: my mother, father, sister, and I.

How many brothers and sisters do you have?

I have one sister, but no brothers.

2 Talking about their ages, marital status, and jobs
談論家人的年齡、婚姻狀態與工作

How old is your brother?
Is he married?
What does he do?

He's twenty years old.
No, he's still single.
He's a waiter.

3 Talking about the relationships between people
談論人與人之間的關係

John

Jenny   Sarah

Who is John?
Who is Sarah?

John is my father.
Sarah is Jenny's sister.

4 Talking about your home 談論住家

How many bathrooms are there in your house?
Do you have any tables in your living room?

There is just one.
Yes, we have a coffee table.

24

II. Vocabulary & Phrases

Hi! I'm Paula.
Let me show you
my family tree.

Family Members

my grandfather 爺爺
my grandmother 奶奶

my aunt 嬸嬸／舅媽
my uncle 叔叔／舅舅

my mother 母親
my father 父親

my father-in-law 公公
my mother-in-law 婆婆

my cousins
堂／表姊妹

my brother-in-law 姊夫
my sister 姊姊
my niece 外甥女 / **my nephew** 外甥

my husband
丈夫　Here I am!

my sister-in-law
小姑

My Home

our son 兒子　**our daughter** 女兒

bedroom 臥室

bathroom 浴室

living room 客廳

dining room 餐廳

kitchen 廚房

- How many people are there in your family?
  There are _three_: _my mother, my father, and I_.
- How many _cousins_ do you have?
  I have _two_.
- How old is your _mother_?
  She's _fifty_.
- Is your sister _married_?
  Yes, she is. / No, she's _single_.
- What does your _father_ do?
  He's a _teacher_.

- Who is _Sandy_?
  Sandy is my _sister-in-law_.
- How many _computers_ do you have at home?
  I have _one_. / I don't have any.
- Do you have any _chairs_ in your _kitchen_?
  Yes, I have _five_. / No, I don't.
- How many _bedrooms_ are there in your house?
  There are _three_. / There aren't any.
- Are there any _towels_ in your _bathroom_?
  Yes, there are _two_. / No, there aren't.

 (032)

**Marital Status
and Relationships**
婚姻狀態與人際關係

She is **single**.
單身的

He's a **bachelor**.
單身漢

He's **in a relationship**.
穩定交往中

She is **engaged**.
訂婚的

They are **married**.
結婚的

They are **divorced**.
離婚的

We are **twins**.
雙胞胎

He's an **only child**.
獨生子／獨生女

He's a **widower**. 鰥夫／
She's a **widow**. 寡婦

He's a **single parent**. 單親爸或媽
She is a **single-parent child**.
單親家庭的孩子

III. Now, Time to Listen!

1 Listen to the CD and complete Paula's family tree. The names of her family members are given.

(033)

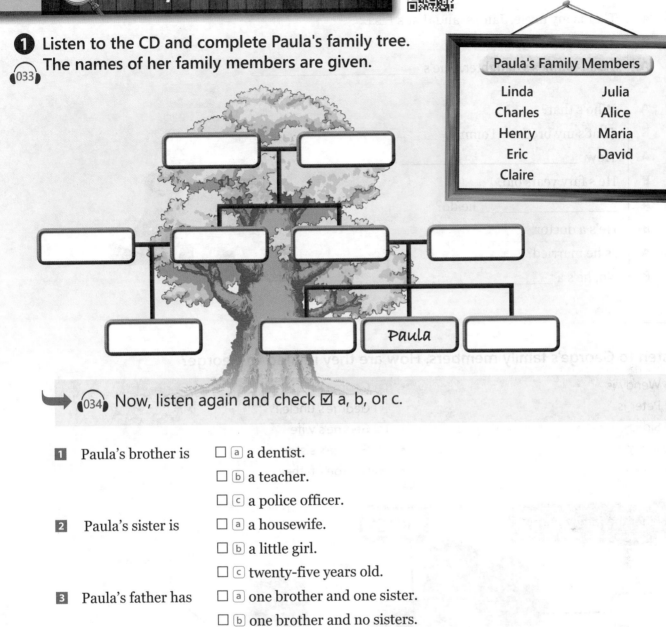

Paula's Family Members

Linda	Julia
Charles	Alice
Henry	Maria
Eric	David
Claire	

Paula

➡ (034) Now, listen again and check ☑ a, b, or c.

1 Paula's brother is
- ☐ ⓐ a dentist.
- ☐ ⓑ a teacher.
- ☐ ⓒ a police officer.

2 Paula's sister is
- ☐ ⓐ a housewife.
- ☐ ⓑ a little girl.
- ☐ ⓒ twenty-five years old.

3 Paula's father has
- ☐ ⓐ one brother and one sister.
- ☐ ⓑ one brother and no sisters.
- ☐ ⓒ one sister and no brothers.

2 Listen to these conversations about families and fill in the blanks.

(035) **1**
A | How many people are there _____?
B | There are five: my grandmother and grandfather, my parents, and I.
     I'm an _____, so I don't have any brothers or sisters.

2
A | How many brothers and sisters _____?
B | I have one sister and no brothers.
A | Is your sister married?
B | No, but she's _____.

3

A That is my uncle, James, and that's Lisa.

B _____ Lisa?

A Lisa is James's daughter. She's _____.

4

A Who's that?

B That's my brother, Tommy.

A How _____ ?

B He's fifty years old.

A _____ he do?

B He's a doctor.

A Is he married?

B No, he's a _____ .

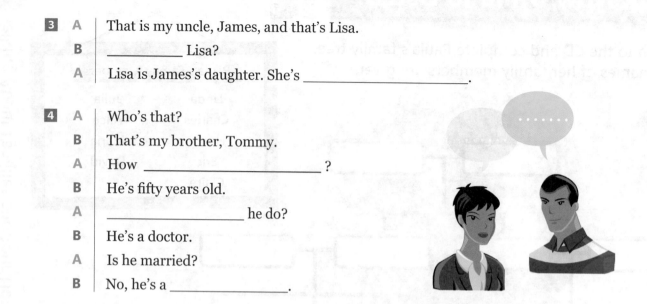

❸ Listen to George's family members. How are they related to George?

(036)

1. Wendy is •
2. Peter is •
3. Sid is •
4. Jenny is •
5. Dora is •

• a George's daughter.
• b George's uncle.
• c George's wife.
• d George's sister.
• e George's father

Now label the family photo!

George

IV. Now, Grammar Time!

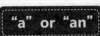

"a" or "an"

Use "**an**" when the next word begins with a **vowel** sound:
當後面接的單字是以母音開頭的時候，要用「**an**」：

an apple [ˈæpl̩]   **an hour** [aʊər]   **an onion** [ˈʌnjən]

Use "**a**" when the next word begins with a **consonant** sound:
當後面接的單字是以子音開頭的時候，要用「**a**」：

a bat [bæt]   **a UFO** [ˈjuɛfˌo]   **a table** [ˈtebl̩]

❹ Write "a" or "an" in front of each word below.

| ___ table | ___ computer | ___ oven | ___ kitchen | ___ umbrella | ___ egg cup | ___ TV |

Articles : "the" or "a/an" 冠詞：the 或 a/an	
a/an	the
referring to something non-specific 指非特定的物品	referring to something specific 指特定的物品
A : What's this? **B** : It's <u>a</u> book.	**A** : What's <u>the</u> book's title? **B** : *The Lord of the Rings.*

❺ Fill in the blanks using the appropriate articles.

1

A	What's on the table?
B	There's _____ pen and _____ pencil.
A	Is _____ pen blue?
B	Yes, it is.
A	Oh, _____ pen is mine, but _____ pencil isn't.

2

A	What do you do?
B	I'm _____ teacher.
A	Where do you work?
B	I work in _____ school.
A	What's _____ school's name?
B	Jamestown High School.

There is / There are		
Affirmative Sentences 肯定句	Negative Sentences 否定句	Yes/No Questions 是非問句
There is <u>a bed</u> in the bedroom.	There isn't <u>a table</u> in my kitchen.	Is there <u>a dog</u> in your family? Yes, there is. / No, there isn't.
There are <u>five people</u> in my family.	There aren't <u>any windows</u> in the bathroom.	Are there <u>any children</u> in your family? Yes, there are two. / No, there aren't.

❻ Pair Work! Look at the picture of Mark's house. Ask and answer questions using the models below.

Household Objects 居家用品

cushion 靠墊   pillow 枕頭   painting 繪畫   mirror 鏡子   sofa 沙發   towel 毛巾

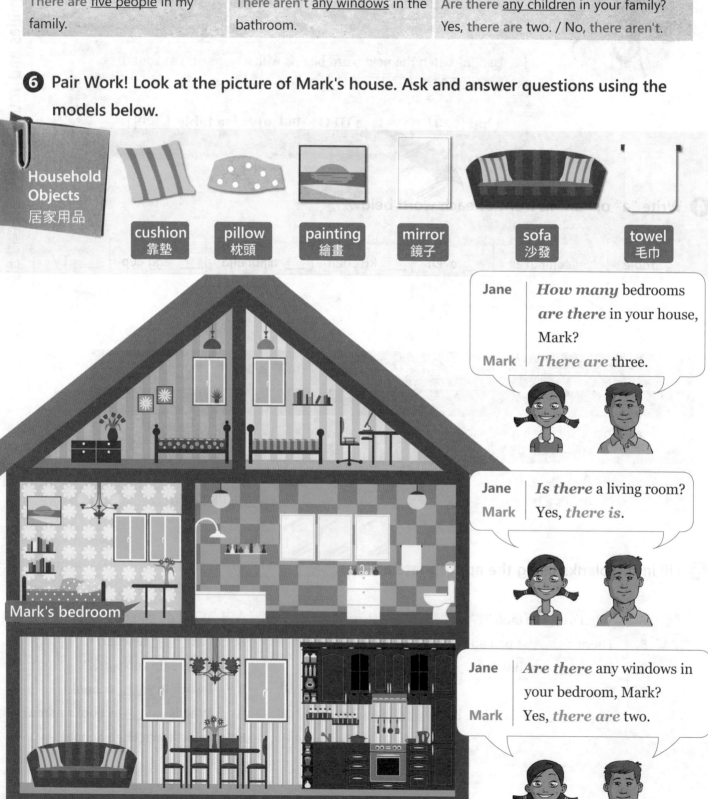

Mark's bedroom

Jane | *How many* bedrooms *are there* in your house, Mark?
Mark | *There are* three.

Jane | *Is there* a living room?
Mark | Yes, *there is*.

Jane | *Are there* any windows in your bedroom, Mark?
Mark | Yes, *there are* two.

	Possessive Adjectives 所有格形容詞		
my	This is my father, Jacob.	your	What's your sister's name?
his	That man over there … What's his name?	her	Jenny's a student, but her sister is a nurse.
our	This is my sister, Amy, and these are our parents.	their	Their names are Peter and Simon.
its	This is my dog. Its name is Benny.	(noun)'s	He is Polly's husband, Leo.

7 **Look at the family tree. Complete the sentences using words from the box.**

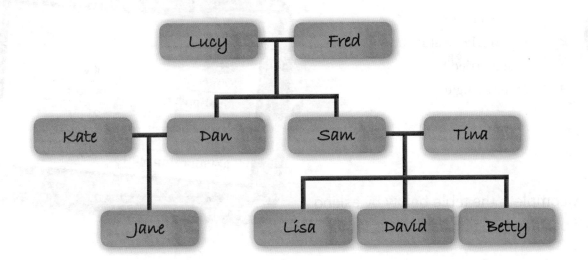

1. Betty's mother is Tina, and _____ cousin is Jane.

2. I'm David. My _____ name is Sam.

3. Sam? He's my brother. _____ wife, Tina, is a hairdresser.

4. Lucy and Fred are married. Sam and Dan are _____ children.

5. Hello, I'm Dan. This is _____ wife, Kate.

6. Nice to meet you. I'm Lucy and my _____ name is Fred.

7. Lisa? She's _____ daughter.

8. David, is this _____ sister Betty?

9. My name's Dan, and this is my brother, Sam. And these are _____ parents, Lucy and Fred.

10. Fred is _____ father-in-law.

Kate's	His
their	father's
her	your
Tina's	husband's
our	my

8 Pair Work! Listen to the dialogue below and practice it with your partner.

A | How many people are there in your family?
B | There are seven: two grandparents, my parents, my uncle, my brother, and I.
A | What are your parents' names?
B | My mom's name is Andrea. My dad's name is Bill.
A | What do they do?
B | My mom is a beautician, and my dad is a mechanic.
A | What's your brother's name?
B | His name's Jim.
A | How old is he?
B | He's 21. He's a student.
A | Is he married?
B | No, he's single.

Name	Jim
Relationship	Brother
Age	21
Job	Student
Relationship Status	Single

Now complete the table below by asking your partner questions about his family.

Name	
Relationship	
Age	
Job	
Relationship Status	

Name	
Relationship	
Age	
Job	
Relationship Status	

Name	
Relationship	
Age	
Job	
Relationship Status	

Name	
Relationship	
Age	
Job	
Relationship Status	

Name	
Relationship	
Age	
Job	
Relationship Status	

Name	
Relationship	
Age	
Job	
Relationship Status	

❾ Describe your house to your partner. Start your sentences with:

There is _____
There are _____ in my living room.
I have _____

➡ Now describe your partner's house to the class.

Example:

John has a TV in his living room.
There are three bedrooms in John's house.

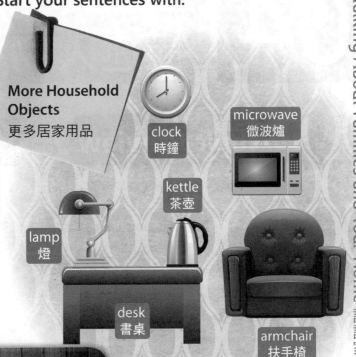

More Household Objects
更多居家用品

clock 時鐘

microwave 微波爐

kettle 茶壺

lamp 燈

desk 書桌

armchair 扶手椅

VI. Now, Time to Pronounce!

Reduced forms of "there is" and "there are"
there is 和 there are 的縮寫

In affirmative sentences, "there is" is often shortened to "there's" in both written and spoken English. In spoken British English, "there are" is often shortened to "there're."

❿ Listen and repeat the words you hear.

(038)
there is	[ðɛr] [ɪz]
there's	[ðɛrz]
there are	[ðɛr] [ɑr]
there're	[ðɛrə]

⓫ Listen to the sentences. Do you hear the long version or the
(039) shortened version of "there is" and "there are"?

1 there is	there's	**2** there are	there're	**3** there is	there's
☐	☐	☐	☐	☐	☐

4 there are	there're	**5** there is	there's	**6** there are	there're
☐	☐	☐	☐	☐	☐

Describing People
描述人物

1 Appearance 外貌

What does Gabby look like?

She's very pretty.

Is Johnny handsome?

No, he's not very attractive.

2 Weight and height 身高體重

How tall are you?

I'm six feet two inches tall.

How much do you weigh?

I weigh about 180 pounds.

3 Hair and eyes 頭髮和眼睛

What color is her hair?
What kind of hair does she have?
What color eyes does she have?

Her hair is brown.
She has straight hair.
She has green eyes.

4 Personality 個性

What's Darren like?

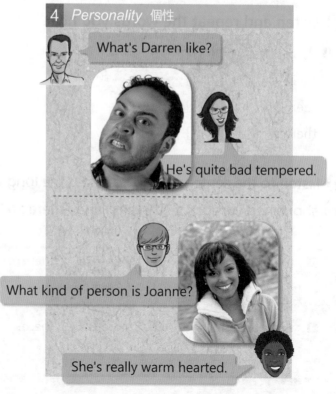

He's quite bad tempered.

What kind of person is Joanne?

She's really warm hearted.

II. Vocabulary & Phrases 041

Describing Appearance 形容外貌

pretty 漂亮的

handsome 英俊的

unattractive 不好看的

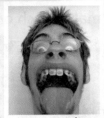
cute 可愛的

average-looking 相貌平庸的

tall / short 高的／矮的

overweight / fat 過重的／肥胖的

slim 苗條的

fit 健康的

young 年輕的

middle-aged 中年的

old 年老的

Describing Hair 形容頭髮

straight 直的

wavy 波浪的

curly 捲的

bald 禿頭的

beard （下巴的）鬍鬚
mustache 小鬍子

black 黑色的

brown 咖啡色的

red 紅色的

blond 金色的

gray 灰色的

long 長的

short 短的

Describing Eyes 形容眼睛

dark / light brown 深棕色的／淡棕色的

gray 灰色的

dark / light blue 深藍色的／淺藍色的

green 綠色的

Sentence Patterns 042

- What does he/she look like?
  He is very *handsome*. / She is quite *cute*.
- How tall are you?
  I'm *five* feet *eleven* inches tall. /
  I'm *five* foot *eleven*. / I'm *five eleven*.
- How much do you weigh?
  I weigh about *150* pounds.
- What color is her hair?
  Her hair is *brown*. / She has *brown* hair.

- What kind of hair does he have?
  He has *curly* hair.
- What color are his eyes?
  His eyes are *blue*. / He has *blue* eyes.
- What's Peter like? /
  What kind of person is Peter?
  He's *warm hearted*.

- 1 foot (1') = 30.48 cm
- 1 inch (1")= 2.54 cm
  (There are 12 inches in a foot.)
- 1 pound (1 lb)= 0.45 kg

1 Listen to the conversations. Then match each one with the person that is being described.

043

1 _____

2 _____

3 _____

4 _____

5 _____

2 First read the questions. Then listen to the description of Mandy and answer them.

044

1 Her hair is ☐ ☐ .

2 Mandy is _____ cm tall.

Mandy is around _____ kg.

3 Mandy is quite ☐ ☐ .

4 Mandy's eyes are ☐ ☐ .

5 She is a ☐ ☐ person.

→ Which of these women is likely to be Mandy? _____

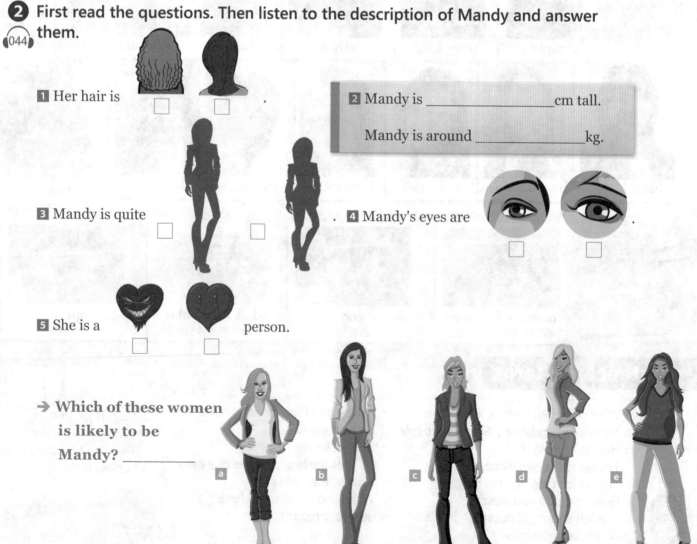

Ways to Describe People 形容人的方式

patient 有耐心的	warm-hearted 熱心的	bad-tempered 脾氣差的	fun-loving 喜歡玩樂的	hard-working 勤奮工作的	shy 害羞的

❸ Listen to the CD. Who is being described? Link the names to the correct pictures.

045

❶ Sam ☐

❷ Jo ☐

❸ Lexie ☐

❹ Tina ☐

❺ Drew ☐

❻ Pat ☐

a

b

c

d

e

f

IV. Now, Grammar Time!

Adjective Position 形容詞的位置	
Before a noun 在名詞之前	*After "be"* 在 be 動詞之後
John is a handsome <u>man</u>. He has a big <u>nose</u>. The old <u>man</u> has green <u>eyes</u>. I have short, brown <u>hair</u>.	<u>John</u> is handsome. <u>His nose</u> is big. <u>The man</u> is old, and <u>his eyes</u> are green. <u>My hair</u> is short and brown.

4 Put the words in the correct order to make sentences. The first one has been done for you.

1 straight / has / hair / Peter
<u>Peter has straight hair.</u>

2 cute / he / baby / is / a
_____.

3 eyes / blue / are / John's
_____.

4 tall / thin / Peter / and / is
_____.

5 woman / beautiful / the / curly / hair / has
_____.

6 short / my / is / mother / and / slim
_____.

Using "and" to separate adjectives (after "be") 在 be 動詞之後用 and 來分隔形容詞
<u>John</u> is tall **and** handsome. <u>His nose</u> is big **and** broad. <u>Sam</u> is short, fat, **and** ugly. <u>My hair</u> is long, wavy, **and** brown.

5 Read the following sentences and insert "and" where necessary. The first one has been done for you.

1 Peter's hair is long black.
         ‿and

2 My friend Jenny is beautiful, warm hearted, fun loving!

3 Is Sally young pretty or old ugly?

4 Stephen's eyes are big, round, green.

5 My sister has short, brown hair, and her nose is long straight.

6 My grandmother's face is small cute.

V. Now, Time to Speak!

6 Pair Work! Listen to the conversation and practice it with a partner.

A   Is **your sister** tall?

B   **Yes, she's** around **five** foot **eleven**.

A   How much does **she** weigh?

B   **She** weighs around **140** pounds.

A   What kind of hair does **she** have?

B   **She** has **long, straight, black** hair.

A   What color are **her** eyes?

B   **Her** eyes are **dark brown**.

A   Is she **pretty**?

B   **Yes, she's quite pretty.**

➡ Then talk about the movie stars below.

Bruce Willis

6'0"
205 lbs

6'2"
193 lbs

Will Smith

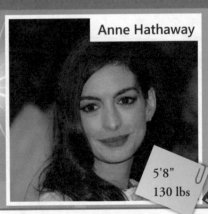

Anne Hathaway

5'8"
130 lbs

Robert Downey Jr.

5'8"
175 lbs

5'3"
126 lbs

Scarlett Johansson

Angelina Jolie

5'6"
131 lbs

7 Describe your partner to the class. Use the vocabulary words below to help you describe his or her face in more detail!

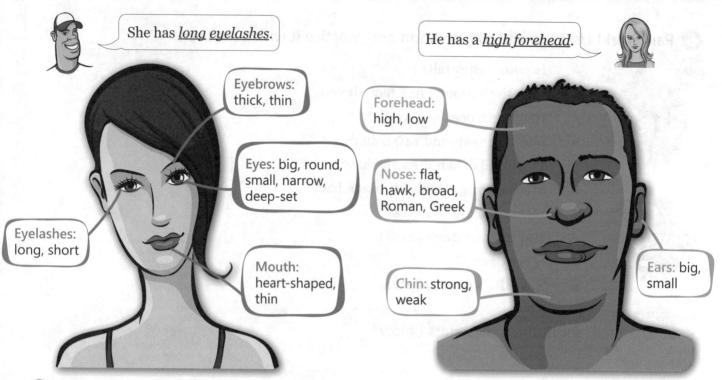

She has *long eyelashes*.

Eyebrows: thick, thin

Eyes: big, round, small, narrow, deep-set

Eyelashes: long, short

Mouth: heart-shaped, thin

He has a *high forehead*.

Forehead: high, low

Nose: flat, hawk, broad, Roman, Greek

Chin: strong, weak

Ears: big, small

8 Group Work! Prepare a description of your ideal man or woman. Compare your answers with those of your classmates.

1 What does he/she look like?

2 What kind of person is he/she?

VI Now, Time to Pronounce!

[p] [t] [k] [f]

[b] [d] [g] [v]

Review of Voiceless and Voiced Consonants
複習無聲子音和有聲子音

9 Listen and repeat the words you hear.

047

Voiceless Consonants

[p]	pull	plant	keep	pop	drop
[t]	teen	tile	lit	foot	ten
[k]	coke	cook	cat	cap	comb
[f]	laugh	fat	flop	fluff	gruff

10 Listen and repeat the words you hear.

048

Voiced Consonants

[b]	ban	bell	boy	black	brown
[d]	dale	damp	do	deep	don't
[g]	gum	grin	gap	frog	yoga
[v]	live	knives	move	vote	give

11 Listen to the following words. Number them from 1 to 10 in the order that you
049 hear them.

ban	dote	vote	file	kite
	1			
plug	dock	tight	ghost	peat

Saying Good-bye, Thanks, and Congratulations
道別、道謝與道賀

Topic Preview (050)

1 Saying good-bye to someone 與人道別

Bye, Rob. Have a good weekend.

Bye, Jo. See you tomorrow.

See you, Tim. Take care.

So long, Doris. You, too!

2 Giving reasons for leaving 說明離開理由

Sorry. I have to go. I'm late for work.

I'd better get going. I have a busy schedule today.

Wow! Is that the time? It's so late.

3 Thanking someone for something 為某事向某人道謝

Wow! What a great gift! Thank you so much.

My pleasure. I'm so glad you like it.

Thanks so much for inviting me to dinner.

Oh, you're welcome. Thank you for coming.

4 Congratulating someone 恭賀他人

Surprise party

Congratulations on getting engaged!

Thank you! What a nice surprise!

5 Wishing someone well 祝福他人

Happy birthday!

Thank you! How thoughtful!

Wish me luck!

Bon voyage!

II. Vocabulary & Phrases

work 工作

class 上課

lunch 午餐

dinner 晚餐

date 約會

meeting 開會

dinner party 聚餐

birthday party 生日派對

farewell party 餞別會

engagement party 訂婚派對

get a new job 找到新工作

pass a test 通過考試

have a baby 生小孩

graduate from school 畢業

get engaged 訂婚

Sentence Patterns

- Bye. / So long. / Have a good _evening_. / See you _later_. / Take care.
- Sorry. I have to go.
- I'm late for a _meeting_.
- Is that the time? It's so late.
- I'd better get going. I have _a date soon_.
- Thank you so much.
  Thank you for _buying me a gift_!
  Thanks so much for inviting me to _your dinner party_.

- My pleasure. / You're welcome. / I'm so glad you like it!
- What a _great party_! / What an amazing dinner!
- Congratulations on _passing your test_!
- Happy Birthday! / Merry Christmas! / Happy New Year!
- Wish me luck! / Good luck!
- Bon voyage! / Have a great trip!

1 Look at the topics below. Write down which ones you hear in each of the following conversations. The first one has been partly done for you.

(053)

> **a** Saying good-bye.
>
> **b** Giving a reason for leaving.
>
> **c** Saying thanks.
>
> **d** Congratulating someone.
>
> **e** Wishing someone well.

1 __b__   **2** _____   **3** _____   **4** _____   **5** _____

2 Now listen again and fill in the blanks.

(054)

1 A | Oh no! I have to go. I'm _____.

   B | Oh, OK. See you later.

   A | _____.

2 A | Wow! Is that the time? _____!

   B | Yes, you're right. It's almost eleven.

   A | I'd better get going. Thank you so much for _____ me to dinner.

   B | Our pleasure. _____!

3 A | _____, Matt!

   B | See you next week!

   A | _____!

4 A | _____ passing your test, Jo!

   B | Thank you! Oh, and _____ to you _____ your test tomorrow!

   A | Haha! Thanks. I need it!

5 **A** _____, Harry!

B Merry Christmas to you, too, Sarah!

A Sorry I have to go so early. I have _____.

B No problem. Thanks for coming to our Christmas party!

A _____ inviting me!

3 Listen to the first half of each conversation. Match each one to the picture that best illustrates it. (055)

1 _____

2 _____

3 _____

4 _____

5 _____

(056) Now listen again and match each one to the most likely response.

1

2

3

4

5

- **a** Thank you for the gift.
- **b** I'm so glad you like it!
- **c** See you.
- **d** Bon voyage! Have a great trip.
- **e** Thanks so much! We are very happy.

IV. Now, Grammar Time!

Exclamatory Sentences 感嘆句	
What (a/an) + [adjective] + [noun]! What (a/an) + 形容詞 + 名詞	**How + [adjective]!** How + 形容詞
• What a wonderful surprise! • What an amazing party! • What great gifts!	• How wonderful! • How amazing! • How great!
. . . such (a/an) + [adjective] + [noun]! . . . such (a/an) + 形容詞 + 名詞	**. . . so + [adjective]!** . . . so + 形容詞
• This is such a wonderful surprise! • This is such an amazing party! • These are such great gifts!	• This is so wonderful! • This is so amazing! • These are so great!

4 **Fill in the exclamatory sentences. Use one of the adjectives below.**

wonderful   strange   beautiful   generous   tasty   thoughtful

Merry Christmas!

Wow! _____ big gift!
How _____!

1

2

I passed my test!

_____ great! That's _____ _____ achievement!

3

Wow! He's _____ cute baby!

I know. He's so _____!

4

HAPPY BIRTHDAY!

Wow! This is so _____! _____ great surprise!

Object Pronouns 受格代名詞			
Singular 單數	me	Thank you for inviting me to your party.	
	you	I want to give you a gift.	
	him	Give the gift to Peter.	Give it to him.
	her	Say thank you to Joan. →	Say thank you to her.
	it	I'm glad you like the party.	I'm glad you like it.
Plural 複數	us	Wish Sam and me luck!	Wish us luck!
	you	It's great to see you and your wife! →	It's great to see you two!
	them	Tell John and Mary I have to go.	Tell them I have to go.

5 Replace the words in **bold** with the correct object pronouns. The first one has been done for you.

1 I have to go and meet Tony. I have a date with **Tony** soon.

him

2 Here's a gift for you. I hope you like **the gift**!

3 Peter and Tony have a test tomorrow. Let's wish **Peter and Tony** good luck.

4 This is such an amazing party! I love **this party**.

5 Jerry and I have to go. Come and say goodbye to **Jerry and me**.

6 Is this your new baby girl? I want to give **your baby girl** a kiss!

7 Garry isn't here? OK, please tell **Garry** I hope he has a great trip.

6 Pair Work! Listen to the conversations below and practice them with a partner. Replace the words in color with ones from the word bank.

WORD BANK

graduating from school	well done	a date	(your / my . . .)
having a baby	bon voyage	class	dinner party
your new job in Japan	all the best	work	brunch
turning 18	happy birthday	a busy day	engagement party
passing your driving test	congratulations	a meeting	farewell party
	have a great trip		birthday party

057 Conversation A

Mandy : Congratulations on getting engaged, Fred!

Fred : Thanks, Mandy.

Mandy : I have a little gift for you to say good luck.

Fred : Oh! How thoughtful! Thank you so much!

058 Conversation B

Andy : I'd better get going. I have a meeting at two o'clock.

Amy : Oh, OK.

Andy : But thank you so much for inviting me to lunch.

Amy : You're welcome. Thank you for coming!

Andy : See you again soon.

Amy : Bye!

059 Conversation C

Jo : Merry Christmas, Pete!

Pete : Thanks, Jo!

Jo : Wow! Is that the time? Sorry, I have to go. I have a date later.

Pete : No problem. Thanks for coming to my Christmas party!

Jo : Thanks for inviting me! See you!

Pete : Bye. Take care.

7 Discuss how you would say good-bye in the following situations. Select one sentence from each box to form a 3-sentence dialogue between two people.

A | I'd better get going.
B | Thanks for coming.
A | Thanks for inviting me.

A
- I'd better get going.
- Is that the time! Sorry, I have to go.
- Bye!
- Wish me luck!

B
- Bye. Have a good day / evening / weekend.
- Bon voyage!
- Thanks for coming.
- Take care.

A
- See you soon.
- You too.
- Bye!
- Thanks for inviting me.

8 Group Work! Ask your classmates to look at the pictures below. Write down what they say to the people in the pictures.

Student 1 : _Mike_

Congratulations on having a new baby!

Student 1 : _____

Student 2 : _Laura_

What a cute baby!

Student 2 : _____

Student 1 : _____

Student 2 : _____

Student 3 : _____

Student 1 : _____

Student 2 : _____

Student 3 : _____

Student 1 : _____

Student 2 : _____

Student 3 : _____

VI. Now, Time to Pronounce!

Voiceless Consonants 無聲子音  [s] [θ]

9 Listen and repeat the words you hear.

(060)

[s]   smell   cell   dance   horse   kiss

[θ]   thank   fifth   month   teeth   thing

(061) Listen and circle the words that you hear.

1 sin | thin   **2** sink | think   **3** sing | thing   **4** miss | myth   **5** sigh | thigh

10 Listen to the words. Fill in the blanks with either [s] or [θ].

(062)

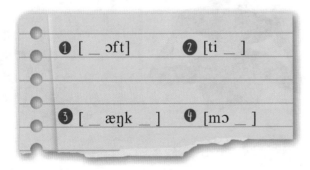

❶ [_ ɔft]   ❷ [ti _]

❸ [_ æŋk _]   ❹ [mɔ _]

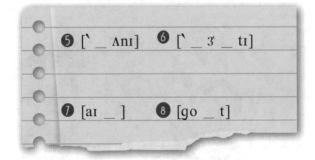

❺ [ˋ _ ʌnɪ]   ❻ [ˋ _ ɝ _ tɪ]

❼ [aɪ _]   ❽ [go _ t]

Expressing How You Feel 表達感受

Topic Preview 063

1 Talking about your mood 談論情緒

You look angry. Are you OK?

Yes. I'm fine. I'm just in a bad mood.

Wow! You look very happy today!

That's because I'm in a good mood!

2 Talking about how you feel 談論感受

How do you feel about tomorrow's exam?

I feel great!

I'm scared!

I don't feel so good.

3 Saying what you think about something 說出對某件事物的想法

What do you think about the book?

I think it's boring!

How do you feel about wearing this hat?

I think that's a silly idea.

4 Expressing surprise/anger/love/frustration 表達驚訝／生氣／愛／沮喪

I don't believe it! What a surprise!

I'm so angry with you right now!

I love you so much!

Argh! I give up!

II. Vocabulary & Phrases

What a **breathtaking** view! 好**壯觀**的景致！

This is a **boring** class. 這是一堂**無聊**的課。
I'm **bored**. 我覺得好**無聊**。

This game is **fun**. 這個遊戲是**有趣**的。

That's a **strange-looking** carrot! 這是一根**長相奇怪**的胡蘿蔔！

What a **terrible** sight! 好**糟糕**的景象！

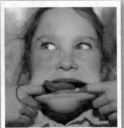

That's a **silly** face. 這是一張鬼臉（**傻氣**的）。

This roller coaster is **exciting**! 這雲霄飛車好**刺激**（**令人興奮**的）！
I'm **excited**! 我覺得好**興奮**啊！

This math problem is **confusing**. 這題數學真**令人困惑**。
I'm **confused**. 我覺得好**困惑**。

This job is **frustrating**. 這份工作真**令人沮喪**。
I'm **frustrated**. 我覺得好**沮喪**。

This movie is **disappointing**. 這場電影真**令人失望**。
I'm **disappointed**. 我覺得好**失望**。

This news is **surprising**! 這個消息真**令人驚訝**！
I'm **surprised**! 我覺得好**驚訝**！

What a **tiring** trip! 好**累人**的一趟旅行！
I'm **tired**. 我覺得好**疲倦**。

This kitten is **adorable**. 這是一隻**可愛**的小貓。

This book is **interesting**. 這是一本**有趣**的書。
I'm **interested**. 我很**感興趣**。

This hamster is very **nervous**! 這隻倉鼠好**緊張**！

Different ways to express how you feel	表達感受的各種方法		
Happy 快樂的	Sad 悲傷的	Good 好的	Bad 差的
over the moon 欣喜若狂	**down in the dumps** 沮喪的	**wonderful** 美好的	**awful** 很差的
on top of the world 開心至極	**blue** 憂鬱的	**amazing** 美妙的	**terrible** 糟糕的
on cloud nine 九霄雲端	**downhearted** 悶悶不樂的	**terrific** 非常棒的	**dreadful** 糟透的

Sentence Patterns

• You look _sad_.
• I'm in a _bad_ mood.
• How do you feel about _getting married_?
  I feel _nervous_! / I don't feel so good. / I'm _excited_!
• What do you think about _the game_?
  I think _it's fun_.

• How do you feel about _this book_?
  I think _it's very interesting_.
• What a _big surprise_! / What an _exciting story_!
• I'm so _tired_ right now.
• I love _you_ so much!
• I give up!

1 Listen to the people expressing their feelings and opinions. Then match each adjective to a picture.

066

1 ☐   **A** silly

2 ☐   **B** wonderful

3 ☐   **C** excited

4 ☐   **D** confusing

5 ☐   **E** strange looking

a

b How are you?   ? ?

c

d

e

2 Listen to the conversations. How does Bob feel in each one? Complete the table below.

067

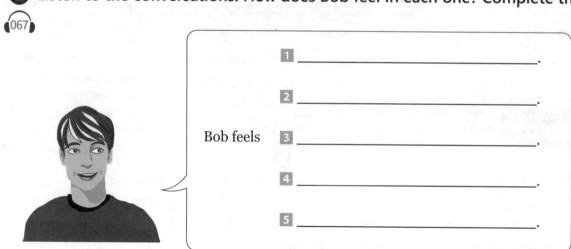

Bob feels

1 _____.

2 _____.

3 _____.

4 _____.

5 _____.

➤ 068 Now listen again and check ☑ a, b, or c.

1 Bob looks …
- a) ☐ down in the dumps.
- b) ☐ over the moon.
- c) ☐ confused.

2 The woman thinks Bob is …
- a) ☐ in a bad mood.
- b) ☐ in a good mood.
- c) ☐ disappointed.

3 Bob thinks the math problem is …
- a) ☐ hard.
- b) ☐ easy.
- c) ☐ fun.

4 Bob looks sad because he heard …
- a) ☐ a sad story.
- b) ☐ an awful song.
- c) ☐ terrible news.

5 Jane looks …
- a) ☐ interested.
- b) ☐ amazing.
- c) ☐ over the moon.

❸ **Listen to the first half of each conversation. Fill in the blanks and then match each**
069 **one to the most likely response.**

1 This video game looks very _____. •

2 I don't believe it! I'm _____! •

3 What do you _____ my new dog? •

4 _____ feel about getting married? •

5 _____! Are you OK? •

• **a** I'm a little bit nervous, actually.

• **b** It's so much fun!

• **c** It's so adorable!

• **d** You got the job? That's wonderful!

• **e** I'm fine. I'm just really bored.

Emotive Verbs and Participial Adjectives
情緒動詞和分詞形容詞

Some verbs that express feelings/emotions can be changed into adjectives by adding -ed or -ing.　有些表達感受或情緒的動詞，可以在字尾加上 ed 或 ing 變成形容詞

Verb 動詞	[verb]-ing → an adjective that describes a thing 動詞+ing→ 描述事物的形容詞	[verb]-ed → an adjective that describes how someone feels 動詞+ed→ 描述人的感受的形容詞
bore	This <u>movie</u> is boring.	I <u>feel</u> so bored in class.
excite	This <u>game</u> is exciting.	<u>I'm</u> really excited about my birthday party!
tire	<u>Running</u> is very tiring.	<u>I'm</u> so tired after working all day.
frighten	<u>Ghosts</u> are very frightening.	<u>I'm</u> frightened of the dark!
confuse	This <u>map</u> is so confusing!	I <u>feel</u> so confused. I don't know where to go.
embarrass	<u>Singing in class</u> is really embarrassing.	<u>I'm</u> so embarrassed! I have food on my face.

❹ **Fill in the blanks below. Use the prompts to help you. Be sure to use the correct adjective endings.**

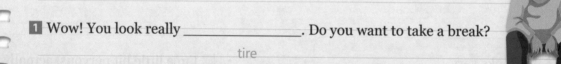

1 Wow! You look really _____. Do you want to take a break?

tire

2 I'm so _____. This book is not _____.

bore　　　　　　　　　　　　　interest

3 Is this gift for me? I'm so _____!

surprise

4 I give up. Math is too _____!

frustrate

5 I'm _____ of flying, but my sister thinks it's _____.

frighten　　　　　　　　　　　　　excite

❺ Look at the pictures below. Choose words from the box to fill in the blanks.

| embarrassing | confusing | disappointing | frightening | exciting | boring | tiring |
| embarrassed | confused | disappointed | frightened | excited | bored | tired |

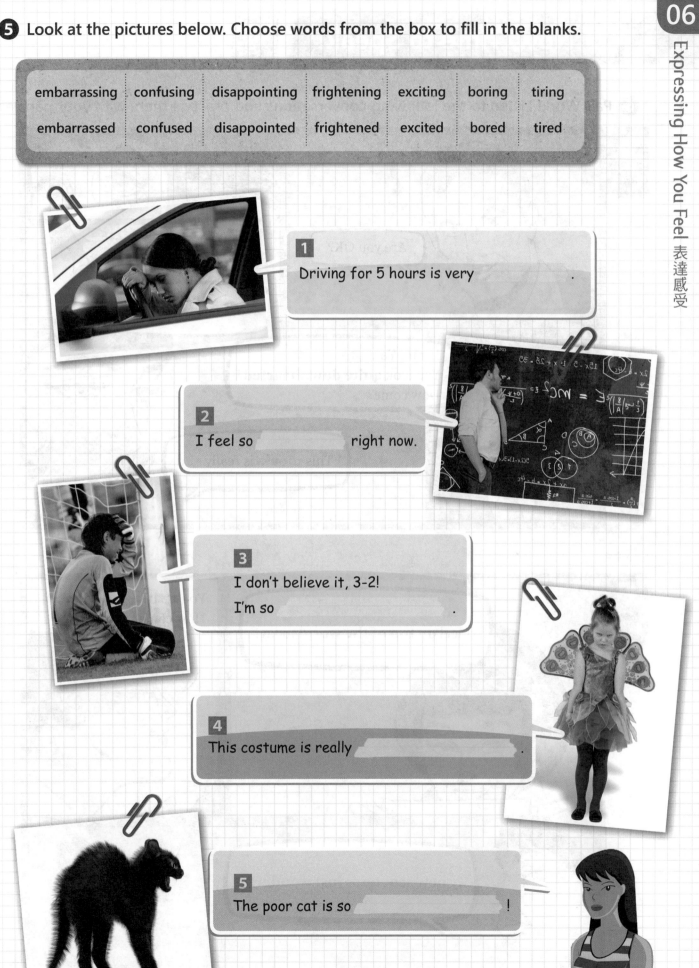

1 Driving for 5 hours is very _____ .

2 I feel so _____ right now.

3 I don't believe it, 3-2!
I'm so _____ .

4 This costume is really _____ .

5 The poor cat is so _____ !

6 Pair Work! Listen to the following conversations and practice them with your partner.

1 070

2 071

Now use the pictures below to have similar conversations.

I / down in the dumps

report / disappointing

I / disappointed

book / boring

I / frustrated

puzzle / confusing

I / terrible

work / tiring

I / over the moon

new video game / exciting

I / nervous

presentation / important

7 With your partner, discuss how to fill in the blanks in the following conversation. Discuss your answers with the class.

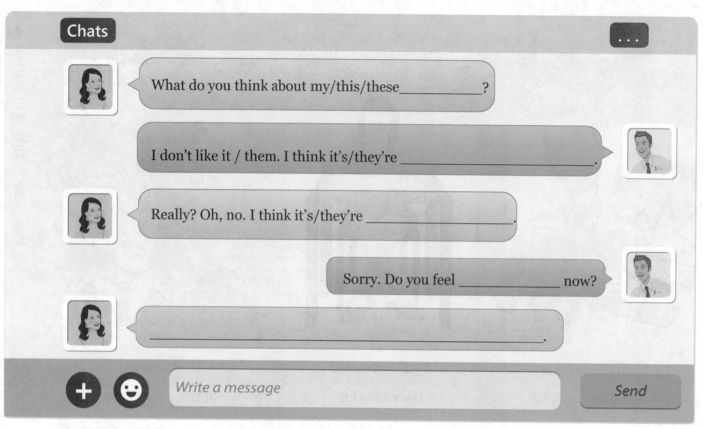

Chats   ...

What do you think about my/this/these_____?

I don't like it / them. I think it's/they're _____.

Really? Oh, no. I think it's/they're _____.

Sorry. Do you feel _____ now?

_____.

+ ☺   *Write a message*   Send

8 Ask your partner how he/she feels about the following items. Ask and answer using the models below. Discuss your answers with the class.

How do you feel about the **carrot**? / What do you think about the **carrot**?

I think it's very **strange looking**. / I feel very **confused** when I look at it.

carrot

roller coaster

city

painting

60

VI. Now, Time to Pronounce!

Voiced Consonants 有聲子音　[z]　[ð]

9 Listen and repeat the words you hear.

072

[z]	zero	buzz	razor	busy	zone

[ð]	there	they	bathe	those	then

10 Listen to the tongue twisters. Then try to say them as many times as you can and 073 as fast as possible.

Zizzi is a zebra. Is Zizzi a zebra?
吉吉是一匹斑馬。吉吉是斑馬嗎？

They make leather together with their father.
他們和父親一起製做皮革。

11 Listen to the words. Fill in the blanks with either [z] or [ð].

074

❶ [___ u]　　❷ [___ ə]

❸ [ˋ ___ ɪpɚ]　❹ [waɪ ___]

❺ [smʊ ___]　❻ [ˋwɛ ___ ɚ]

❼ [___ ɪs]　　❽ [___ æp]

Asking What Time and Day It Is
詢問時間與星期

Topic Preview
(075)

1 Asking about the day 詢問今天星期幾

Is today Wednesday?

No, it isn't.

What day is it today?

Today's Monday.

2 Asking about the date 詢問日期

Is today the twelfth?
What's the date today?

No, I don't think so. It's March (the) fourteenth.

3 Asking about an important date 詢問重要日期

When is your birthday?
When's Jenny's birthday?

It's on July (the) tenth. October (the) third.

4 Asking the time 詢問時間

Excuse me. What time is it?

Excuse me. Do you have the time?

Yes, it's three fifteen.

It's one o'clock.

5 Asking what time it is in a different time zone 詢問不同時區的時間

It's 7 p.m. in Las Vegas. What time is it in Taipei?

It's eleven o'clock in the morning here.

6 Asking what time something happens 詢問某件事發生的時間

When does the supermarket open?

What time is dinner?

It opens at eight thirty.

COME IN WE ARE OPEN

Dinner is at seven o'clock.

62

II. Vocabulary & Phrases 076

twelve o'clock　midday　midnight
12 點鐘　　正午　　午夜

twelve fifty eight
two minutes to one　12 點 58 分

twelve o three
three minutes past twelve　12 點 3 分

twelve o five
five past twelve　12 點 5 分

twelve fifty
ten to one　12 點 50 分

twelve ten
ten past twelve　12 點 10 分

twelve forty-five
(a) quarter to one
12 點 45 分

twelve fifteen
(a) quarter past twelve
12 點 15 分

twelve forty-three
seventeen minutes to one
12 點 43 分

twelve eighteen
eighteen minutes past twelve
12 點 18 分

twelve thirty-five
twenty-five to one　12 點 35 分

twelve thirty
half past twelve　12 點半

twelve twenty-five
twenty-five past twelve　12 點 25 分

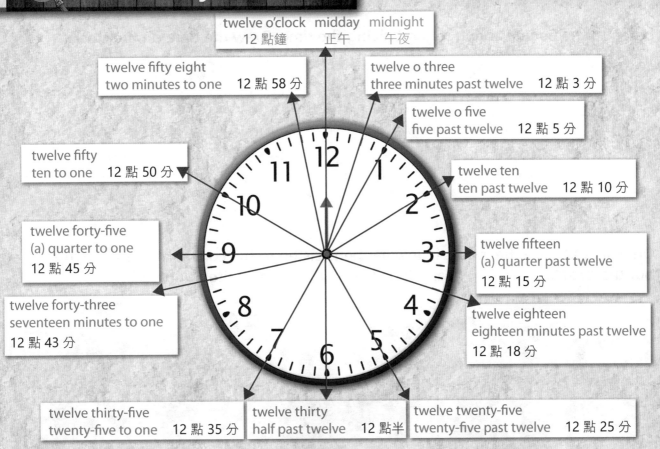

Months 月份	January 一月	February 二月	March 三月	April 四月	May 五月	June 六月
	July 七月	August 八月	September 九月	October 十月	November 十一月	December 十二月

Sunday 星期日	Monday 星期一	Tuesday 星期二	Wednesday 星期三	Thursday 星期四	Friday 星期五	Saturday 星期六
	1 first	2 second	3 third	4 fourth	5 fifth	6 sixth
7 seventh	8 eighth	9 ninth	10 tenth	11 eleventh	12 twelfth	13 thirteenth
14 fourteenth	15 fifteenth	16 sixteenth	17 seventeenth	18 eighteenth	19 nineteenth	20 twentieth
21 twenty-first	22 twenty-second	23 twenty-third	24 twenty-fourth	25 twenty-fifth	26 twenty-sixth	27 twenty-seventh
28 twenty-eighth	29 twenty-ninth	30 thirtieth	31 thirty-first			

Sentence Patterns 077

- Is today _Saturday_? / What day is it today?
  Today is _Monday_.
- Is today _March (the) tenth_? / What's the date today?
  It's _April_ (the) _seventh_.
- When is _your birthday_?
  It's on _January (the) ninth_.
- Do you have the time? / What time is it? / What's the time?
  It's _five past one_.

- It's _8 a.m._ in _London_. What time is it in _Tokyo_?
  It's _five o'clock_ in the _evening_ here.
- What time/When does _the movie start_?
  The movie starts at _eight o'clock_.
- What time/When is the party?
  The party is at _seven thirty_.

1 Listen to the people asking for and giving the time. Draw the time on the clocks.

078

1   2   3   4   5

2 On what dates do the events below happen? Listen to the conversations and write
out the date like this: You hear: "June the first" → You write: "June 1"

079

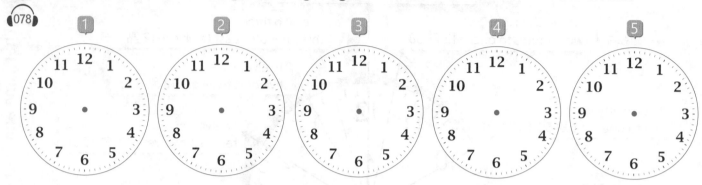

a

Mother's Day
Date : _____

b

**Wedding
Anniversary**
Date : _____

c

Midterm Exam
Date : _____

d

**American
Father's Day**
Date : _____

e

Jane's Birthday
Date : _____

3 Listen to the conversations. Choose the calendar that has the correct day and date.

080

1

a

MARCH

S	M	T	W	T	F	S
		1	2	3	4	5
6	7	8	9	10	11	12
13	14	15	16	17	18	19
20	21	22	23	24	25	26
27	28	29	30	31		

b

MARCH

S	M	T	W	T	F	S
	1	2	3	4	5	6
7	8	9	10	11	12	13
14	15	16	17	18	19	20
21	22	23	24	25	26	27
28	29	30	31			

c

MARCH

S	M	T	W	T	F	S
					1	2	3
4	5	6	7	8	9	10
11	12	13	14	15	16	17
18	19	20	21	22	23	24
25	26	27	28	29	30	31

2

a

APRIL

S	M	T	W	T	F	S
		1	2	3	4	5
6	7	8	9	10	11	12
13	14	15	16	17	18	19
20	21	22	23	24	25	26
27	28	29	30			

b

APRIL

S	M	T	W	T	F	S
	1	2	3	4	5	6	7
8	9	10	11	12	13	14
15	16	17	18	19	20	21
22	23	24	25	26	27	28
29	30					

c

APRIL

S	M	T	W	T	F	S
					1	2	3
4	5	6	7	8	9	10
11	12	13	14	15	16	17
18	19	20	21	22	23	24
25	26	27	28	29	30	

IV. Now, Grammar Time!

Prepositions Used with Time 與時間連用的介系詞

at giving the exact time 提供精確時間 holidays 節日	at 7 : 15 a.m. at eight o'clock at Christmas
in parts of the day 一日中的各時段 long periods 較長的時間 (months / years / seasons … etc.)（月分／年分／季節等）	in the morning in 2012 in January
on days / dates 星期／日期	on Sunday on March 15 on Christmas day

4 Fill in the blanks with the correct prepositions.

1 I finish class _____ three o'clock.

2 The movie starts _____ five fifteen.

3 He always gives me a gift _____ my birthday.

4 I like to take a walk _____ the afternoon.

5 Their anniversary is _____ February 8.

6 I want to visit Japan _____ 2015.

7 What do you do _____ Monday mornings?

8 Do you do homework _____ the evenings?

9 Do you visit your family _____ Chinese New Year?

10 The train leaves _____ nine thirty.

What time / When + "be" + [subject]? What time / When + be 動詞 + 主詞？	*What time / When + do/does + [subject] + [verb]?* What time / When + do/does + 主詞 + 動詞？
What time is dinner? What day is the party? What date is Mother's Day this year? When is Christmas Day?	What time does the train leave? What days do you go to class? What date do you celebrate Father's Day? When does the show finish?

⑤ Pair Work! Ask and answer questions using the prompts and phrases below. Be sure to use the correct preposition in your answer.

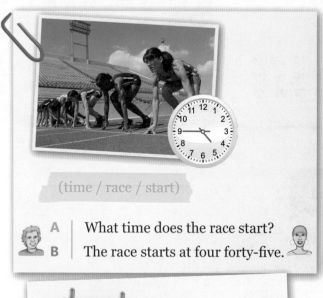

(time / race / start)

A What time does the race start?
B The race starts at four forty-five.

1 (time / the museum / close)

2 (your birthday)

3 (day / the exam)

4 (date / your anniversary)

5 (the train / arrive)

66

Now, Time to Speak!

6 Pair Work! Draw different times on each of the clocks. Then ask for the time using each of the following expressions:

Excuse me. What time is it?

Do you have the time?

Excuse me. What's the time?

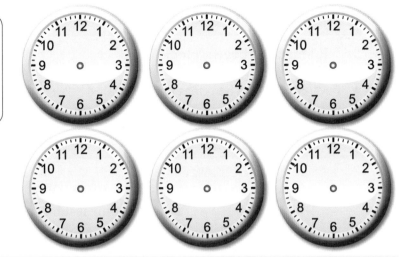

Now read the following dialogue and practice it with your partner. Then use the calendar to replace the words in bold with ones of your own.

A	What's the date today?
B	It's **December (the) twelfth**. What day is it today?
A	Today's **Thursday**.

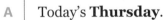

January						
S	M	T	W	T	F	S
		1	2	3	4	5
6	7	8	9	10	11	12
13	14	15	16	17	18	19
20	21	22	23	24	25	26
27	28	29	30	31		

February						
S	M	T	W	T	F	S
					1	2
3	4	5	6	7	8	9
10	11	12	13	14	15	16
17	18	19	20	21	22	23
24	25	26	27	28		

March						
S	M	T	W	T	F	S
					1	2
3	4	5	6	7	8	9
10	11	12	13	14	15	16
17	18	19	20	21	22	23
24	25	26	27	28	29	30
31						

April						
S	M	T	W	T	F	S
	1	2	3	4	5	6
7	8	9	10	11	12	13
14	15	16	17	18	19	20
21	22	23	24	25	26	27
28	29	30				

May						
S	M	T	W	T	F	S
			1	2	3	4
5	6	7	8	9	10	11
12	13	14	15	16	17	18
19	20	21	22	23	24	25
26	27	28	29	30	31	

June						
S	M	T	W	T	F	S
						1
2	3	4	5	6	7	8
9	10	11	12	13	14	15
16	17	18	19	20	21	22
23	24	25	26	27	28	29
30						

July						
S	M	T	W	T	F	S
	1	2	3	4	5	6
7	8	9	10	11	12	13
14	15	16	17	18	19	20
21	22	23	24	25	26	27
28	29	30	31			

August						
S	M	T	W	T	F	S
				1	2	3
4	5	6	7	8	9	10
11	12	13	14	15	16	17
18	19	20	21	22	23	24
25	26	27	28	29	30	31

September						
S	M	T	W	T	F	S
1	2	3	4	5	6	7
8	9	10	11	12	13	14
15	16	17	18	19	20	21
22	23	24	25	26	27	28
29	30					

October						
S	M	T	W	T	F	S
		1	2	3	4	5
6	7	8	9	10	11	12
13	14	15	16	17	18	19
20	21	22	23	24	25	26
27	28	29	30	31		

November						
S	M	T	W	T	F	S
					1	2
3	4	5	6	7	8	9
10	11	12	13	14	15	16
17	18	19	20	21	22	23
24	25	26	27	28	29	30

December						
S	M	T	W	T	F	S
1	2	3	4	5	6	7
8	9	10	11	12	13	14
15	16	17	18	19	20	21
22	23	24	25	26	27	28
29	30	31				

7 Listen to the following dialogues and practice them with your partner. Then create new dialogues using the information given.

news	9:15 a.m. – 9:30 a.m.
department store	10 a.m. – 9 p.m.
ballet	6:30 p.m. – 8:00 p.m.
art gallery	8:30 a.m. – 6:15 p.m.
concert	8:00 p.m. – 10:40 p.m.

081 **1**

A What time / When does the **movie start**?

B It **starts** at **three o'clock**.

A What time / When does it end?

B It **ends** at **five thirty**.

082 **2**

A It's **1 a.m.** in London right now. What time is it in **Taipei**?

B It's **eight o'clock** in the **morning** in Taipei.

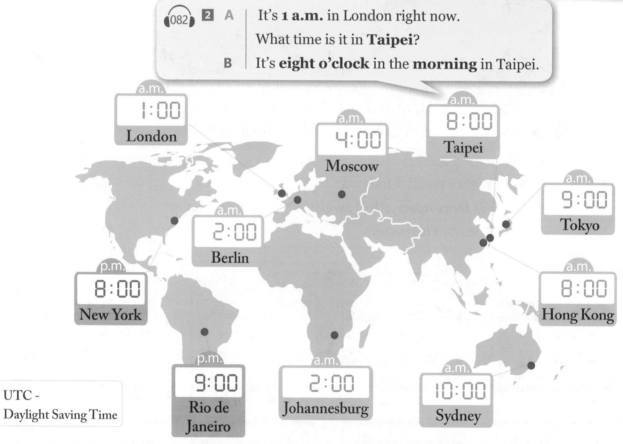

a.m. **1:00** London

a.m. **4:00** Moscow

a.m. **8:00** Taipei

a.m. **9:00** Tokyo

a.m. **2:00** Berlin

p.m. **8:00** New York

a.m. **8:00** Hong Kong

p.m. **9:00** Rio de Janeiro

a.m. **2:00** Johannesburg

a.m. **10:00** Sydney

UTC - Daylight Saving Time

8 Group Work! Use the model below to ask your classmates when their birthdays are. Write the information in the table below.

A When is your birthday?

B October the first. When is yours?

A April the second.

Name : _____
Date : _____

Name : _____
Date : _____

Name : _____
Date : _____

Name : _____
Date : _____

VI. Now, Time to Pronounce!

Review of Voiceless and Voiced Consonants
複習無聲子音和有聲子音

[z] [ð] [s] [θ]

9 Listen and repeat the words you hear.

083

[z]	zoom	rides	hides	toes	zip
[ð]	them	that	brother	together	weather
[s]	smile	sell	miss	seven	voice
[θ]	thin	fourth	north	thumb	mouth

10 Listen and repeat the following sentences. Circle the words that contain the **[z]** sound.

084

The seven wives sell shells by the sea.
Does Delia's Sweet Shop supply toffees?

085 ➡ Listen again and underline the words that contain the **[s]** sound.

11 Listen and repeat the following sentences. Circle the words that contain the **[ð]** sound.

086

My mother's brother is thirty-three.
I hope the weather doesn't thunder on my birthday.

087 ➡ Listen again and underline the words that contain the **[θ]** sound.

12 Plural Nouns

088 Plural nouns end with either [s], [z], or [ɪz].
Listen and repeat what you hear.

[s]	books	cups	cats	shops	coats
[z]	tables	apples	dogs	ears	shoes
[ɪz]	watches	kisses	dresses	boxes	wishes

Make the words into plural nouns and then read them aloud. Then write [s], [z], or [ɪz] in the Pronunciation column.

Word	Plural Form	Pronunciation
1 friend	friends	[z]
2 thing		
3 page		
4 drink		
5 key		
6 match		
7 nose		
8 roof		

Topic Preview (089)

1 Describing the temperature 描述溫度

It's freezing!

It's boiling!

Yes, it's twenty degrees (Fahrenheit)!

It's 100 degrees (Fahrenheit) outside.

2 Describing the weather 描述天氣

What's the weather like in New York?

It's rainy and windy.
What about Bangkok?

Bangkok

New York

The sun is shining, but it's very humid.

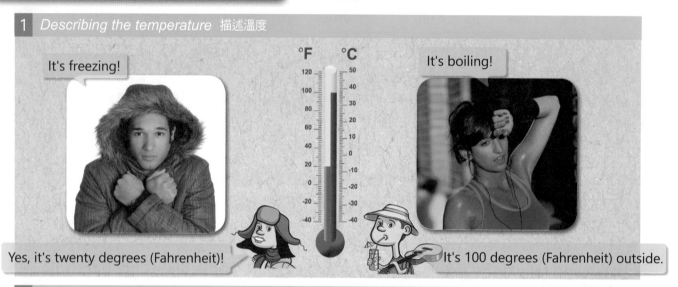

3 Making small talk about the weather 關於天氣的閒聊

This weather is terrible!

I know.
It's awful.

I'm glad I'm wearing a coat.

4 Describing the seasons 描述季節

What's autumn like in England?

It's very pleasant. The weather is cool, and the leaves turn brown. It sometimes rains though.

5 What are you doing in this weather? 這種天氣下你愛做些什麼事？

The weather's beautiful! What are you doing?

I'm sunbathing! You?

I'm eating ice cream!

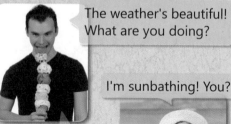

II. Vocabulary & Phrases

sunny 天晴的

cloudy 多雲的

windy 風大的

snowy 下雪的

rainy 下雨的

stormy 暴風雨的

cold 冷的

hot 熱的

humid 潮濕的

cool 涼爽的

warm 溫暖的

spring
春

summer
夏

autumn / fall
秋

winter
冬

Sentence Patterns

- It's very _humid_. / It's so _cold_. / It's _thirty_ degrees.
- What's the weather like?
  It's rainy. / It's raining. / It's sunny. / The sun is shining.
- This weather is _beautiful_!
- I'm glad _I'm wearing a hat_!

- What's _summer_ like in _Florida_?
  The weather is _hot_, and the _sun shines all day long_.
- What are you doing?
  I'm _building a snowman_!

Describing the weather
描述天氣

Using Adjectives	Using Verbs
It's rainy.	It's raining.
It's snowy.	It's snowing.
It's sunny.	The sun is shining.
It's windy.	The wind is blowing.

In the United States, people use Fahrenheit (°F). In other English-speaking countries, people use Celsius (°C).

美國一般使用華氏溫度（°F），其他的英語系國家則使用攝氏溫度（°C）。

$$°F = °C \times \frac{9}{5} + 32$$

$$°C = (°F - 32) \times \frac{5}{9}$$

III. Now, Time to Listen!

1 Listen to the people describing the weather on different days. Match each description to a day of the week.

(092)

1 _____ 2 _____ 3 _____ 4 _____ 5 _____

NEWS 5

WEEKEND FORECAST

| Monday | Tuesday | Wednesday | Thursday | Friday | Saturday | Sunday |

2 Listen to the conversation about the weather. What adjectives does the speaker use to describe each season? Write the adjectives in the table below.

(093)

SPRING   SUMMER   AUTUMN   WINTER
Windy   _____   _____   _____

_____   _____   _____   _____

(094) Now listen again. Listen for the sentences below and fill in the blanks.

_____ like in your country?

It's usually very _____. But every _____ is different.

Sometimes _____, though.

The _____ every day.

What about _____? Is it usually warm or _____?

It's snowy, and the _____ is usually around twenty _____ Fahrenheit.

3 Listen to the following people talking about the weather and what they're doing. Then fill in the table below. The first one has been done for you.

(095)

	Name	Weather	Activity
1	Tina	rainy	
2	Mick		
3	Charles		
4	Sarah		
5	Sam		

IV. Now, Grammar Time!

Present Continuous (be + V-ing) 現在進行式（be 動詞 + 現在分詞）	
Use the present continuous to describe what is happening now. 用現在進行式來說明正在發生的事情。	
Affirmative Sentence 肯定句	I *am* hiding from the rain. You *are* building a snowman!
Negative Sentence 否定句	John *is* not doing homework. The sun *is* not shining.
Yes/No Questions 是非問句	*Is* it snowing outside? *Are* they playing soccer in the rain?

Present Continuous:
Rules for Verb Endings
現在進行式：動詞字尾變化的規則

play	+ ing	play**ing**
run	+ _ ing	run**ning**
die	ie + ying	d**ying**
shine	e + ing	shin**ing**

❹ **Look at the picture and rewrite the sentences below with the correct information.**

Actions you see in the Picture.

 sit

eat

 watch

 sleep

 put on

 talk on the phone

 make

1 ✗ It's raining outside. → O It's snowing outside _____.

2 ✗ The boy is playing in the snow. → O _____.

3 ✗ The man is sitting on his coat. → O _____.

4 ✗ The woman is reading a book. → O _____.

5 ✗ The girl is sleeping on the sofa and making cookies.

→ O _____.

5 Describe the pictures below using the present continuous tense and the prompts given. The first one has been done for you.

1

It's snowing.
snow

2

The sun _____ . shine
The wind _____ . blow

3

_____ . rain
_____ . drive

4

_____ .
fall

5

_____ .
eat

6

_____ .
not rain

7

_____ .
sleep

8

_____ .
sunbathe

V. Now, Time to Speak!

6 Select one sentence from each box to form a 3-sentence dialogue between two people.

A | What's the weather like?
B | This weather is terrible!
A | I'm glad I have my coat.

A
- What's the weather like?
- Wow! What amazing weather!
- Is it raining?
- Oh no. It's cloudy!

B
- I'm glad I'm wearing a T-shirt!
- It's cloudy. But it isn't raining.
- This weather is terrible!
- The sun is shining!

A
- I'm glad I have my coat.
- It's snowing here.
- That's lucky!
- I want to get some ice cream.

7 Listen to the following dialogue and practice it with your partner. Create new dialogues using the information given.

A	What's the weather like in **Paris** today?
B	It's **sunny, but cloudy too.**
A	What's the temperature there?
B	It's **seventy-five** degrees.
A	That's **nice and warm**.

Some extra vocabulary . . . 補充詞彙			
hot 炎熱的 →	boiling 沸騰的	scorching 燒焦的	sweltering 悶熱的
cold 寒冷的 →	freezing 極冷的	icy 冰冷的	frosty 嚴寒的
warm / cool 暖的／涼的 →	pleasant 宜人的	comfortable 舒服的	lovely 美好的

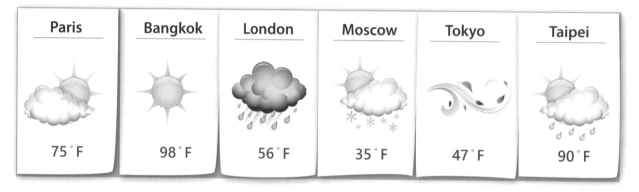

Paris	Bangkok	London	Moscow	Tokyo	Taipei
75°F	98°F	56°F	35°F	47°F	90°F

8 With a partner, take turns asking and answering the following questions. Make more questions by replacing the words in color with ones of your own.

What's spring like in Taiwan?

It's windy in March, but in April it's . . .

What's the weather like today in London?

What's the temperature today in Taipei?

Is it very cold in winter here?

Is it raining today?

VI. Now, Time to Pronounce!

Voiceless Consonants 無聲子音　[ʃ]ᶜ　[tʃ]ᶜ　[h]ᶜ

9 Listen and repeat the words you hear.

(097)

[ʃ]ᶜ　　shoe　　dish　　shine　　ship　　fish

[tʃ]ᶜ　　chip　　pitch　　choose　　chop　　rich

(098) ➡ Listen and circle the words that you hear.

1 shop | chop　**2** ship | chip　**3** shoes | choose　**4** sheep | cheep　**5** shin | chin

10 Listen to the following tongue twisters. Then try to say them as many times as you can and as (099) fast as possible.

Shelly shops at cheap shoe shops.
雪莉在一間便宜的鞋店買鞋。

Charlie the chimp chomps chocolate chips.
黑猩猩查理大嚼巧克力脆片。

11 Listen and repeat the words you hear.

(100)

[h]ᶜ　　help　　hole　　he　　hello　　hair

(101) ➡ Listen to the words. Number them from 1 to 10 in the order that you hear them.

hoot	chap	hot	shell	shoot
happy	watch	chimp	wash	him

Activities 活動

I Topic Preview

 102

1 *Talking about how often/long you do something*
談論做某一件事的頻率和時間

How often do you go to the dentist?

I go every six months.

How long do you work for on Saturdays?

I work for five hours on Saturdays.

2 *Describing your daily routine*
描述每天的例行公事

I wake up at seven o'clock.
I take a bus to work at eight.
At six o'clock in the evening,
I watch TV for an hour. I go to
bed at eleven thirty at night.

3 *Talking about things you do regularly*
談論固定行事

I work every day from 9 a.m. to
5 p.m. On Saturday mornings,
I usually exercise. Sometimes
I take a nap in the afternoon.
I always hang out with my
friends on weekends.

4 *Talking about what you do in your free time*
談論閒暇時間的活動

What do you do in your free time?

I usually go online.
How about you?

I usually go shopping, but sometimes I go to
museums or art galleries.

II. Vocabulary & Phrases

wake up / get up
醒來／起床

brush (one's) teeth
刷牙

**have breakfast /
lunch /dinner /
supper**
吃早餐／午餐／晚餐

get dressed
穿衣服

go to work/school
上班／上學

come home
回家

**go online /
surf the Web**
上網

watch TV 看電視

take a bath/shower
洗澡

listen to music
聽音樂

go shopping
購物

hang out with friends
和朋友出去

exercise
運動

**play the guitar/
piano/violin**
演奏吉他／鋼琴／小提琴

go to bed
就寢

Sentence Patterns

- How often do you *exercise*?
  I *exercise* *twice a week*.
- How long do you *watch TV* (for) *every day*?
  I *watch TV* for *two hours every day*.
- I *take a shower* at *seven thirty*.
  I *have breakfast* at *eight o'clock*.

- I always *play the piano in the afternoon*.
  I usually *go shopping on Saturdays*.
  Sometimes I *listen to music before I go to bed*.
- What do you do in your free time?
  Sometimes I *hang out with friends*. /
  I *usually go online*.

Here are some expressions you can use when talking about how often / how long you do something . . .
以下是常用來表達做事情的頻率或持續時間的用語。

- every day
- once a week
- twice a month
- three times a day
- on Friday afternoons
- thirty minutes
- an hour
- two hours
- a while

1 Listen to James describing his daily routine. Fill in the table below with the missing information.

105

James's Day

Activity	Time
get up	7 : _____ a.m.
have _____	7 : 45 a.m.
go to work	8 : _____ a.m.
come _____	5 : _____ p.m.
have _____	6 : 00 p.m.
have a snack	_____ p.m.
take _____	9 : 30 p.m.
go to _____	10 : 00 p.m.

2 Read the questions below. Then listen again and answer them.

106 **1** What does James do between getting up and having breakfast?
☐ ⓐ Brushes his teeth and gets dressed.
☐ ⓑ Takes a shower.

2 How long does James work for every day?
☐ ⓐ Eight hours.
☐ ⓑ Nine hours.

3 What does James do after he has dinner?
☐ ⓐ Watch TV.
☐ ⓑ Exercise.

4 How often does James play the guitar?
☐ ⓐ Never.
☐ ⓑ Sometimes.

3 Mei Ling wants Peter to teach her English. They are trying to arrange a day to have
107 class. Listen to their conversation and fill in the blanks in their schedules.

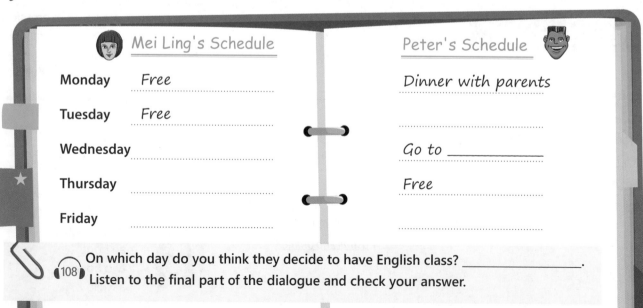

	Mei Ling's Schedule	Peter's Schedule
Monday	Free	Dinner with parents
Tuesday	Free	
Wednesday		Go to _____
Thursday		Free
Friday		

On which day do you think they decide to have English class? _____.
108 Listen to the final part of the dialogue and check your answer.

4 Listen to Polly and Simon discussing what they do in their free time. Match each activity to how often <u>Simon</u> does it.

(109)

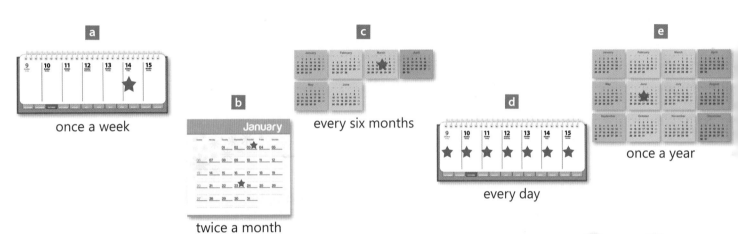

once a week

twice a month

every six months

every day

once a year

(110) Now listen again and fill in the blanks.

Polly	What do you do in your _____, Simon?
Simon	Oh, lots of things. I like to go to the movies.
Polly	Oh, me too. I go about _____ a month.
Simon	I go once a _____! I love the movies. I love music, too. I listen to music _____.
Polly	What about outdoor activities, like camping?
Simon	I do like camping. But I hardly ever go. Maybe _____ a year. So how about you? What do you do in your free time?
Polly	Me? I _____ just hang out with friends. And we go out for a meal maybe _____ a week.
Simon	That's a lot! I hang out with my friends quite often. But we only _____ go out for a meal, maybe twice _____.
Polly	Haha! I think they're embarrassed to go out with you. Your hair is so messy! _____ do you get a haircut? Once every ten years?
Simon	Hey! I get a haircut every six months!

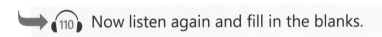

81

IV. Now, Grammar Time!

Asking About Frequency and Duration
詢問事情發生的
頻率與持續時間

Frequency 頻率	Duration 持續時間
• How often do you exercise? 　I exercise once a week.	• How long do you exercise (for)? 　I exercise for two hours.
• How often do you surf the Web? 　I surf the Web three times a day.	• How much time do you spend surf<u>ing</u> the Web <u>each time</u>? 　I spend thirty minutes surfing the Web each time.
• How many times a <u>week</u> do you work at the store?	• How many <u>hours</u> do you work (for) <u>each day</u>?
I work at the store every day.	I work for ten hours each day.

Frequency Adverbs 頻率副詞

100%	always	▸	I **always** brush my teeth in the morning.
	usually	▸	Peter **usually** goes online in the evenings.
	often	▸	She **often** goes camping on the weekend.
	sometimes	▸	We **sometimes** go out for a meal.
	hardly ever	▸	I **hardly ever** go shopping.
0%	never	▸	We **never** exercise.

5 Pair Work! Takes turns asking and answering questions using the prompts. The first one has been done for you.

1 often/ take / shower?

<u>How often do you take a shower?</u>

　I take a shower twice a day.

2 much / time / spend / showering / each time
_____?

　I spend . . .

3 times / week / study English
_____?

　. . .

4 many / hours / study / each time
_____?

　. . .

5 often / take / nap / afternoon
_____?

　. . .

6 long / sleep / each time
_____?

　. . .

7 times / week / exercise
_____?

　. . .

8 much / time / spend / exercising / each time
_____?

　. . .

sometimes and usually

The words "sometimes" and "usually" can also be placed <u>before</u> the subject.

「sometimes」和「usually」也可以放在主詞的前面。

e.g. Usually, Peter goes online in the evenings.

Sometimes we go out for a meal.

6 Rewrite the following sentences using frequency adverbs. The first one has been done for you.

1 I eat breakfast every morning. (**always**)

<u>I always eat breakfast in the morning.</u>

2 I watch TV in the evening four times a week. (**often**)

_____

3 I go camping once a year. (**hardly ever**)

_____

4 I take a shower in the morning twice a week. (**sometimes**)

_____

5 I go to the movies every Saturday. (**always**)

_____

6 I go out for a meal twice a week, but I eat at home five times a week. (**Sometimes, usually**)

_____

7 I go shopping zero times a year. (**never**)

_____

7 Fill in the schedule below with the activities that you do every week. Then use the model to describe your schedule to your partner. Discuss each other's schedule with the class.

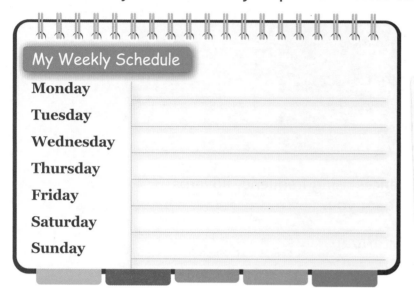

My Weekly Schedule

Monday
Tuesday
Wednesday
Thursday
Friday
Saturday
Sunday

" On Monday I practice the piano after school. On Tuesday evening I hang out with friends. On Wednesday I usually go to the park in the morning for a walk . . . "

8 Ask your partner how often he/she does the following activities. Use the model below to answer.

A | *How often do you take the bus to work?*
B | *I sometimes take the bus to work. I take the bus to work twice a week.*

go abroad for vacation

eat eggs for breakfast

take the bus to work / school

go shopping for new clothes

go out with friends on the weekend

sing in the shower

go to a museum in your free time

go for a picnic on a sunny day

9 Look at Alice's daily routine. Use the model to have a conversation with your partner.

Time	Activity
7:10 - 7:20 a.m.	take a shower
7:45 - 8:00 a.m.	read the newspaper
9:00 a.m. - 6:00 p.m.	work
7:00 - 7:30 p.m.	watch TV
7:45 - 8:15 p.m.	play the piano
8:20 - 9:10 p.m.	go online
9:15 - 10:30 p.m.	read
10:15 - 11:00 p.m.	listen to music

A | *Alice usually reads the newspaper at 7:45.*
B | *How long does she read the newspaper for?*
A | *She reads the newspaper for about fifteen minutes.*

VI. Now, Time to Pronounce!

Voiced Consonants 有聲子音   [ʒ]   [dʒ]   [l]

10 Listen and repeat the words you hear.

111

[ʒ]   television   pleasure   usual   measure

[dʒ]   age   joke   gin   large

112 → Now listen and repeat the following sentences. Then write the underlined words in the correct box.

Jenny usually eats jam before going to the gym.
In July I found some treasure in my garage.

[ʒ]	[dʒ]

11 Listen and repeat the words you hear.

113

[l]   light   long   late   leaf   like

[l]   belt   salt   fool   pale   pull

Pay Attention:
When it comes at the end of a word or before a consonant, [l] can sound a little different from the way it sounds before a vowel. Try to recognize both sounds.
請注意:
「l」位於單字的字尾或子音的前面時,發音會與位於母音前面有些微的不同。試著辨識這兩種發音。

12 Listen to the words. Fill in the blanks with either [ʒ], [dʒ], or [l].

114

❶ [ˋvɪ___ən]   ❷ [___un]   ❸ [ru___]   ❹ [spɪ___]   ❺ [___aɪm]

❻ [ˋ___i___ɚ]   ❼ [ˋbæ___ɚ]   ❽ [___ɪ___i]   ❾ [___ʌ___]   ❿ [fɔ___]

Topic Preview

 115

1 *Talking about sports you play* 談論你所從事的運動

Do you play soccer?
How about tennis?

Yes, I play for my college team.
No, I'm not very good at tennis.

2 *Expressing your sporting ability*
表達你的運動能力

Can you play baseball?
Can you play ice hockey?

No, I can't. I can't hit the ball!
Yes, I can. I'm good at ice hockey.

3 *Describing athletes* 描述運動員

 Kobe Bryant is a professional basketball player.

 Which team does he play for?

 He plays for the Los Angeles Lakers.

4 *Saying which team you support* 說出你支持的隊伍

Which soccer team do you support?

I support Manchester United.

Me too!

5 *Saying what you think about a sport*
談論你對一項運動的看法

Tennis is so easy.
Soccer is a very competitive sport.
I think surfing is really exciting.

II. Vocabulary & Phrases (116)

basketball 籃球　**swimming** 游泳　**baseball** 棒球　**golf** 高爾夫球　**hockey** 曲棍球　**soccer** 足球　**tennis** 網球

cycling 騎自行車　**surfing** 衝浪　**American football** 美式足球　**rowing** 划船　**a professional athlete** 職業運動員　**play for a team** 效力於某隊伍　**play for fun** 為休閒而運動　**support a team** 支持某支隊伍

Talking about sports 談論運動

Noun 名詞	Verb 動詞	Athlete 運動員
basketball / soccer / baseball / hockey / tennis	play basketball	basketball player
rowing / swimming / surfing	row / swim / surf	rower / swimmer / surfer
golf	play golf	golfer
cycling	cycle	cyclist

Sentence Patterns (117)

- Do you *play baseball*? Yes, I play for *my school team*. / No. I don't.
- Can you *swim*? Yes, I can *swim*. / No, I can't.
- I can't *surf*. I always *fall off*!
- I can't *play American football*. I can't *catch the ball*.

- *David Beckham* is a *great soccer player*.
- Which team does Tim *play* for? He *plays* for the *Bears*.
- Which *basketball* team do you *support*? I *support* *the New York Nicks*.
- *Tennis* is so *easy*. / *Basketball* is a very *competitive* sport. / I think *baseball* is really *hard*.

Verbs Used With Sports
運動常用動詞

shoot the ball 射籃

miss the shot 沒進

score 得分

hit the ball 擊球

miss the ball 撲球失敗

catch the ball 接球

drop the ball 漏接

win the game 獲勝

1 Listen to the conversations about sports. Then match each one to the picture that best illustrates it. (118)

1 _____ **2** _____ **3** _____ **4** _____ **5** _____

 a

 b

 c

 d

 e

➡ (119) Now listen again and fill in the blanks.

1 A | _____ you play golf?
B | _____.
A | Do you play often?
B | Yes, I _____ every Saturday.

2 A | Does Matt play basketball?
B | Yes, he's an excellent basketball player.
A | Is he a _____?
B | No, he only plays _____.

3 A | Do you know my friend Simon?
B | No, what does he do?
A | He's a professional _____.
B | Which _____ does he play for?
A | He plays for the Michigan Monsters.

4 A | _____ golf?
B | No, _____.
It's too _____.
I always _____ the ball!

5 A | _____ hockey team do you _____?
B | Italy. It's the team wearing green.

88

2 Listen to the following people talking about their teams. Fill in the table below with the missing information. Use the words in the box to help you.

120

| basketball | Toronto Devils | France | Chicago Bulls |
| hockey | cycling | United States | rowing |

Name	Sport	Athlete / Supporter		Team
Sam		☐	☐	
Abby		☐	☐	
Lucy		☐	☐	
David		☐	☐	

121 Now listen one more time. Listen for the following phrases and correct the mistakes.

1 I am a rower and I play for the United States.

2 I don't play, but I always watch it on TV.

3 I run to work every day, but I'm not a professional runner.

4 Which team do I support ?

3 Listen to the conversation between Fred and Mindy. Then write the correct names in the spaces.

122

1 _____ thinks surfing is too hard. He/She can't stand up on the board.

2 _____ thinks surfing is easy.

3 _____ can't play tennis. He/She always misses the ball.

4 _____ can play tennis, but he/she only sometimes hits the ball.

IV. Now, Grammar Time!

Modal Auxiliary Verbs: Can
情態助動詞 *can*

Use "can" to express ability 用 **can** 來表示能力		
Affirmative Statements 肯定句	Negative Statements 否定句	Yes/No Questions 是非問句
Mary **can** play hockey. Darren **can** dance.	Mary **can't** play hockey. Darren **can't** dance.	Can Mary play hockey? Yes, she can. Can Darren dance? No, he can't.

4 Pair work. Look at the pictures below. Ask and answer questions using "can."

A	Can he play soccer?
B	Yes, he can.
A	Can she play soccer?
B	No, she can't.

play soccer

catch the ball

speak Chinese

hit the ball

swim

Which [noun] . . . ? Which 名詞……?	
Use "Which [noun] . . . ?" when you have a limited number of choices in mind. 當你已經預設了幾個選項的時候，可以用「Which 名詞……？」的句型	

Questions about the predicate 關於述語的問句		Questions about the subject 關於主詞的問句
I can play hockey and tennis. → **Which sports** can you **play?**	I support England. → **Which team do** you **support,** England or France?	David Beckham is a soccer player. → **Which athlete** is a soccer player, David Beckham or Kobe Bryant?
He is from France. → **Which country** is he from?	He wants the red shirt. → **Which shirt does** he want?	Baseball uses a bat and a ball. → **Which sport** uses a bat and a ball?

5 Look at the answers on the right. Write questions with "Which [noun]" about the words in bold.

1 <u>Which team do you play for</u> _____ ? I play for **the Taipei Tigers**.

2 _____ ? **The United States** is wearing red.

3 _____ ? I can speak **Chinese and French**.

4 _____ ? I play **soccer and baseball** at school.

5 _____ ? **American football** is from the United States.

More Sports
更多運動

bowling
保齡球

boxing
拳擊

ice-skating
溜冰

dancing
跳舞

skiing
滑雪

cricket
板球

volleyball
排球

table tennis
桌球

motor racing
賽車

6 Group Work! Fill in the table with sports you CAN'T play. Try to find a classmate who CAN play that sport. Use the model to help you.

Sports you CAN'T play	Classmates who CAN
❶	
❷	
❸	
❹	
❺	
❻	

A | Can you play baseball, James?

B | Yes, I can.

➤ Now report your findings to the class. Use the model below.

I can't play baseball, but James can.

7 Practice dialogues A and B with a partner. Then have similar conversations by replacing the words in **bold** with ones of your own.

A

A | Which sports do you play?

B | I **play baseball**. I'm quite good at it, too.

A | Do you **play baseball** for a team?

B | Yes, I **play baseball** for *the Boston Red Sox*.

Some possible team names . . .

The Chicago Bulls

The Houston Rockets

The New York Yankees

The San Francisco Giant

The Dallas Cowboys

The Pittsburgh Stealers

Manchester United

Real Madrid

B

A | Can you **play hockey**?

B | No, I can't. I can't **hit the puck**, and I always **fall over**.
 I watch it on TV though.

A | Which team do you support?

B | I support the *Los Angeles Kings*.

Some verbs for sports . . . 運動常用動詞

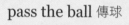

pass the ball 傳球	serve the ball 發球	pitch 投球	dribble 運球；盤球
tackle （橄欖球）擒抱；（足球）鏟球	keep one's balance 保持平衡	foul 犯規	fall over 跌倒

8 **Look at the athletes below. Choose one and describe him/her to a partner.**

A | He's a professional soccer player. He plays soccer for Paris Saint-Germain.
 He can **shoot the ball** very <u>accurately</u>.

B | Is it **David Beckham**?

A | Yes, it is.

Mercedes

Michael Schumacher
drive car / fast

Yani Tseng
hit the ball / far

Roger Federer
serve the ball / well

Miami Heat

Toronto Blue Jays

Chien-Ming Wang
pitch the ball / straight

Paris Saint-Germain

David Beckham
shoot the ball / accurately

LeBron James
jump / high

92

VI. Now, Time to Pronounce!

How to pronounce "can" and "can't"
can 與 can't 的發音

9 Listen and repeat the words you hear.

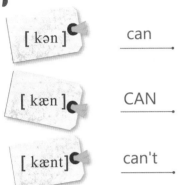

[kən] can

[kæn] CAN

[kænt] can't

➡ 124 We use [kæn] when we want to add emphasis. Listen to the dialogue.
Pay attention to the underlined words.

A	What sports can you play?
B	I **can** play soccer and volleyball.
A	You can't play soccer!
B	I **CAN** play soccer!

➡ 125 Did you hear the difference?
Did you hear [kən], [kæn], or [kænt]? Check ☑ the correct box.

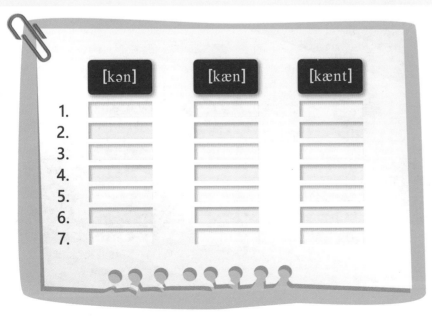

	[kən]	[kæn]	[kænt]
1.			
2.			
3.			
4.			
5.			
6.			
7.			

Identifying and Describing Objects
辨識與描述物品

Topic Preview

 126

---

1 *Describing something that is lost/stolen* 描述遺失或被偷的物品

Oh no! I can't find my wallet!

My camera! It's gone!

Where's my phone? It's not here.

---

2 *Describing what color something is* 描述物品的顏色

What color is your camera?

It's blue and white.

3 *Describing something's size/shape*
描述物品的大小與形狀

How big is your phone? Is it slim or bulky?

It's quite small, about ten centimeters long. It's slim. And it's square, too.

---

4 *Describing something in detail* 描述物品的細節

What does your wallet look like?

It's a small, black leather wallet with a red dragon on the front.

5 *Saying whom something belongs to*
說明物品的所有人

Whose mug is this? It's white and heart-shaped.

What does it look like? Oh! It's mine!

II. Vocabulary & Phrases

round 圓的

square 方的

heart-shaped 心形的

slim 纖細的

bulky 笨重的

leather 皮革製的

plastic 塑膠製的

metal 金屬製的

wooden 木製的

woolen 羊毛的

retro 復古的

new 新的   **old** 舊的

small 小的   **big** 大的

Sentence Patterns

- Oh no! I can't find my *purse*! / My *suitcase*! It's gone!
  Where are my *glasses*?
  They're not here.
- What color is your *bag*?
  It's *blue*.
- How big is your *suitcase*?
  It's quite *big*, about *ninety* *centimeters* tall/long/wide.
- Is it *square*?
  Yes, it's *square* and *bulky*.

- What does your *mug* look like?
  It's a *red*, *heart-shaped* *mug* with *my name* on the side/front/back/top/bottom.
- Whose *watch* is this?
  It's *mine*.
- Whose *glasses* are these?
  They're Tony's.

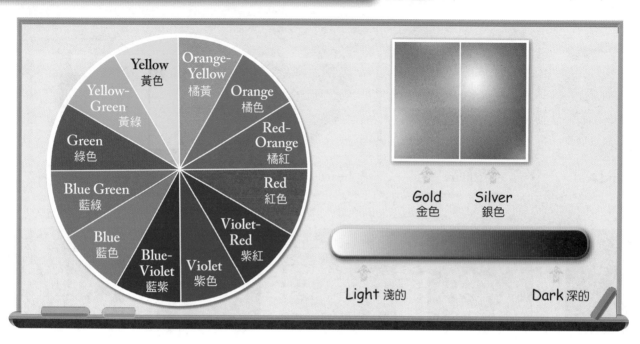

① Listen to the people describing their belongings. Choose the object they're describing and write the adjectives you hear in the box on the right.

2 Emma can't find her purse. Listen to the conversation and check ☑ what Emma says.

(130)

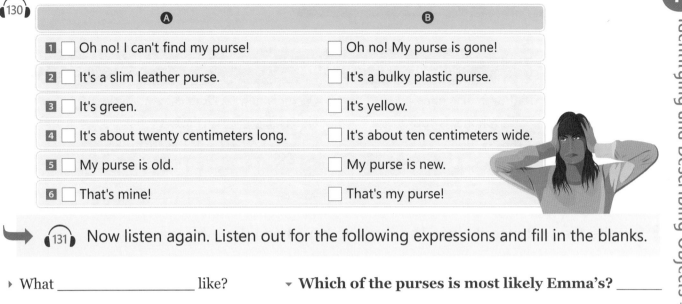

	A	**B**
1	☐ Oh no! I can't find my purse!	☐ Oh no! My purse is gone!
2	☐ It's a slim leather purse.	☐ It's a bulky plastic purse.
3	☐ It's green.	☐ It's yellow.
4	☐ It's about twenty centimeters long.	☐ It's about ten centimeters wide.
5	☐ My purse is old.	☐ My purse is new.
6	☐ That's mine!	☐ That's my purse!

➡ (131) Now listen again. Listen out for the following expressions and fill in the blanks.

▸ What _____ like?

▸ What _____ it?

▸ How _____ it?

▸ _____ your purse?

▸ No, that's _____.

▾ **Which of the purses is most likely Emma's?** _____

a b c d e

3 Listen to Ella and Roy discussing their belongings. Write the correct person's name under each object.

(132)

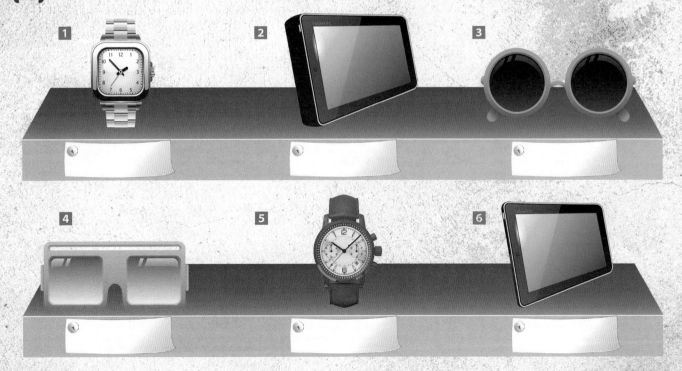

1 2 3

4 5 6

IV. Now, Grammar Time!

Possessive Pronouns 所有格代名詞	
That's _my watch_. ➡ That (watch) is mine. This is _your phone_. ➡ This (phone) is yours. They're _his glasses_. ➡ They're his. _Her camera_ is blue. ➡ Hers is blue.	_Our car_ is new. ➡ Ours is new. Fido is _their dog_. ➡ Fido is theirs. Is this _Jerry's bag_? ➡ Is this (bag) Jerry's?

4 Rewrite the sentences below. The first two have been done for you.

1. Is this your pen? ➡ <u>Is this pen yours?</u>

2. These books are hers. ➡ <u>These are her books.</u>

3. Is this mug mine? ➡ _____

4. This is Polly's cat. ➡ _____

5. Are these his glasses? ➡ _____

6. I think that's my coat. ➡ _____

7. This CD is not Mary's. ➡ _____

8. Your friend is also my friend. ➡ _____

9. Our phones are slim and black. ➡ _____

10. This is their car. ➡ _____

Adjective Order 形容詞的順序	Opinion 評價	Size 尺寸	Age 年齡	Shape 形狀	Color 顏色	Origin 來源	Material 材質	Noun 名詞
	beautiful		new		purple		leather	bag
		slim			brown	Italian		wallet
	cool	big		round				sunglasses
			antique				metal	mug

98

5 Put these adjectives in the correct boxes.

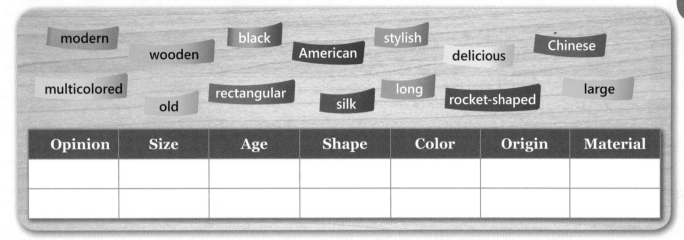

modern wooden black American stylish delicious Chinese multicolored old rectangular silk long rocket-shaped large

Opinion	Size	Age	Shape	Color	Origin	Material

➥ Pair Work. Take turns describing the following objects to your partner.

Where's my
This is my
Whose
Look at my

+ adjective(s) + noun +

?
.
is this?
.

1 flag

2 scarf

3 dress

4 clock

5 ice pop

V. Now, Time to Speak!

6 Pair Work! With a partner, try to fill in the blanks in the following short dialogue. Discuss your answers with the class. Then practice the dialogue with your partner.

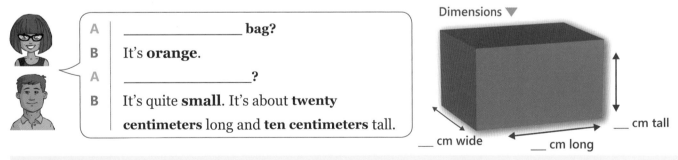

A | _____ bag?
B | It's **orange**.
A | _____ ?
B | It's quite **small**. It's about **twenty centimeters** long and **ten centimeters** tall.

Dimensions ▼

__ cm tall
__ cm wide
__ cm long

➥ Now look at the pictures below and create similar conversations.

suitcase

hat

package

book

7 Listen to the dialogue and practice it with a partner.

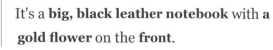

A	Oh no! I can't find my **notebook**!
B	What does it look like?
A	It's a **big, black leather notebook** with **a gold flower** on the **front**.

Locations ▼

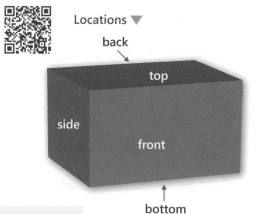

back

top

side

front

bottom

➤ Now make up similar conversations by replacing the words in bold with ones of your own. Use the pictures below to help you.

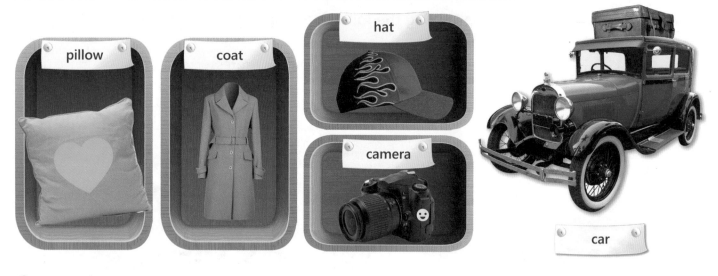

pillow

coat

hat

camera

car

8 Group work! Choose some of your belongings and write them down in the table. Compare your belongings with those of your classmates. Fill in the table with the information they give you.

| A | My phone is bulky and old. How about yours, Peter? |
| B | Mine is slim and new. |

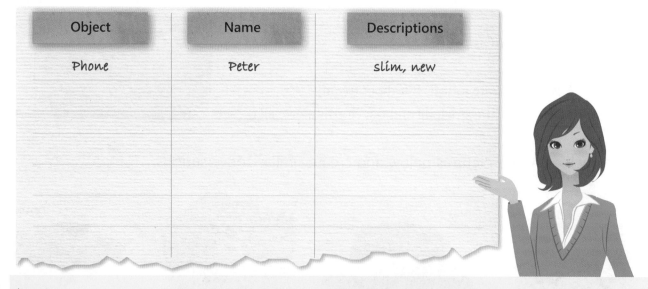

Object	Name	Descriptions
Phone	Peter	slim, new

➤ Now report your findings to the class.

VI Now, Time to Pronounce!

Review of Voiceless and Voiced Consonants
複習無聲子音和有聲子音

9 Listen and repeat the words you hear.

(134) **Voiceless Consonants**

[ʃ]	wish	shop	cash	shape	shell

[tʃ]	chain	which	chair	chart	chick

[h]	hole	hat	high	happy	horse

10 Listen and repeat the words you hear.

(135) **Voiced Consonants**

[ʒ]	beige	garage	Persia	casual	visual

[dʒ]	page	jail	jelly	juice	edge

[l]	lace	light	lamp	lily	long

11 Listen to the words. Number them from 1 to 10 in the order that you hear them.

(136)

age	Asia	leech	lair	hill
pleasure	pledge	chair	leash	chill

Apologizing 道歉

Topic Preview

1 Saying you're sorry and accepting an apology 向人道歉與接受道歉

I'm so sorry for breaking your mug.

I'm really sorry for keeping you waiting.

Oh, don't worry. I can get a new one.

That's OK.

2 Apologizing for something serious 為嚴重的事情道歉

You really hurt my feelings.

Please forgive me. I promise not to do it again. I'm so sorry for upsetting you.

3 Turning down an invitation 拒絕他人的邀約

Sorry, Jill. I can't see you later because I'm really busy at work.

Thank you for the invitation, but I'm not feeling very well.

I don't think I can make it. I have plans that night. Sorry to turn you down.

II. Vocabulary & Phrases (138)

upset someone
讓某人心煩

break something
打破某物

keep someone waiting
讓某人等

forget something
忘記某件事

bother someone
打擾某人

give someone bad news
告知某人壞消息

be late 遲到

spill something
打翻某物

insult someone
羞辱某人

lose something
遺失某物

make a mistake
犯錯

call so late/early
太晚／太早打電話

interrupt someone / something
打斷某個人／某件事

forgive someone
原諒某人

turn someone down
拒絕某人

Sentence Patterns (139)

Offering an Apology 向人道歉		Accepting an Apology 接受道歉
I'm sorry to interrupt your meeting.	That's OK.	
I'm sorry for losing your keys.	Don't worry about it.	
Sorry to keep you waiting.	No problem.	
Sorry for breaking your camera.	That's all right.	
I want to apologize for insulting you.	I accept your apology.	
Sorry. My mistake.	It happens.	
I'm terribly sorry!	Don't feel bad.	
Please forgive me for spilling coffee on you.	Just don't let it happen again.	

- I can't *come for lunch* because *I'm really busy at work*.
- Thank you for the invitation, but *I'm not feeling very well*.
- I don't think I can make it. I *have plans that night*.

1 Listen to the people offering apologies. Match each conversation with the picture that best illustrates it.

(140)

1 _____   2 _____   3 _____   4 _____   5 _____

(141) Now listen again and fill in the blanks.

1 A | Sorry to _____ your phone call, but I need to ask you a question.

B | _____. Go ahead.

2 A | _____ for being late to class, Mrs. King.

B | That's all right. Just don't let it _____.

3 A | Do you want to go out for dinner with me later?

B | Oh no! I can't. I have plans. Sorry to _____.

A | Don't _____. Maybe we can go out another time.

4 A | Mr. Fredrick, I want to _____ making a mistake in my report.

B | _____ your apology, but you need to be more careful next time.

5 A | I'm so sorry for _____ your birthday, Sandra.

B | It happens. _____.

2 Listen to the conversation between Mary and Bill. Check ☑ true or false.

(142)

True	False	
_____	_____	**1** Bill wants to apologize to Mary.
_____	_____	**2** Bill is angry.
_____	_____	**3** Bill accepts the apology.
_____	_____	**4** Mary asks Bill out for lunch.
_____	_____	**5** Bill accepts the invitation.

I am Sorry

143 ➡ Listen one more time. Listen for the following expressions and correct the sentences. The first one has been done for you.

1 Bill, sorry to ~~interrupt~~ you.
     bother

2 I want to say "sorry" for losing your mug.

3 Oh, that's OK. No problem.

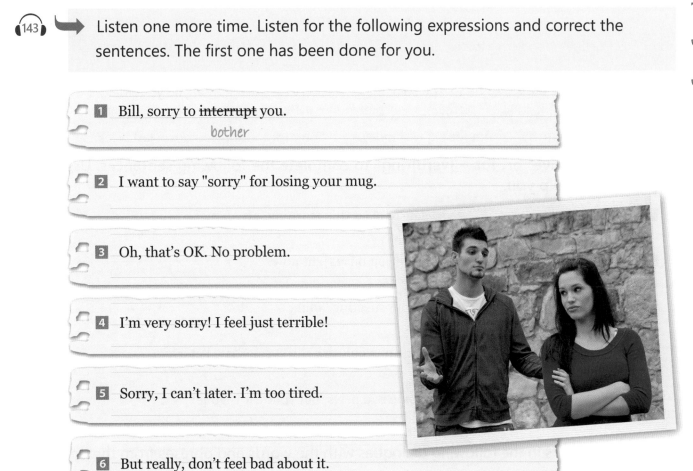

4 I'm very sorry! I feel just terrible!

5 Sorry, I can't later. I'm too tired.

6 But really, don't feel bad about it.

3 Listen to the first half of each conversation, then match each one to the most
144 appropriate response.

1

2

3

4

5

• [a] I understand. Thanks for letting me know.

• [b] Don't feel bad! I forgive you.

• [c] I accept your apology. But you really hurt my feelings.

• [d] That's all right. What's the problem?

• [e] Sorry, I can't. I don't feel very well.

"Sorry + to-infinitive" or "Sorry for + [verb]-ing" 「Sorry + 不定詞」或「Sorry + 動名詞」	
Use "sorry + to-infinitive" to apologize for the current situation. 用「sorry + 不定詞」為當前狀況致歉	Use "sorry for + [verb]-ing" to apologize for things in the past. 用「sorry + 動名詞」為過去的事致歉
• Sorry to interrupt you, but I need to ask you something.	• Sorry for interrupting you yesterday.
• Sorry to call you so late. Are you busy now?	• Sorry for calling you so late last night.
• Sorry to turn you down, but I'm not feeling well today.	• Sorry for turning you down last week.

4 Use "to-infinitive" or "for + [verb]-ing" to complete the following sentences. Use the prompts to help you.

1 I'm sorry _____ late to class this morning, Mr. James.
   (be)

2 Sorry _____ you. Are you busy right now?
   (bother)

3 I'm so sorry _____ our meeting, John.
   (forget)

4 I'm sorry _____ wine on your new shirt yesterday, Peter.
   (spill)

5 Sorry _____ you some bad news, but your car is gone!
   (give)

5 Fill in the blanks in the following dialogues with the words and phrases from the box.

to correct	to shout	for interrupting	to interrupt	for shouting	for correcting	Online ✓

1 I'm sorry _____ you earlier, Lisa. You're right. Father's Day is tomorrow, not today.

That's all right, Mr. Smith. Everyone makes mistakes.

2 Sorry _____, Ben. I just want to apologize for losing your report.

That's OK. I'm sorry _____ at you earlier, too.

3 Sorry _____ you in the meeting, Jim.

Don't worry about it. I was talking too much anyway.

4 Today is Tuesday, March twenty-fifth.

Sorry _____ you, but it's the twenty-sixth.

5 I'm sorry_____, but it's very loud in here.

Sorry, I still can't hear you.

6 Look at the pictures below. Select one sentence from each box to form a 3-sentence dialogue between two people.

A | I feel terrible. Please forgive me.
B | Don't feel bad. I accept your apology.
A | Can I take you to dinner to apologize?

A
- Can you come to my party tonight?
- I'm sorry for losing your camera.
- I feel terrible. Please forgive me.
- I want to apologize for upsetting you.

B
- That's all right. It happens.
- I forgive you. Just don't let it happen again.
- Sorry, I can't. I'm not feeling well today.
- Don't feel bad. I accept your apology.

A
- I promise to be more careful next time.
- OK. Don't worry about it.
- Can I take you to dinner to apologize?
- Here's a gift to say I'm sorry.

7 With a partner, practice offering and accepting apologies for the situations below. Use what you learned in the Sentence Patterns section to help you.

VI. Now, Time to Pronounce!

The Different Pronunciations of "The"
the 的不同發音

8 Listen and repeat the different pronunciations of "the."

(145)

Before a consonant sound 在子音之前 [ðə]

the man　　the film　　the desk　　the report　　the chair

Before a vowel sound 在母音之前 [ði]

the hour　　the idea　　the eye　　the athlete　　the egg

9 Listen to each word and circle (C) if it starts with a consonant sound or (V) if it
(146) starts with a vowel sound. Then fill in the blanks with the correct phonetic symbols:
[ðə] or [ði].

1 [_____] onion	**2** [_____] elephant	**3** [_____] day	**4** [_____] omelet	**5** [_____] peach
(C)(V)	(C)(V)	(C)(V)	(C)(V)	(C)(V)
6 [_____] orange	**7** [_____] people	**8** [_____] gift	**9** [_____] ape	**10** [_____] inside
(C)(V)	(C)(V)	(C)(V)	(C)(V)	(C)(V)

(147)   Now listen and check your answers.

Asking for and Giving Directions
詢問與指引方向

Topic Preview

1 *Asking for and giving directions* 詢問與指引方向

Excuse me. I'm looking for the City Hotel.

Go straight for two blocks. Then turn right onto George Street. The hotel is on your left.

I'm trying to find the Royal Bank. Do you know where it is?

Do you know how to get to the train station from here?

Take the first left. Walk straight to Bond Street. And it's across the street.

Take the second left. Then go along Kent Road for about 200 meters. It's opposite the post office.

2 *Not being able to give directions* 無法指引方向

I'm sorry, but I don't know this area very well.

Sorry. I'm not from here.

3 *Suggesting a means of transportation* 建議交通方式

Excuse me. How do I get to the airport from here?

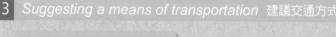 

The airport? You can take a taxi or bus number 5. It's about 30 minutes away.

II. Vocabulary & Phrases

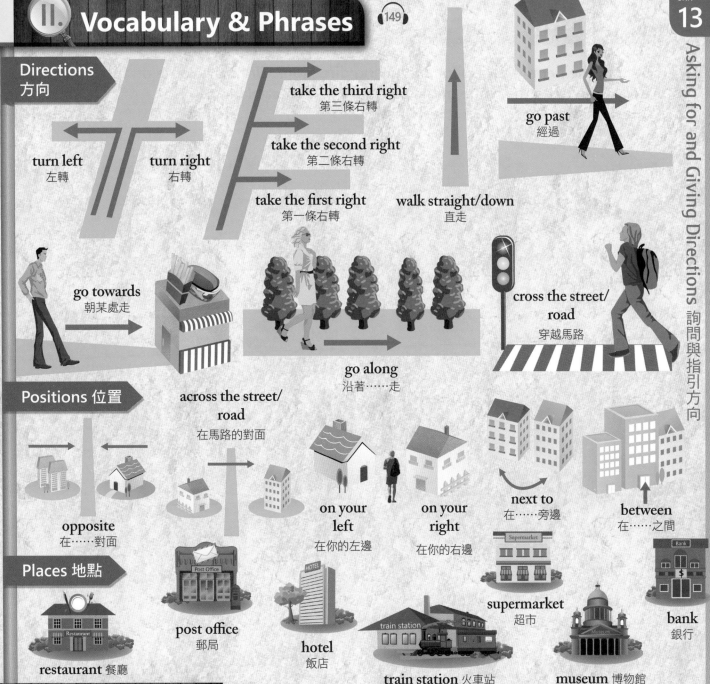

Directions 方向

take the third right
第三條右轉

take the second right
第二條右轉

take the first right
第一條右轉

turn left
左轉

turn right
右轉

walk straight/down
直走

go past
經過

go towards
朝某處走

cross the street/
road
穿越馬路

go along
沿著……走

Positions 位置

across the street/
road
在馬路的對面

opposite
在……對面

on your
left
在你的左邊

on your
right
在你的右邊

next to
在……旁邊

between
在……之間

Places 地點

post office
郵局

hotel
飯店

supermarket
超市

bank
銀行

restaurant 餐廳

train station 火車站

museum 博物館

Sentence Patterns

- I'm looking for the _bank_. /
  Do you know how to get to the _museum_ from here? /
  I'm trying to find the _train station_. Do you know where it is?
- Go straight (down _Peter Street_) for _two blocks_ to _Charles Street_.
- Turn _right_ onto _Charles Street_.
- Take the _second left_.
- Walk towards _the bank_.

- Go past the _train station_.
- The hotel is _on your left_. /
  The _restaurant_ is _opposite_ the _bank_. /
  The _post office_ is _next to_ the _supermarket_.
- I don't know this area very well. /
  I'm not from here.
- Take _bus number 47_. It's about _20 minutes_ away.

Now, Time to Listen!

1 Listen to the people asking for and giving directions. Draw the route on the map as you listen. Then write the name of the place in the correct blank.

151

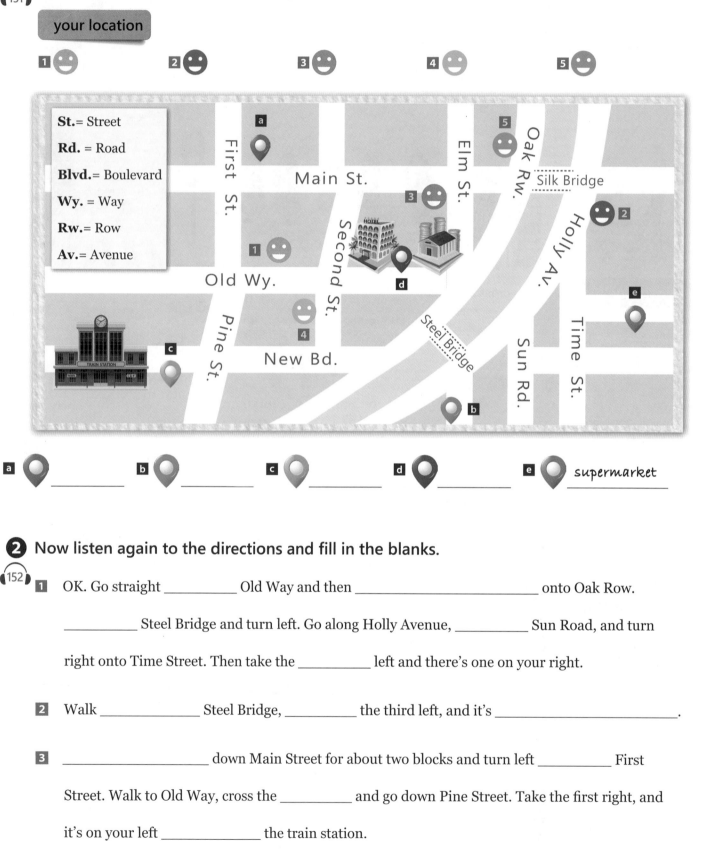

St. = Street
Rd. = Road
Blvd. = Boulevard
Wy. = Way
Rw. = Row
Av. = Avenue

a _____   b _____   c _____   d _____   e _supermarket_

2 Now listen again to the directions and fill in the blanks.

152

1 OK. Go straight _____ Old Way and then _____ onto Oak Row. _____ Steel Bridge and turn left. Go along Holly Avenue, _____ Sun Road, and turn right onto Time Street. Then take the _____ left and there's one on your right.

2 Walk _____ Steel Bridge, _____ the third left, and it's _____.

3 _____ down Main Street for about two blocks and turn left _____ First Street. Walk to Old Way, cross the _____ and go down Pine Street. Take the first right, and it's on your left _____ the train station.

4 Walk down this _____, Second Street, to Main Street. _____, walk for

one _____, and it's on your right.

5 Go _____ Oak Row for about 200 _____. Turn right onto Old Way.

Go straight on Old Way for about half a block, and the museum is _____ right.

It's _____ a big hotel and a bank.

Transportation 交通工具

take a bus 搭公車　　take a taxi 搭計程車　　take a train 搭火車　　walk 走路

3 Listen to the following conversations. Match each place with the picture that best
illustrates how to get there.

153

1　　2　　3　　4　　5

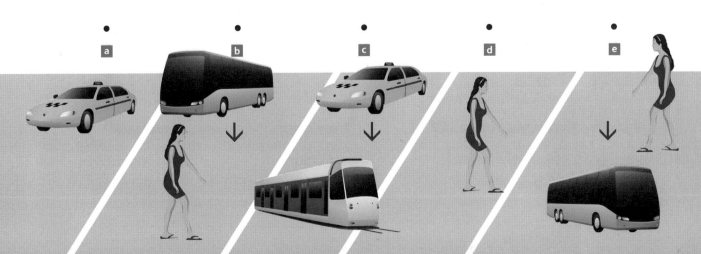

a　　b　　c　　d　　e

IV. Now, Grammar Time!

Prepositions Used With Directions 用來描述方向的介系詞	
at	Turn right at the end of the street.
on	The bank is on your left.
to	Go straight to Church Boulevard and turn left.
onto	Turn left onto Old Kent Road.
between	The post office is between the bank and the restaurant.
next to	The hotel is next to the park.
opposite	The restaurant is opposite the train station.
down	Walk down this road for five minutes.
towards	Walk towards Taipei 101, and take the second left.
past	Go past the museum. Then take a right.

4 Look at the pictures and complete the sentences using the correct prepositions. The first one has been done for you.

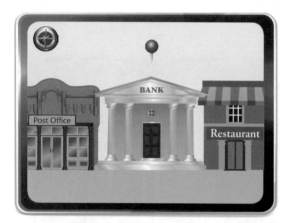

1 The bank is <u>between the post office and the restaurant.</u>

2 The supermarket is _____ the hotel.

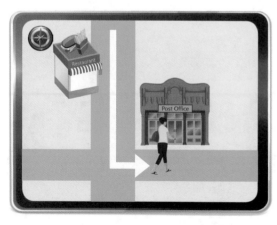

3 Walk _____ the restaurant and turn left _____ the post office.

4 Go straight _____ Church Street. Then turn right _____ Main Street.

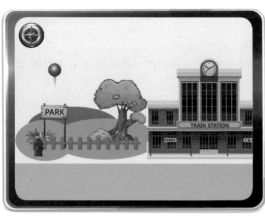

5 The park is _____ the train station.

6 Walk _____ the hotel. The supermarket is _____ your left.

Imperatives
祇使語氣

| Use imperatives to give directions or instructions 用祇使語氣來指引方向或下指令 ||
Affirmative Sentences 肯定句	Negative Sentences 否定句
Take the first left.	Don't take the first left.
Turn right at the end of the street.	Don't turn right.
Go straight for five minutes.	Don't go straight.
Take a bus to Peter St. Then walk to the hotel.	Don't take a bus.

5 Match each sentence with the correct picture.

1 ☐ Take the second right.

2 ☐ Don't take a taxi to the airport.

3 ☐ Take bus number 10 to the museum.

4 ☐ Don't walk to the zoo. It's too far.

5 ☐ Go straight down Duke Street.

a b c

d e

V. Now, Time to Speak!

6 Pair Work! Ask for and give directions to the places on the map! Use the model to help you.

A *Excuse me. Do you know how to get to the bus station from here (Delicious Dan's Restaurant)?*

B Yes, I do. Go straight to Oak Row. Turn Right. Go along Oak Row for about 300 meters. The bus station is on your right opposite Steel Bridge.

First St.   Main St.   Elm St.   Oak Rw.   Silk Bridge   Holly Av.   Second St.   Old Wy.   Time St.   Pine St.   Steel Bridge   Sun Rd.   New Bd.

Central Bank   Post Office   Delicious Dan's Restaurant   Rich Hotel

History Museum   Supermarket   Bus Station

7 Listen to the following conversation and practice it with your partner. Then use the prompts to have similar conversations.

(154)

A *Excuse me. How do I get to the zoo from here?*

B Take bus number 34 to Bishop Road. It's about thirty minutes away. Then walk for about five minutes to get to the zoo.

ZOO

🚌 bus 34 ⇨ Bishop Road (30 minutes)
🚶 walk ⇨ zoo (5 minutes)

1 department store

🚶 walk ⇨ bus station (2 minutes)
🚌 bus 453 ⇨ department store (20 minutes)

2 airport

🚕 taxi ⇨ train station (15 minutes)
🚆 train ⇨ airport (1 hour)

3 theater

🚕 taxi ⇨ theater (10 minutes)

4 city center

🚌 bus 35 ⇨ Bond Street (5 minutes)
🚌 bus 569 ⇨ city center (40 minutes)

VI. Now, Time to Pronounce!

Voiced Consonants 有聲子音 [m] [n] [ŋ] [j] [w] [r]

8 Listen and repeat the words you hear.

🎧155

[m]	meet	may	moan	mute	mine
	team	swim	ham	time	dream

[n]	gnome	never	knight	nail	note
	pants	then	train	sign	bin

[ŋ]	sing	ring	drink	thing	wink

Pay Attention :

When they come at the end of a word or before a consonant, [m], [n], and [r] can sound a little different to the way they sound before a vowel. Make sure you can recognize both sounds.

🎧156 ➡ Listen and circle the words that you hear.

1 kin | king **2** gnat | mat **3** run | rum **4** sun | sung **5** win | whim

6 knit | mitt **7** pin | ping **8** tan | tang **9** need | mead **10** nice | mice

9 Listen and repeat the words you hear.

🎧157

[j]	you	yellow	yuck	yawn	year

[w]	what	when	win	want	swim

[r]	read	rim	reel	rain	from
	bar	party	market	chart	shark

🎧158 ➡ Listen to the words. Do you hear [j], [w], or [r]? Check ☑ the box that corresponds to the sound you hear.

	[j]	[w]	[r]
1.			
2.			
3.			
4.			
5.			
6.			
7.			
8.			
9.			
10.			

Asking for and Giving Instructions
詢問與提供指示

Topic Preview

1 Asking for instructions 請求指示

Can you show me how to send an email?

How do you make orange juice?

Sure, no problem. First ...

Well. First ...

2 Giving step-by-step instructions 提供逐步指示

First click on "compose." Then write the person's email address here. Next ...

First warm some milk in a pan. Then you have to stir in the chocolate. Next ...

3 Emphasizing something important 強調重要事項

Don't forget to check the address before you press send.

You must wash your hands after you touch raw chicken.

4 Asking people if they understand 詢問對方是否明白

Do you understand?   Yes. I do.

Is that clear?   Sorry. I still don't understand.

II. Vocabulary & Phrases 🎧160

then
接著；然後

next
接下來

after that
之後

first
第一

finally
最後

**send an email /
a text message**
寄電子郵件／傳簡訊

**click on / select /
type**
點擊／選取／打字

**brainstorm / plan /
revise**
集思廣益／計畫／修改

cook/make a dish
做菜

 fry 炸   **boil** 煮

 bake 烘；烤   **cut** 切

 spread
塗抹

work a machine
操作機器

 press 壓按   **plug in** 插電

 turn on 開啟    **remote**
遙控的

**read the
instruction
manual**
閱讀操作手冊

**write
(a formal letter)**
書寫（正式信件）

**put something
together**
組合物品

 screw A into B
把 A 用螺絲拴進 B

 glue A to B
把 A 黏在 B 上

attach A to B
把 A 貼或附加在 B 上

Sentence Patterns 🎧161

**Asking for instructions
詢問指示**

- Can you show me how to make a cheese omelet?
- How do you make a cheese omelet?

Giving instructions 給予指示

- First crack the eggs into the bowl and add one cup of milk.
- Then (you have to) beat the eggs and fry them in a pan.
- Next add the cheese.
- And finally, fold the omelet in half and enjoy!
- Don't forget to season it with salt and pepper.

**Asking if he/she understands
詢問對方是否明白**

- Do you understand?
- Have you got that?
- Is that clear?
- Are you with me so far?

Saying you understand 表示了解

- Yes, I think so.
- Yes, It makes sense now.
- Yes, I follow you.
  I'm with you.

Saying you don't understand 表示不了解

- I'm sorry. I still don't get it.
- I'm not quite clear on the last part.
- I don't follow.
  I'm not with you.

III. Now, Time to Listen!

1 Listen to the people giving instructions. Match each set of instructions with the question you think the person is replying to.

(162)

1. _____

2. _____

a How do you make a good ham sandwich?

c How do you work the TV?

3. _____

4. _____

b How do you send a text message?

d How do you write a good story?

(163) Listen to the conversations again. Circle what the person says.

1 *First / Finally* select "menu."

2 *After that / Then* you have to press the round black button to turn it on.

3 *Finally / After that* bake the sandwich in the oven for 15 minutes.

4 *Then / Next* write your first draft, and after that *ask your teacher to correct it / revise it.*

2 Listen to Bill telling Kelly how to make the perfect cup of English tea. Put the steps in order from 1-6.

(164)

(165) Listen again. Pay attention to what Kelly says and fill in the blanks below.

Kelly | Bill, can you _____ to make a cup of English tea?

Kelly | OK. I _____.

Kelly | Yes, I'm _____.

Kelly | That _____. You _____ wait for it to cool down, right?

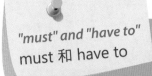

IV. Now, Grammar Time!

"must" and "have to"
must 和 have to

"must," "must not," "have to" → *express necessity*
"must," → *give orders; "have to"* → *give instructions*
must、must not 和 have to → 表示必要性
must→ 下命令；have to→ 提供指示

* You must be careful with boiling water.
* You must not add pepper to the cake!
* You have to press the red button to turn it on.

must not = mustn't

"don't have to" → *express something that is unnecessary*
don't have to → 表示某件事是不必要的

* You don't have to put sugar in your tea, but you can if you want.
* You don't have to brainstorm your ideas, but it helps if you do.
* You don't have to make dinner for me. I can make it myself.

3 Look at the pictures and fill in the blanks using "must," "must not," "have to," or "don't have to."

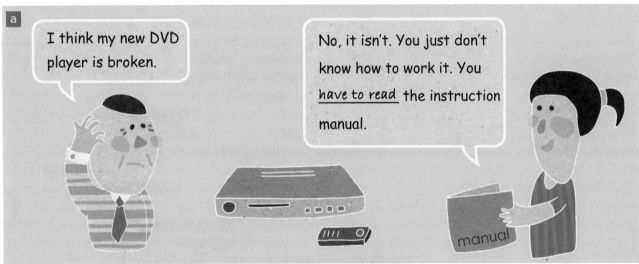

4 Look at the pictures below and match the two halves of the sentences.

1 You must not •   • **a** glue the wings to the plane.

2 You must •   • **b** feed the animals.

3 You don't have to •   • **c** make a face, but I think it's fun.

4 Then you have to •   • **d** finish this report before 5 p.m.

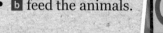

V. Now, Time to Speak!

5 Pair Work! Listen to the conversation below and practice it with your partner.

A	Can you show me how to use this camera?
B	Sure. _First (you have to)_ push the small silver button to turn it on. _Then_ press this button and select "flash." **Are you with me so far?**
A	Yes, I'm with you.
B	_Next_ press the red button to take a photo. And _finally_, press this green button to check your photo.
A	Wait, I'm not quite clear on that last part.
B	Here, let me show you. You take a photo, and then press this green button to check if it is OK.
A	**Oh, I get it!** Thanks.
B	No problem.

Now have similar conversations using the instructions below. Remember to ask if your partner understands your instructions.

How do you make a boiled egg?

1 Fill a pot with water and put an egg into the pot.

2 Boil the water.

3 Take the pot off the heat and cover the pot.

4 Wait for six minutes.

5 Take out the egg and enjoy!

Eggs

Can you show me how to work the washing machine?

1. Press the "power" button.
2. Put your clothes into the machine.
3. Add the detergent.
4. Close the lid.
5. Select "regular wash," and then press "start."

How do you make a call with a public phone?

1. Pick up the receiver.
2. Insert your money.
3. Dial the number.
4. Have your conversation.
5. Insert more money if you need to.

6 Read the hotel notice below. Take turns to tell your partner what you must or mustn't do.

Example: You must not give your room key to strangers.

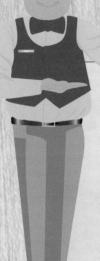

We want you to enjoy your stay! Please remember:

1 Do not give your room number to people you don't know.

2 Turn off the lights when you leave the room.

3 Close the windows when you leave the room.

4 Do not smoke in your room.

5 Do not cook anything in your room.

6 Put dirty towels in the bathtub.

7 Return your key when you leave.

VI. Now, Time to Pronounce!

Rising and falling intonations of instructions
指令語的音調上揚或下降

7 Listen and pay attention to the rising and falling intonations throughout the instructions.

1 First pick up the receiver. Then insert your money. Next dial the number. Then start talking.

2 First you have to heat the water. It needs to be 80 degrees. Are you with me? Next you put in the egg. Remember to choose a fresh one.

3 First press "on". Then press "open" and put in your DVD.

Suggestions and Advice 提議和建議

Topic Preview 168

1 Suggesting a specific activity
提議一項特定的活動

What shall we do today?
OK. Where shall we go?

Let's go out!
Why don't we go to the park for a picnic?

2 Giving someone advice for their problem
針對他人的問題提出建議

I can't sleep.
What should I do?

You should drink a glass of warm milk before bed.

3 Giving a list of suggestions
提出好幾項建議

Where shall we go for my birthday?

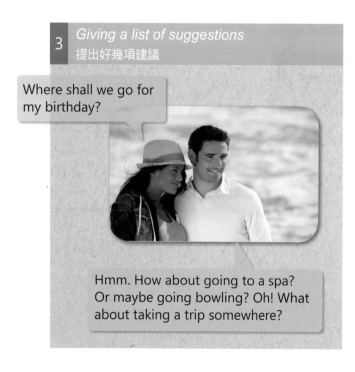

Hmm. How about going to a spa?
Or maybe going bowling? Oh! What about taking a trip somewhere?

4 Warning someone against doing something bad
告誡某人別做某件不好的事

You shouldn't smoke.
It's bad for your health.

You shouldn't drive so fast.
It's dangerous.

II. Vocabulary & Phrases 169

take a trip 旅行

go for a coffee 喝咖啡

go to an arcade 去遊樂場

go to a spa 做水療

get a massage 按摩

go to a night market 逛夜市

go to the beach 去海灘

play a board game 玩桌遊

go to the zoo 去動物園

go hiking 健行

smoke 抽菸

complain 抱怨

eat fast food 吃速食

cheat 作弊

lie 說謊

Sentence Patterns 170

▼ **Asking for suggestions** 尋求提議 ▼ **Giving suggestions** 給予提議

Asking for suggestions	Giving suggestions
• What *shall* we <u>do</u>?	**Why don't we** <u>have</u> pizza?
• When *shall* we <u>meet</u>?	**How about** <u>meeting</u> at 7 o'clock?
• Where *shall* we <u>go</u>?	**Let's** <u>go</u> to an arcade.
• Who *shall* we <u>invite</u>?	**What about** <u>inviting</u> Tina and Maria?
• Which car *shall* we <u>buy</u>?	**Shall we** <u>buy</u> the red one?

▼ **Asking for advice** 尋求建議   ▼ **Giving advice** 給予建議

Asking for advice	Giving advice
• What *should* I <u>do</u>?	**My advice is you should** <u>see</u> a doctor.
• When *should* I <u>tell my mom</u>?	**You should** <u>tell</u> her right away.
• Where *should* I <u>hang this painting</u>?	**You shouldn't** <u>hang</u> it in the bathroom.
• Who *should* I <u>talk to about my problem</u>?	**I recommend** <u>talking</u> to the school nurse.
• Which pet *should* I <u>choose</u>?	**I think** <u>getting</u> a cat **is a good idea.**

III. Now, Time to Listen!

1 Listen to the conversations. Are the people asking for advice or suggestions? Write (A) for advice or (S) for suggestions in the space given. Then match each one to the best response.

171

Sugestion (S) / Advice (A)		Response
1 _____ ·	· **a**	You should practice with me. I can help you.
2 _____ ·	· **b**	I recommend getting a nice relaxing massage to calm down.
3 _____ ·	· **c**	No, we shouldn't lie to him.
4 _____ ·	· **d**	Let's go to the little coffee shop across the street.
5 _____ ·	· **e**	Why don't we play a board game?

2 Listen to the conversations and fill in the blanks.

172

1

A Do you want to hang out this weekend?

B Yeah, sure. What _____ we do?

A _____ going to the zoo?

B That's a good idea. But the zoo is always busy on weekends.

A _____ about _____ hiking, then?

B OK. That sounds great.

2

A I really want to get healthy, Doctor. What _____ I do?

B Well, my _____ you should stop smoking.

A OK. Should I change my diet, too?

B Yes. You _____ fast food, and you should exercise everyday.

3   A   Do you want to go for a coffee with me later?

     B   Sure, that _____. Which coffee shop shall we go to?

     A   _____ go to Pop's Café? They have very good cappuccinos.

4   A   The weather here is always terrible.

     B   We shouldn't _____. At least we don't have typhoons!

     A   Shall we go inside? I'm getting wet.

     B   Yes. _____ going inside is a _____.

❸ Listen to Kevin and Bella talking about what to do for dinner. Circle the correct answer.

DINNER

1   Kevin suggests eating *hamburgers / pizza* for dinner.

2   Bella thinks they shouldn't *eat fast food / go out for dinner*.

3   Kevin *suggests / advises* going to Burger King.

4   *Bella / Kevin* suggests they go at 7:30.

Dinner

❹ Diane and Jimmy are talking about their math test. Listen to their conversation and check ☑ true (T) or false (F).

True	False	
_____	_____	**1** Diane suggests that Jimmy cheat.
_____	_____	**2** Jimmy thinks Diane should cheat.
_____	_____	**3** Jimmy advises Diane to talk to the teacher.
_____	_____	**4** Jimmy advises Diane not to throw the answers away.

WH-word
WH 開頭的字

What objects / ideas / actions 物品／想法／動作	What is that? What do you want to eat? What shall we do?
Which choices 選擇	Which shoes should I buy? Which watch is yours?
When time 時間	When does the movie start? When should we meet?
Where places 地點	Where are you from? Where shall we go?
Who people 人物	Who is John Doe? Who shall we invite?
Why reason 原因	Why is he angry? Why should I listen to you?
How manner 方式	How do you work the washing machine? How are you today?

5 Pair Work! Look at the pictures. What questions do you think the people are asking? Take turns asking and answering questions.

1

A | *Where shall I go?*
B | *Why don't you go to the museum?*

What should I do?

How do you do that?

Where shall I go?

Why are you crying?

Who are you?

When does the plane leave?

WH-Questions
WH 開頭的問句

Questions about the predicate 關於述語的問句		Questions about the subject 關於主詞的問句
You should **get a massage**. →What should I do?	The bookshop opens **at 9 o'clock**. →When does the bookshop open?	**The park** is a good place for a picnic. →Where is a good place for a picnic?
Let's go to **Pop's Café**. →Where shall we go?	He lives in **London**. →Where does he live?	**John** works in an office. →Who works in an office?
The weather is **rainy** today. →How is the weather today?	I want to talk to **Jim**. →Who do you want to talk to?	**Sad movies** make me cry. →What makes you cry?

❻ Look at the answers below. Write WH-questions about the words in bold.

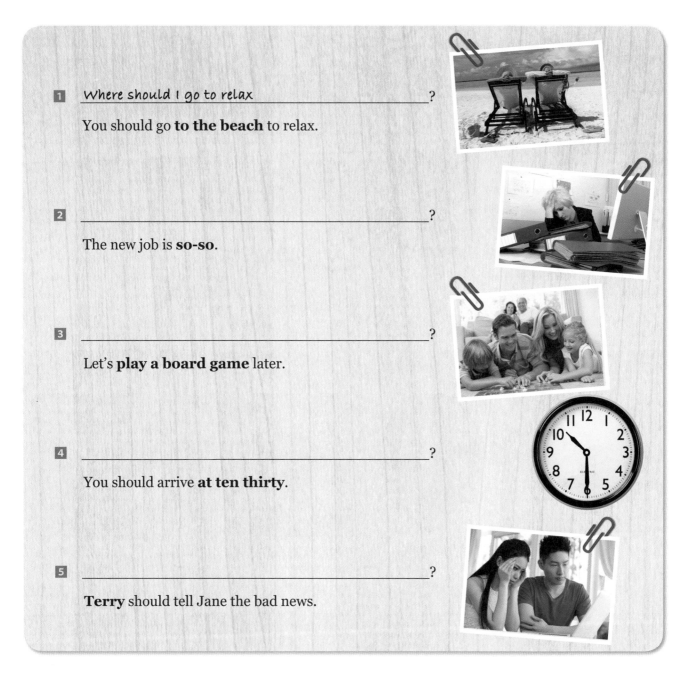

1 Where should I go to relax _____?

You should go **to the beach** to relax.

2 _____?

The new job is **so-so**.

3 _____?

Let's **play a board game** later.

4 _____?

You should arrive **at ten thirty**.

5 _____?

Terry should tell Jane the bad news.

7 Pair Work! Listen to the dialogue below and practice it with your partner.

A	When shall we go on vacation?
B	How about next week?
A	No, that is too soon.
B	OK. What about next summer?
A	That is too far away!
B	Hmm. Oh! I know. Let's go at Chinese New Year.
A	Yes, OK. Chinese New Year is perfect!

➡ Now have similar conversations using the information below.

1 Where shall we go for dinner?

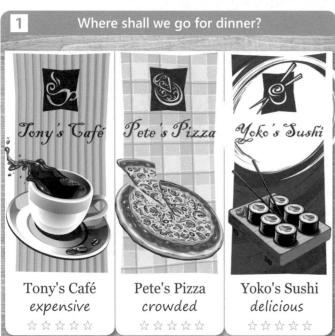

Tony's Café
expensive
☆☆☆☆☆

Pete's Pizza
crowded
☆☆☆☆☆

Yoko's Sushi
delicious
☆☆☆☆☆

2 What shall we do this afternoon?

play a board game
boring
☆☆☆☆☆

go to the beach
hot
☆☆☆☆☆

go to the zoo
interesting
☆☆☆☆☆

3 Who shall we invite to the party?

Ben
serious
☆☆☆☆☆

Sam
silly
☆☆☆☆☆

Jenny
fun
☆☆☆☆☆

4 Which movie shall we watch?

Ghost House 5
scary
☆☆☆☆☆

Fairytale 2
childish
☆☆☆☆☆

Action Hero 3
exciting
☆☆☆☆☆

8 With your partner take turns giving advice to the people in the pictures below. Compare your advice with that of your classmates.

> **Example** | *You shouldn't eat fast food.*
> *I recommend eating more vegetables.*
> *My advice is you should . . .*

"I'm overweight. I always eat fast food and I never exercise."

"My boss always makes me do too much work. I'm so stressed!"

"I always go shopping in my free time. I spend way too much money on clothes!"

"I hate my mom. She is so unfair and she never lets me do what I want!"

"I smoke 40 cigarettes a day. My friends say I always smell of smoke!"

"Sometimes I cheat at poker. But I only cheat my friends. That's OK, right?"

VI. Now, Time to Pronounce!

Rising and falling intonations of suggestions and advice
提議和建議時的語調上揚與下降

176 **9** Listen and pay close attention to the rising and falling intonations throughout the conversation.

Henry	What shall we do this weekend?
Vanessa	How about taking a trip?
Henry	No. That's too much trouble. Let's just go to the zoo.
Vanessa	OK. We should invite Fred and Alice, too.
Henry	Shall we call them now?
Vanessa	Sure. What's their phone number?

Topic Preview 🎧177

1 Saying how you celebrate a particular holiday/festival 描述如何慶祝某個特定的節日或節慶

How do you celebrate Christmas?

We decorate the house.
The whole family gets together.
We exchange gifts.
We have Christmas dinner.
We pull Christmas crackers.

2 Talking about the special foods you eat at a particular holiday/festival
談論某個特定的節日或節慶會吃的特殊食物

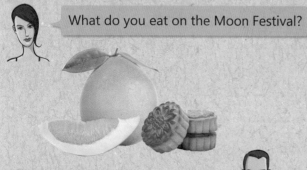

What do you eat on the Moon Festival?

We eat moon cakes and pomelos.

What do you eat on Halloween?

We eat lots of candy!

3 Saying why you celebrate a particular holiday/festival
說出為何要慶祝某個特定的節日或節慶

Why do you celebrate Thanksgiving?

We celebrate Thanksgiving to give thanks for all the good things in our lives.

4 Explaining your country's customs to a visitor
向訪客說明自己國家的習俗

It's rude to slurp your food in this country.

It's polite to tip about 10%.

You should bow when you greet someone.

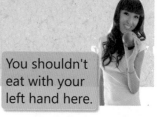

You shouldn't eat with your left hand here.

II. Vocabulary & Phrases 178

decorate
裝飾

exchange gifts
交換禮物

have a feast
享用盛宴

watch fireworks
觀賞煙火

dress up
穿上盛裝

watch a parade
看遊行

remember
回憶起

celebrate
慶祝

pray
祈禱

give thanks
表達感謝

bow
鞠躬

spit 吐痰

shake hands
握手

 tip 給小費

kiss someone on the cheek
親吻某人的臉頰

cut in line
插隊

belch / burp
打嗝

slurp 吃出聲音

Sentence Patterns 179

- How do you celebrate *Thanksgiving*?
  What do you do at/on *Thanksgiving*?
  We *have a special meal* and *watch a parade*.

- Why do you celebrate *Chinese New Year*?
  To *celebrate a new year beginning* and to *pray for good luck*.

- What do you eat on/at *Easter*?
  We eat *chocolate Easter eggs*.

- You should *tip* when you *pay the check*.
- You shouldn't *cut in line*.
- It's rude to *spit* in this country.
- It's polite to *kiss someone on the cheek* when you *greet them*.

1 Listen to Oscar and Mei Ling talking about St. Patrick's Day and the Moon Festival. Then answer the questions below by checking ☑ the correct box.

Words About St. Patrick's Day and the Moon Festival

Guinness 健力士啤酒　　barbecue 烤肉　　shamrock 三葉草　　Holy Trinity 三位一體

A

180

1 Which of the following do people NOT do on St. Patrick's Day?

　ⓐ Dance and play music ☐
　ⓑ Dress up in green ☐
　ⓒ Have a barbecue ☐

2 Which of the following is a reason for celebrating St. Patrick's Day?

　ⓐ To celebrate Irish culture ☐
　ⓑ To pray for prosperity ☐
　ⓒ To give thanks for Irish mothers ☐

3 People wear a shamrock to _____.

　ⓐ remember the teachings of St. Patrick ☐
　ⓑ give thanks for Guinness ☐
　ⓒ pray for good luck ☐

B

181

4 Which of the following is the reason for celebrating the Moon Festival?

　ⓐ To celebrate families coming together ☐
　ⓑ To pray for good health ☐
　ⓒ To give thanks for a new year beginning ☐

5 On Moon Festival, people _____.

　ⓐ have a barbecue ☐
　ⓑ dress up in red ☐
　ⓒ exchange gifts ☐

6 Which of the following do people NOT do on the Moon Festival?

　ⓐ Eat pomelos ☐
　ⓑ Look at the moon ☐
　ⓒ Watch a parade ☐

More Words about Holidays
更多與節慶相關的詞彙

trick or treating
不給糖就搗蛋

eat dumplings
吃水餃

rhyming couplets
春聯

Christmas lights
聖誕燈飾

red envelope
紅包

tinsel
聖誕彩帶

❷ Listen to the following people describing a festival or holiday. Match each
182 description to the correct festival.

1 _____ 2 _____ 3 _____ 4 _____

a b c d

183 Listen again. Some of the things below are mentioned by the speaker.
Check ☑ the things that are mentioned.

1 | a ☐ | b ☐ | c ☐ | d ☐ | e ☐

2 | a ☐ | b ☐ | c ☐ | d ☐ | e ☐

3 Listen to the following conversations. Fill in the blanks in the guidebook with the information you hear.

THINGS TO REMEMBER WHEN YOU VACATION IN THE UNITED STATES.

1 You should _____ _____ at least _____ percent in cafés, restaurants and taxis.

2 You should _____ _____ when you meet someone. Don't _____ _____.

3 Don't _____ in public. It's_____!

4 You should never _____ _____. Wait your turn!

INDOOR   OUTDOOR

5 Don't _____. Go _____ if you need a cigarette.

IV. Now, Grammar Time!

Countable and Uncountable Nouns
可數與不可數名詞

Countable Nouns 可數名詞	Uncountable Nouns 不可數名詞
Affirmative Sentences 肯定句	
I am eating a dumpling. There *are* ten gifts under the tree. Here *are* some Christmas cards for you.	I'm eating some cake. There *is* some tinsel on the tree. It's just some fun. It's not really scary.
Negative Sentences 否定句	
There *isn't* a star on the tree. There *aren't* any cookies in the jar.	There *isn't* any food in the refrigerator. There *isn't* any candy left.
Yes/No Questions 是非問句	
Is there a plate on the table? *Are* there any Christmas lights in the attic?	*Is* there any rice in the bowl? Can you see any snow?
WH-Questions　WH 問句	
How many candles *are* there? → There *are* a few. How many cards do you send at Christmas? → I send a lot of cards!	How much turkey is left? → There *is* a little left. How much money do you usually get for Chinese New Year? → I get a lot of money!

❹ Look at the pictures and fill in the blanks in the following sentences with the words from the box.

a few
a/an
a little
any
a lot of
how much
some
how many

1 At Christmas, we decorate our house with _____ tinsel!

2 _____ candy do you have in your bucket? I only have _____.

3 Do you have _____ red envelope for me?

4 There are only _____ _____ dumplings left. _____ do you want?

5 Here's _____ pumpkin pie for you. Enjoy!

6 Oh no! There aren't _____ gifts under the tree!

139

Measure Words 量詞

We can make uncountable nouns countable by adding a countable word before the noun.

在不可數名詞的前面加上可以計量的詞彙，就可以計算不可數名詞。

a bottle of water	一瓶	There are <u>three bottles of water</u> on the table.
a cup of tea	一杯	I want <u>two cups of tea</u>, please.
a bowl of rice	一碗	I usually eat <u>a few bowls of rice</u> for dinner.
a bar of chocolate	一條	Are there <u>any bars of chocolate</u> left?
a piece of cake	一塊	Here's <u>a piece of</u> cake for you.
a slice of turkey	一片	Please cut <u>two slices of turkey</u> for me.
a jar of jam	一罐	How <u>many jars of jam</u> do you want me to make?
a bag of candy	一袋	There's <u>a bag of candy</u> for you, and one for you brother.
a sheet of paper	一張	I need <u>a few sheets</u> of paper.

❺ Change the following **uncountable** sentences to **countable** ones using the prompts given. The first one has been done for you.

1 There is some coffee for you on the table. *(cup)*

→ There are two cups of coffee for you on the table.

2 Please get me some milk from the fridge. *(carton)*

⊃ _____

3 Is there any cake left? *(piece)*

⊃ _____

4 How much turkey do you want? *(slice)*

⊃ _____

5 We usually drink some wine with Thanksgiving dinner. *(bottle)*

⊃ _____

6 Put some tinsel on the tree. *(piece)*

⊃ _____

V. Now, Time to Speak!

6 Pair Work! Listen to the conversation below and practice it with a partner. Then replace the words in color with words from the word bank to have similar conversations.

WORD BANK

- Christmas
- Thanksgiving
- Halloween
- St. Patrick's Day
- The Moon Festival

- decorate the house
- wear shamrocks
- have a big meal
- look at the moon
- watch fireworks/ a parade
- exchange gifts
- go trick-or-treating
- drink Guinness
- dress up as ghosts and monsters
- have a barbecue

- turkey and pumpkin pie
- mince pies and Christmas cake
- moon cakes and pomelos
- Irish stew and Guinness pudding
- candy, lots of candy

- give thanks for all the good things in our lives
- celebrate Irish culture
- celebrate our families coming together
- remember the birth of Jesus
- have some fun

A : How do you celebrate Chinese New Year?
B : We dress up in red and exchange red envelopes.
A : Do you eat any special food at Chinese New Year?
B : Yes, we eat fish, dumplings, and sticky rice cake.
A : Why do you celebrate Chinese New Year?
B : To celebrate a new year beginning.

7 Fill in the table below with information about your country's customs. Discuss your answers with the rest of the class.

Things that are rude	Things that are polite
Talking while eating.	

NO

YES

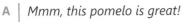

Role-play! Choose one of the things you listed and create a short dialogue around it. Student A is a local, and student B is visiting the country from abroad.

A | *Mmm, this pomelo is great!*
B | *I'm sorry. In England, it's rude to talk while you're eating.*
A | *Oh, I'm so sorry. How embarrassing.*

8 Look at the pictures below. Select one sentence from each box to form a 3-scentence dialogue between two people.

A | What are you doing?
B | I'm bowing goodbye.
A | Oh, I see. Here we just shake hands.

A
- Mmmm. These noodles are delicious.
- Out of my way! Two tickets please.
- What are you doing?
- Hello, I'm Jane. Nice to meet you!

B
- Shhh. It's rude to slurp in this country.
- Hey! Don't cut in line!
- I'm bowing goodbye.
- I want to buy a movie ticket.
- I'm enjoying my noodles.
- Oh! Here you should bow when you meet someone.

A
- I'm sorry. I'm not from here.
- Oh, I see. Here we just shake hands.
- You should wait your turn.
- Oh I'm so sorry. It's different where I come from.
- You shouldn't do that here. It's rude.

VI. Now, Time to Pronounce!

Silent Letters and Homophones

不發音的字母與同音異義字

9 **Listen and repeat the words you hear.**

 186

Silent Letters	Words		
B	lamb	debt	climb
D	edge	Wednesday	handsome
G	design	sign	foreign
H	honest	ghost	rhyme
K	knife	know	knee
L	talk	calm	salmon
T	watch	often	castle
U	guest	biscuit	guide
W	who	answer	write

➡ Now read each word in the table below aloud. Write down the silent letters.

Word	Silent Letters	Word	Silent Letters
1 hour		**4** sword	
2 knight		**5** listen	
3 half		**6** doubt	

10 **Look at the homophones below.**
 187 **Listen and repeat them aloud.**

➡ Try to think of some homophones of your own. Complete the table below.

/ sʌn /	son	sun
/ baɪ /	by	buy
/ hɪr /	hear	here
/ pis /	peace	piece
/ aʊr /	our	hour
/ plen /	plane	plain
/ dɪr /	dear	deer

1 son   *sun*

2 weak

3 sum

4 write

5 flour

6 sea

7 for

8 know

英語力 1

16堂流利英語聽說訓練課

Listening and Speaking in Everyday Life

作　　者	Owain Mckimm
翻　　譯	丁宥榆
英文審訂	Judy Majewski / Zachary Fillingham
企劃編輯	葉俞均
校　　對	歐寶妮
編　　輯	王鈺婷
內文排版	蔡怡柔／丁宥榆
封面設計	林書玉
插　　畫	陳太乙（P. 73, 81, 121, 122）
製程管理	洪巧玲
發 行 人	黃朝萍
出 版 者	寂天文化事業股份有限公司
電　　話	+886-(0)2-2365-9739
傳　　真	+886-(0)2-2365-9835
網　　址	www.icosmos.com.tw
讀者服務	onlineservice@icosmos.com.tw
出版日期	2024 年 8 月 初版再刷（寂天雲隨身聽 APP 版）(0102)

郵撥帳號 1998620-0 寂天文化事業股份有限公司
訂書金額未滿 1000 元，請外加運費 100 元。

【若有破損，請寄回更換，謝謝】

英語力 . 1：16 堂流利英語聽說訓練課（寂天雲隨身聽 APP）/ Owain Mckimm 作；丁宥榆譯 . -- 初版 . -- [臺北市]：寂天文化，2024.04 印刷

　冊；　公分

ISBN 978-626-300-250-0（菊 8K 平裝）

1.CST: 英語 2.CST: 讀本

805.18　　　　　　　　　　113005024

Unit 01

■ Topic Preview p. 8 (001)

1. What have you learned so far on your cookery course?
   Well, so far we've learned how to make the perfect scrambled eggs and how to make French fries.

▸ 你們上烹飪課到現在學到了什麼？
喔，到目前為止，我們學會炒出完美的炒蛋，還有做薯條。

2. How long have you studied Japanese?
   I've studied for two years altogether.
   Have you ever been to Japan to study?
   Yes, I studied in Japan for a few months last year.

▸ 你日文學了多久？
我一共學了兩年。
你有去日本唸書嗎？
有啊，我去年在日本唸了幾個月的書。

3. I find keeping my balance really difficult.
   Keep at it. I practiced for a long time before I could do it.

▸ 我覺得保持平衡真的好難喔。
繼續練習，我練了好久才做得到。

4. The first time I drove, I almost crashed!
   Why did that happen?
   Because I didn't use my mirrors.
   What about now? Have you improved?
   Definitely. I've learned a lot in a short time.

▸ 我第一次開車的時候，差點撞車！
怎麼會？
因為我沒看後照鏡。
那現在呢？你有沒有進步？
當然有，我在很短的時間就學了很多。

Sentence Patterns (003) p. 9

- 你們上舞蹈課到現在學到了什麼？
  我們到現在已經學會跳騷莎舞了。
- 你學做法式料理多久了？
  我（一共）學了六個月。
- 你學過唱歌嗎？
  學過，我年輕的時候學的。
- 我發現記舞步好難／有挑戰性喔。
- 唱歌最難的就是維持音準。

- 我需要加強練習發聲。
- 繼續努力！／堅持下去。／繼續練習。
- 我學了很久才學會。
- 我第一次唱歌時，唱得五音不全。
  怎麼會這樣？
  因為我不曉得如何正確呼吸。
- 你有進步嗎？／你改進了哪些地方？
  （有。）我學會了如何呼吸和控制聲音。

III Now, Time to Listen! p. 10

1.
   2 passed his test → almost crashed (004)
   3 park → steer
   4 fly a plane → ride a motorcycle
   5 steering → keeping his balance
   6 long time → few weeks

Script & Translation

Jack

When I was 17, I learned how to drive. I took driving lessons for about three months with my dad. The first time I drove, I almost crashed because I couldn't steer properly! But I got better, and I passed my test.
Now I'm learning how to ride a motorcycle. It's a lot easier than learning to drive a car, but I still find some things difficult, like keeping my balance. I've been practicing for a few weeks now, and I think I'm improving a lot.

傑克

我十七歲的時候學開車，我爸爸教我大約三個月。第一次開車的時候，我差點撞車，因為我駕駛的方式不對！但是後來就進步了，也通過考試。
現在我正在學騎機車，這比學開車容易得多了，但還是有些地方很難，像是保持平衡。我現在已經練習幾個禮拜了，我覺得我進步很多。

2.
   1 Maggie   2 Jim, Maggie   (005)
   3 Maggie   4 Maggie
   5 Jim   6 Jim

Script & Translation

Jim	Hi, Maggie. How are your singing lessons going?
Maggie	Hi, Jim. They're going well.
Jim	What have you learned so far?
Maggie	I've learned how take care of my voice and warm up properly. How long have you been studying now?
Jim	About six months. You?
Maggie	Only a few weeks.
Jim	Are you having any problems?

Maggie	Well, I'm finding projecting my voice quite difficult. My teacher says it's because I'm not breathing properly.
Jim	Oh, right. Well, hang in there. I practiced for a long time before I could project my voice well.
Maggie	Do you think you've improved a lot in six months?
Jim	Oh, yes, definitely. I remember the first day in class, I sang horribly out of tune. But now I can really control my voice, and I never sing out of tune anymore!
Maggie	Sounds like you're ready for the stage!
Jim	I hope so!
吉姆	嗨，瑪姬，你的歌唱班上得怎麼樣？
瑪姬	嗨，吉姆，還不錯呀。
吉姆	你到目前為止學了些什麼？
瑪姬	我已經學會保護嗓子，還有正確地開嗓。你現在上課多久了？
吉姆	大概六個月，你呢？
瑪姬	才幾個禮拜而已。
吉姆	有沒有遇到什麼問題？
瑪姬	嗯，我覺得要發聲挺難的。老師説這是因為我呼吸的方式不對。
吉姆	喔，沒錯。不過別灰心，我也是練習了很久才能正確發聲。
瑪姬	你覺得你在這六個月內進步很多嗎？
吉姆	喔，對啊，一定的。我記得上課的第一天，我唱得好爛，五音不全的。但是現在我完全可以控制我的聲音，再也沒走音了！
瑪姬	聽起來你已經可以上台表演了！
吉姆	希望如此！

③　1 a, c　2 b, c　3 a, b　4 a, c　(006)

1 first time I tried, burned　(007)
2 studied, for, altogether
3 find, in sync, challenging
4 work, on, breathing

Script & Translation

1　W　The first time I tried French cooking, I burned everything I cooked! I also found slicing and dicing very difficult because I couldn't hold a knife properly.

女　我第一次嘗試做法國菜的時候，我把煮的東西全部燒焦了！我還發現把食材切片和切塊好困難，因為我連刀子都握不好。

2　M　I've studied German for 10 years altogether, and I'm quite fluent now. Once, though, I accidentally asked

for a küssen, meaning a kiss, when actually I wanted a kissen—a pillow. I also found pronouncing new words quite difficult in the beginning.

男　我學德文一共學了十年，現在可以説得挺流利的。不過有一次，我不小心跟人家討了一個 küssen，也就是「親吻」的意思，其實我要説的是 kissen「枕頭」才對。還有，一開始學新單字的發音時，滿困難的。

3　W　I've taken dance classes for a long time, but I still find dancing in sync with others very challenging, especially if the music is very fast. I've also fallen over a few times, too!

女　我上舞蹈課有一段時間了，但是要跟別人動作一致還是很困難。尤其是音樂非常快的時候。我也摔倒過好多次！

4　M　I love singing, but I find singing on key really hard. I need to work more on my breathing as well. I've improved a lot since I first started, but I still need many more singing lessons before I can sing in front of an audience.

男　我愛唱歌，但是要把音唱準還真難，我的呼吸也需要再調整。從我開始學到現在，已經進步很多了，但是要能在聽眾面前演唱，還有很多課要上。

IV Now, Grammar Time!　p. 12

4　1 sautéing, haven't, flambéing, sauces
2 English folk, studied, yet, So far, have, swing, tap
3 have (already), still, light and shadow, landscapes

VI Now, Time to Pronounce!　p. 15

8　1 peas　2 cave　3 five　(009)
4 sits　5 leave　6 prove　7 knees

9　1 stair　2 mime　3 beer　(011)

10　1 S　2 F　3 S　4 F　5 S　(012)
6 F　7 S　8 S　9 F　10 S

Script & Translation

1　M　He's improved a lot recently.
男　他最近進步很多。

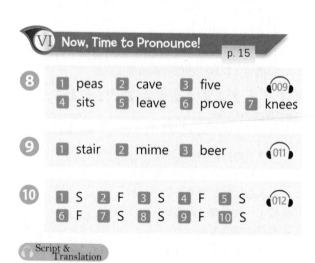

2 | W | She is a very fast learner.
女 | 她學得很快。

3 | M | Do you know if they're studying Spanish or French?
男 | 你知道他們在學西班牙文還是法文嗎？

4 | W | I have studied salsa dancing before.
女 | 我以前學過騷莎舞。

5 | M | We're starting our class next week.
男 | 我們下週開始上課。

6 | W | He has never learned to drive.
女 | 他從來沒有學過開車。

7 | M | I'm not happy with my progress.
男 | 我對我的進展不太滿意。

8 | W | I've been finding dicing quite difficult.
女 | 我發現把食材切塊還挺難的。

9 | M | They are very talented students.
男 | 他們是很有才華的學生。

10 | W | You've really worked hard this week.
女 | 你這週真的工作很認真。

Unit 02

I Topic Preview p. 16 013

1 | I visited my hometown last summer.
Oh yeah? Had anything changed since your last visit?
Yes. They had built a new hotel next to the beach and taken down the statue in the town square.

▶ 我去年夏天回去我老家一趟。
喔，是嗎？跟你上次回去比起來，有什麼改變嗎？
有，他們在海灘旁邊蓋了一間新的飯店，也把市中心廣場的雕像拆除了。

2 | Tell me about John's party last week.
OK. We'd already hidden and turned off the lights when John opened the door. Then we all shouted, "Surprise!"

▶ 跟我說說約翰上週的派對。
好啊。約翰開門的時候，我們已經躲好，並且把電燈關掉。然後我們一起大喊：「意想不到吧！」

3 | I saw you limping yesterday, Kim.
I was limping because I'd crashed my scooter into a tree.

You look very tanned in this photo, Brian.
Yeah. I'd just come back from a vacation.

▶ 金，我昨天看到你一跛一跛的。
對啊，我騎車撞到樹，所以才會一跛一跛的。

布萊恩，你在這張照片裡看起來曬得很黑。
對啊，我那時才剛度假回來。

4 | Sorry I'm late for the meeting. I forgot to set my alarm clock last night. By the time I got to the station, my train had already left.

▶ 對不起，我開會遲到了。我昨天晚上忘了設鬧鐘，趕到車站的時候，火車已經開走了。

Sentence Patterns 015 p. 17

• 我到的時候，火車已經開走了。
• 我到的時候，火車才剛開走。
• 我趕不上火車，所以遲到了。

III Now, Time to Listen! p. 18

1 A 1, 3   B 2, 3   016

Script & Translation

A Karen

I first met David in 1996. He was single, had short hair, wore dull clothes, and seemed very quiet. I met him again a year later. He had completely changed. He had grown his hair, and he had become much more talkative. But he still wore the same dull clothes. I think he was still single, too.

凱倫
我和大衛初次見面是 1996 年時，當時他單身，留著短髮，穿著乏味，看起來很文靜。隔年我又遇見他，他簡直是改頭換面。他把頭髮留長了，也變得健談得多，但是他還是穿著單調。而且我覺得他應該還是單身。

B Ivy

I graduated from college in 2008, but I went back to visit last year. So much had changed. They'd converted the old library into a cafeteria, and my old classmate had become a professor. They still hadn't taken down that weird statue though, and the dorms were still pretty basic.

艾薇
我 2008 年大學畢業，不過去年回母校參觀時，發現變了好多。他們把舊圖書館改建為自助餐廳，我的老同學也當上了教授。但是那座奇怪的雕像還沒被拆掉，宿舍也還是很簡陋。

2   **Ⓐ** **1** c **2** a   **Ⓑ** **1** b **2** a   (017)
Ⓒ **1** c **2** b

  Ⓐ just sat, when, gave   (018)
  Ⓑ had gone, been, for
  Ⓒ by the time, spoke, already given

Script & Translation

Ⓐ **M** | Let me tell you about the interview I had yesterday.

W | OK. I'm listening.

M | Well, before I went to the interview, I'd bought a new suit and studied hard for the company test. I had just sat down outside the boss's office when he came out and gave us the bad news. He had already hired his son the day before.

W | No way!

男 | 我跟你說我昨天面試的事。

女 | 好，我洗耳恭聽。

男 | 我去面試之前，買了一套新西裝，也認真準備了該公司的考試。結果我才剛在老闆辦公室外面坐下，他就走出來跟我們說了一個壞消息，就是他前一天已經雇用他兒子了。

女 | 不會吧！

Ⓑ **M** | Why did Jacob leave the dinner party last night?

W | Because you had served him beef, and he's a vegetarian.

M | Oh, but what about Josie? She likes beef, right? Why did she leave?

W | Because the beef had gone bad. It had been in the fridge for about two years.

男 | 雅各昨天晚上為什麼離開聚餐？

女 | 因為你為他準備牛肉，可是他吃素。

男 | 噢，那裘西呢？她很愛吃牛肉不是嗎？她怎麼也走了？

女 | 因為牛肉壞了，那牛肉在冰箱放兩年了耶。

Ⓒ **Sarah** | Did you manage to get tickets for the concert, Mike?

Mike | No. Sorry, Sarah. I called the ticket office, but they had already sold out.

Sarah | Oh, well. We could ask Jenny if she has some spare tickets.

Mike | I asked her last night, but by the time I spoke to her, she had already given them to someone else.

莎拉 | 麥克，你買到演唱會的票了嗎？

麥克 | 莎拉，對不起，我沒買到。我打電話到售票處，他們說已經賣完了。

莎拉 | 喔，好吧。我們可以問珍妮有沒有多的票。

麥克 | 我昨天晚上問過她了，但是我問她的時候，她已經把票給別人了。

3   **ⓐ** 1 **ⓑ** 2 **ⓒ** 3 **ⓓ** 5 **ⓔ** 4   (019)

Script & Translation

Lisa

Let me tell you about my vacation nightmare. I arrived at the airport with lots of time to spare because I'd already packed my suitcase and prepared everything the night before. When I was at the check-in desk, I realized I'd left my passport in the taxi. I called the taxi company, but by the time I got my passport back, my plane had already left.

麗莎

我跟你說我這次度假的惡夢。因為我前一天晚上就已經打包行李，也把所有東西都準備好，所以我很早就到了機場。但是我到了報到櫃檯，才發現我把護照忘在計程車上。我打電話給計程車公司，但等我把護照找回來的時候，我的飛機已經起飛了。

Ⅳ Now, Grammar Time!   p. 20

4   **2** had already read the book, saw the movie

3 had just brushed her teeth, offered her a snack

4 got home, had already finished eating dinner

5 had just gone home, started serving coffee

6 went to China, had already studied Chinese

Ⅵ Now, Time to Pronounce!   p. 23

9   **1** F **2** S **3** F **4** S **5** S   (021)
   6 F **7** F **8** S **9** S **10** S

Script & Translation

1 By the time he finished his dinner, it had already started raining.

他吃完晚餐前就已經開始下雨了。

2 I'd already studied college math before I left high school.

我還沒高中畢業就已經學過大學數學了。

3 She had just arrived at the airport when the plane took off.

飛機起飛時，她才剛抵達機場。

4 Before they left the party, they'd given me a gift.

他們離開派對之前，已經把禮物給我了。

5 Matt looked unhappy last night because he'd just been fired.

麥特昨晚看起來心情不好，因為他剛被開除。

6 We had already decorated the house by the time they arrived.

他們來的時候，我們已經把房子布置好了。

7 When he was five, he had already learned how to read and write.

他五歲的時候，就已經會閱讀和寫字。

8 By the time I ate the cake, it'd already gone bad.

我吃蛋糕的時候，蛋糕已經壞了。

9 When I visited my mom, she'd thrown away all my old books.

我去找我媽的時候，她已經把我的舊書都丟掉了。

10 We'd already studied some Italian before we went to Italy.

我們去義大利之前，已經學了一些義大利文。

Unit 03

 **Topic Preview** p. 24 022

1 When I was a kid, my family used to go skiing every winter.
What about in the summer?
In the summer, we would always go to the seaside.
That sounds great. I wish I had gone on trips with my family when I was younger.

▸ 我小的時候，每到冬天全家人都會去滑雪。
那麼夏天呢？
夏天的時候，我們都會去海邊。
聽起來好棒喔，我真希望年輕的時候也跟家人一起出遊。

2 Have you always had a dog?
No, I used to have a cat when I was a kid.
- -
Have you always been so slim?
No, I used to be overweight when I was a teenager.

▸ 你一直都有養狗嗎？
沒有，我小的時候養過貓。
- -
你一直都這麼瘦嗎？
沒有，我青少年時期很胖。

3 You look very fit these days!
I used to sit in front of the TV all day, but now I work out five times a week.

▸ 你身材最近看起來很棒耶！
我以前整天都坐在電視機前面，但是現在我一個禮拜運動五次。

4 Do you like tennis?
I used to like tennis, but now I prefer soccer.

▸ 你喜歡網球嗎？
我以前喜歡，但是現在比較喜歡足球。

5 How has your life changed since you got married?
Well, I used to hang out a lot with my friends, but I don't anymore.
- -
John never used to come home late.
He comes home late all the time since he got that new job.

▸ 結婚之後，你的生活有什麼轉變？
喔，我以前常常和朋友出去，結了婚就再也沒有這樣了。
- -
約翰以前從來不會晚回家。
他換了那份新工作之後，就一直很晚才回家。

6 I used to believe in Santa when I was younger, and I used to have an imaginary friend.

▸ 我小的時候相信有聖誕老公公的存在，我還有一位想像出來的朋友喔。

Sentence Patterns 024 p. 25

- 我小的時候，每到聖誕節全家都會一起玩大富翁。
- 每到夜晚，我們總會去看星星。
- 我真希望小的時候能和家人一同旅行。
- 你一向都這麼勇敢嗎？
不，我小的時候很怕黑。
- 我以前都把頭髮染成粉紅色，但是現在染成藍色。
- 我以前喜歡喝白酒，但是現在喜歡喝紅酒。
- 你升職了之後，人生有什麼改變？
我以前會擔心錢的問題，但是現在不會了。
- 麗莎以前從不看小說，自從她加入那個讀書會之後，每晚都會看一本書。

Now, Time to Listen! p. 26

1 a, d, e 025

1 get pocket money, week 026
2 argue 3 aren't 4 go camping, summer 5 play Monopoly 6 never

Charlotte	Did you have a happy childhood, Ben?
Ben	Oh, yes. I had a great childhood. I used to get pocket money every week, so I could always buy the toys I wanted.
Charlotte	I'm so jealous! I never got any pocket money. Do you have any brothers or sisters?
Ben	Yes, I have a brother. We don't talk much now, but we used to be really good friends when we were younger.
Charlotte	I always used to argue with my sister. We're best friends now, but back then we would fight like crazy! I used to hate her!
Ben	Did you ever go on family trips?
Charlotte	Yeah, we used to go camping every summer. Actually, I really loved going camping with my family. We would always play Monopoly by the campfire, talk, and look at the stars. Those trips were great. How about you?
Ben	No, we never went on trips. I wish we had, though. They sound like lots of fun.

夏綠蒂	班，你的童年愉快嗎？
班	喔，愉快啊，我有一個美好的童年。我每個星期都有零用錢，所以我想要什麼玩具都可以買。
夏綠蒂	好羨慕喔！我從來沒有拿過零用錢。你有兄弟姊妹嗎？
班	有，我有一個哥哥。我們現在比較少說話，但是我們小的時候非常要好。
夏綠蒂	我以前經常和我妹妹吵架，我們現在是最要好的朋友，但以前的時候，我們吵架吵翻天了！我以前好討厭她！
班	你們會去家庭旅遊嗎？
夏綠蒂	會啊，我們以前每年夏天都會去露營，說真的，我很愛跟家人去露營。我們總是圍著營火玩大富翁、談天說地、看星星，那些旅遊真美好。你呢？
班	我們從來不會出去旅行，真希望我們有去旅遊，因為聽起來好像很好玩。

2   a Richard   b Janet
      c Ellie   d Tina   e Mark

1	**M**	You've known Tina since she was little. Has she always been so popular? She has so many friends now.
	W	Well, when Tina was little, she used to have an imaginary friend named Charlie. He was Tina's only friend for years!
	男	你跟蒂娜從小就認識了，她以前的人緣就這麼好嗎？她現在的朋友好多喔。
	女	喔，蒂娜小的時候，有一個想像出來的朋友叫作查理，曾經好多年他是蒂娜唯一的朋友呢！
2	**M**	Richard is such a good student. Has he always been like this?
	W	Oh, no. He used to be a troublemaker when he was in elementary school.
	男	理查真是一位好學生，他一直都是這樣嗎？
	女	噢，不是。他國小的時候很會惹麻煩。
3	**W**	Mark never used to be a fussy eater, but he has really changed over the last few years.
	M	Oh, really? How?
	W	Well, he just won't eat anything these days. He used to be a bit overweight, but now he's so thin!
	女	馬克吃東西一向不挑食，可是他近幾年真的改變了很多。
	男	喔，真的嗎？怎麼說？
	女	嗯，他現在什麼都不吃。他以前有一點胖，可是現在好瘦！
4	**M**	Ellie's usually quite brave, but she doesn't like horror movies. I wonder why.
	W	That's nothing. When she was little, she used to be so afraid of the dark that she slept with the light on.
	男	艾麗一向都很勇敢，可是她不喜歡看恐怖片，不知道是為什麼。
	女	這沒什麼，她小的時候會怕黑，都要開燈睡覺。
5	**M**	Janet used to dye her hair blue when she was a teenager, didn't she? She used to think she was so cool.
	W	Yeah, but it was better than her current hairstyle. Now her hair is even worse than before.
	男	珍妮特青少年的時候，頭髮都染成藍色，對嗎？她以前自以為很酷呢。
	女	對啊，不過以前那樣還算好呢，她現在的頭髮真是有過之而無不及。

3 then ① d ② g ③ H ④ e ⟨028⟩
now ① f ② a ③ b ④ c

 Script & Translation

Oliver

My friend Simon has changed a lot over the years. We used to go out for dinner a lot, but we don't see each other very often since he got married. He usually stays at home now. He also used to love playing soccer, but he prefers golf since he got promoted at work. Oh, and last year, he went to India for a vacation. Let me tell you, he never used to like Indian food, but since he got back, he eats Indian food once a week.

One more thing. Recently he's taken up salsa dancing. He used to think that dancing was embarrassing, but since he joined that dance class, he loves to watch dancing shows on TV.

奧利弗

我的朋友賽門這幾年來改變了好多。我們以前經常一起出去吃晚飯，自從他結婚之後，我們就很少碰面了，他現在通常都待在家裡。他以前也很愛踢足球，但是自從升遷之後，就改打高爾夫球了。

喔，還有去年，他去印度度假。我跟你説，他以前從來不愛吃印度菜，自從他回來之後，他每週都要吃一次印度菜。

還有一件事，最近他在學騷莎舞。以前，他覺得跳舞很尷尬，但是他開始上舞蹈課之後，變得很愛看電視上的舞蹈節目。

Ⅳ Now, Grammar Time! p. 28

4 ⓑ didn't use(d) to exercise
ⓒ used to make cookies
ⓓ used to have a dog
ⓔ is not used to flying
ⓕ am used to the noise

5 ① know ② used to give / would give
③ used to own ④ use/used to like
⑤ would play / used to play
⑥ use/used to have
⑦ would read / used to read

Ⅵ Now, Time to Pronounce! p. 31

10 ① play, soccer, brother, day, school ⟨031⟩
② takes, train, work, morning
③ eaten, restaurant, before
④ grandpa, fall, asleep, chair
⑤ know, get, museum

Ⅰ Topic Preview p. 32 ⟨032⟩

1 Hi guys, sorry to interrupt.
That's all right, Joe.
So, what are we talking about?
Jim's telling us about his date last night.
- -
Hey, guys. What's going on?
We're just talking about the game last night.

▸ 嗨，各位，抱歉打斷你們説話。
沒關係的，喬。
那麼，説到哪裡了？
吉姆正在説他昨晚的約會。
- -
嘿，大家好，你們在説什麼？
我們只是在聊昨晚的球賽而已。

2 OK. So, we'd arranged to meet at seven . . .
Uh-huh.
But she turned up about an hour late . . .
No way!
Yeah, and then she ordered the most expensive thing on the menu.
Oh my God! Seriously?

▸ 好，所以呢，我們就約了七點碰面……
嗯嗯。
結果她大約遲到了一個小時……
不會吧！
對啊，然後她又點了菜單上最貴的一道菜。
噢，天啊！真的假的？

3 OK, so what happened next?
Well, next we went for a walk.
Then what?
Well, then we kissed.

▸ 好，接下來呢？
嗯，接著我們就去散步。
然後呢？
喔，然後我們就接吻了。

4 Anyway, it was really terrible.
I bet it was. Actually, the same thing happened to me two years ago . . .

▸ 總之，那真的很恐怖。
那是一定的。老實説，我兩年前也發生過這種事。

Asking to join a conversation 要求加入對話

- 不好意思打斷你們。
- 你們介意我加入一起聊嗎？
- 你們介意我跟你們聊一會兒嗎？

Getting up to speed 趕上對話進度

- 我們在講什麼？
- 發生什麼事？
- 怎麼回事？
- 最近有什麼八卦？

Showing interest 表現出興趣

- 喔，真的嗎？
- 喔，是嗎？
- 喔，對。

Showing you follow 表示有在聽

- 嗯嗯。
- 嗯嗯。

Showing surprise/disbelief 表示驚訝／難以置信

- 喔，哇！
- 不會吧！
- 噢，天啊！
- 真的嗎？
- 你不是在開玩笑吧？

Continuing a conversation 延續對話

- 然後呢？
- 然後怎麼了？
- 接著發生了什麼事？
- 然後發生了什麼事？

Ending your turn 結束自己的話題

- 總之……
- 所以總之……
- 對啊，所以……
- 所以對啊……

Starting your turn 展開對話

- （這是一定的。）老實說……
- （我同意你的看法。）但重點是……
- （哇。）嗯……
- （是，沒錯。）但是……
- （嗯，我也不知道。）我覺得……

Ⅲ Now, Time to Listen!
p. 34

① ① c ② a ③ b 035

Script & Translation

1

W	Hi, guys. Sorry to interrupt.
M	That's OK.
W	Do you mind if I join you?
M	No, not at all.
W	Cool. So, what's going on?

女	嗨，各位，抱歉打斷你們。
男	沒關係。
女	你們介意我加入你們嗎？
男	一點也不介意。
女	太棒了。那麼，你們在聊些什麼？

2

M	We were winning.
W	Uh-huh.
M	And then Simon fouled and got a red card.
W	No way! Then what happened?

男	那時我們就快要贏了。
女	嗯嗯。
男	結果賽門犯規，被舉紅牌。
女	不會吧！然後呢？

3

W1	I told him he shouldn't talk to people like that.
W2	Uh-huh.
W1	Then I walked out of his office and slammed the door. So anyway, that's how I quit.

女1	我跟他說他不應該那樣跟人說話。
女2	嗯嗯。
女1	然後我就走出他的辦公室，把門甩上。總而言之，我就是那樣辭職的。

② ① b ② a ③ a ④ b ⑤ a ⑥ b ⑦ a 037

Script & Translation

Harry	So, anyway, it just made me feel really uncomfortable, you know?
Kate	I bet. Actually, something similar happened to me two weeks ago.
Harry	Oh, really?
Kate	Yeah. I was taking the subway, and there was an old woman sitting next to me.
Harry	Uh-huh.
Kate	Then she just started singing really loudly.
Harry	Oh my God! Seriously?
Kate	Yeah. And then she tried to make me stand up and dance with her.
Harry	Ha-ha! That's so weird.
Kate	Yeah, so I know how you feel.
Harry	Right. Well, the thing is, now I'm really nervous about taking the bus.

哈利	總之，那件事真的讓我很不舒服，你知道嗎？
凱特	那是一定的啊。老實說，我兩個禮拜前也發生過類似的事。
哈利	喔，真的嗎？
凱特	對啊，我在坐地鐵的時候，有一個老女人坐在我旁邊。
哈利	嗯嗯。
凱特	然後她開始大聲唱歌。
哈利	喔，天啊！真的嗎？
凱特	對啊，然後她還叫我站起來跟她一起跳舞。

哈利	哈哈！那樣好奇怪喔。
凱特	對啊，所以我知道你的感受。
哈利	沒錯。所以問題是，我現在真的很怕搭公車。

3 ❶ a ❷ c ❸ a, b ❹ b ❺ a (038)

🎧 Script & Translation

Julie	I don't know. I think they'll probably break up soon.
Grant	Hmm. I don't know. I think . . . Oh, hi, Phil.
Phil	Hi, guys. Sorry to interrupt. You don't mind if I join you, do you?
Julie	No, no. Grant and I were just talking about Terry and June.
Phil	Oh, yeah? What's the latest gossip?
Julie	Well, Terry told me they've been arguing a lot recently, so I think they're going to break up soon.
Phil	Right. The thing is they're just such different people.
Julie	Mm-hm.
Phil	And they don't enjoy spending time with each other. So, yeah, I don't think they'll last much longer.
Julie	I totally agree with you. They're just not suited to each other. So, anyway, Phil, how are things with you?
Phil	Not too bad, thanks, Julie. I just got promoted at work, so that was nice.
Julie	Oh, wow! That is good news. Congratulations.

茱莉	我不知道，我覺得他們可能快分手了。
葛蘭特	嗯，我不知道，我覺得……喔，嗨，菲爾。
菲爾	嗨，兩位，抱歉打斷你們，我可以一起聊嗎？
茱莉	好啊，葛蘭特和我正聊到泰瑞和茱恩的事。
菲爾	喔，是嗎？最新的八卦是什麼？
茱莉	嗯，泰瑞跟我說他們最近吵得很凶，所以我覺得他們快要分手了。
菲爾	沒錯，問題就在於他們根本是兩個世界的人。
茱莉	嗯嗯。
菲爾	而且他們不願意花時間陪對方。所以，沒錯，我覺得他們不會撐太久。
茱莉	我完全同意，他們根本不適合彼此。所以，對了，菲爾，你最近過得怎麼樣？
菲爾	還不錯，謝謝，茱莉。我上個禮拜剛升職喔，所以滿不賴的。
茱莉	喔，哇！那是好消息耶，恭喜。

IV Now, Grammar Time! p. 36

4 otherwise, even so, in addition, So, as a result, In short, then, for example

V Now, Time to Speak! p. 37

5

🎧 Translation (039)

威爾	嗨，各位，抱歉打斷你們。
葛瑞絲	沒關係，一起聊啊。
威爾	謝謝。發生什麼事了？
葛瑞絲	我正在跟傑克說我上星期的約會，超糟的。
威爾	喔，真的嗎？
葛瑞絲	對啊，我們去市區那家新開的法國餐廳。
威爾	嗯嗯。
葛瑞絲	然後我不小心點了田螺。
威爾	田螺？什麼是田螺？
葛瑞絲	就是蝸牛啊！
威爾	不會吧！你開玩笑吧？
葛瑞絲	才沒有。所以我在吃的時候，就覺得非常、非常想吐。
威爾	嗯嗯，然後呢？
葛瑞絲	喔，我就吐在桌上了。
威爾	喔，天啊！真的假的？
葛瑞絲	真的啊。總之，那是我這輩子最糟的一件事了。
威爾	一定的啊，不過老實說，我幾個禮拜前也發生過類似的事。

VI Now, Time to Pronounce! p. 39

7
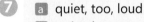

- a quiet, too, loud
- b arrived, store, already, closed.
- c Grandma, always, send, card, birthday.
- d have, imaginary, friend, younger?

Unit 05

I Topic Preview p. 40

1 Why do you always interfere in my business?
You never listen to me!
It's so annoying when you talk down to me.

▸ 你為什麼老是要干涉我的事？
你每次都不聽我的！
我真的很不喜歡你用高高在上的口氣跟我講話。

2 | You always make me clean the house. It's not fair.
　 | Excuse me? When do you ever clean the house?

> 你每次都叫我打掃房子，這樣不公平。
不好意思喔？你什麼時候打掃過房子了？

3 | You're always so mean to me.
　 | Are you kidding me? I'm never mean to you.

> 你總是對我這麼壞。
你開什麼玩笑？我哪有對你壞過。

4 | It's not my fault.
　 | Then whose fault is it?
　 | Jerry made me do it.
　 | Don't try to blame someone else.

> 那又不是我的錯。
那是誰的錯？
是傑瑞叫我那樣做的。
你不要推卸責任。

5 | You're so unreasonable!
　 | Just take it easy for a second.

> 你很不講理耶！
你可以冷靜一下嗎？

Sentence Patterns　(046)　p. 41

Complaining and defending yourself
抱怨並為自己辯護

* 你從不讓我用電腦。
你在開什麼玩笑？我都有讓你用。
* 你為什麼每次都要我照顧弟弟？
我什麼時候要你照顧弟弟了？
* 你為什麼總是這麼自私？
我哪有自私？
* 我受夠了你老是用高高在上的口氣對我說話。
我幾時用高高在上的口氣對你說話了？
* 你老是碎碎唸叫我打掃房間。
你錯囉，我沒有對你碎碎唸喔。
* 你那樣霸著電視真的很討厭耶。
喔，是嗎？那你又好到哪裡去？
* 你為什麼一定要這麼不負責任？
你竟敢說我不負責任。

Passing the blame 推卸責任

* 那不是我的錯。　　　* 又不是我，是約翰。
* 他／她叫我那樣做的。

Trying to end an argument 試著停止爭吵

* 冷靜。　　* 冷靜一下。　　* 不要大發雷霆。

---

① | ⓐ 4 　ⓑ 2 　ⓒ 5 　ⓓ 1 　(047)
　 | ⓔ 6 　ⓕ 3

② | ❶ Are you kidding me　(048)
　 | ❷ What about
　 | ❸ blow a fuse　❹ not fair, interfere in
　 | ❺ take advantage　❻ my fault, nag me

Script & Translation

1 | Mother | You never help around the house. You're so selfish.
　 | James | Are you kidding me? I always help around the house.
　 | 母親 | 你都不幫忙做家事，太自私了。
　 | 詹姆斯 | 你開什麼玩笑？我都有幫忙做家事。

2 | Mother | Why do you insist on talking down to me like that?
　 | James | What about you? You talk to me like I'm a child.
　 | 母親 | 你為什麼要用那種高高在上的口氣對我說話？
　 | 詹姆斯 | 你還不是一樣？你說話的口氣好像我是三歲小孩一樣。

3 | Mother | You're irresponsible. You always make a mess. You never listen. You always . . .
　 | James | OK, OK. Don't blow a fuse.
　 | 母親 | 你太不負責任了，老是弄得一團亂，講也講不聽，你老是……
　 | 詹姆斯 | 好啦，好啦，不要生氣啦。

4 | Mother | That's it. You're not going out with your friends this weekend.
　 | James | That's not fair. Why do you always interfere in my business?
　 | 母親 | 不用說了，你這個週末不准和朋友出去。
　 | 詹姆斯 | 不公平，為什麼你每次都要管我？

5 | Mother | I'm tired of you taking advantage of me and your father.
　 | James | When do I ever take advantage of you?
　 | 母親 | 我受夠了你這樣利用我和你爸。
　 | 詹姆斯 | 我哪有利用你們？

6 | Mother | You always cause trouble in this house.
　 | James | It's not my fault. You always nag me to do things I don't want to do.

10

母親	你每次都在家裡惹麻煩。
詹姆斯	又不是我的錯，是你一直嘮叨叫我做我不想做的事。

3	1 Max	2 Jane	3 Max		049
	4 Max	5 Jane	6 Jane	7 Max	

b, c, f, g, i   050

Script & Translation

Jane	Max, can I talk to you for a second.
Max	Yeah, sure. What's up?
Jane	Look. You have to stop making a mess in the office kitchen. You never clean up your things.
Max	Whoa, Jane. Just take it easy for a second.
Jane	Excuse me? How dare you speak to me like that?
Max	Hey! Why do you always try to cause trouble in the office?
Jane	Huh? Since when do I cause trouble? You're the one who always talks behind people's backs.
Max	Oh, please! When do I ever talk behind people's backs?
Jane	I heard you talking about Paula yesterday.
Max	That wasn't me. That was Simon.
Jane	Don't try to blame Simon. I heard you. I'm tired of you insulting my friends.
Max	Oh, yeah? What about you? You always talk down to Jimmy.
Jane	Are you kidding me? I'm always nice to Jimmy.
Max	OK. I'm not going to listen to this anymore. I'm leaving.
Jane	Fine. Whatever.
珍	邁克斯，我可以跟你說一下話嗎？
邁克斯	好啊，可以。什麼事？
珍	我跟你說，你能不能不要再把公司的廚房搞得一團亂了，你都不清理你自己的東西。
邁克斯	齁，珍，別激動。
珍	什麼？你竟敢那樣對我說話！
邁克斯	嘿！你為什麼總是要在公司裡惹麻煩？
珍	啥？我幾時開始惹麻煩了？每次在背後說別人壞話的是你吧？
邁克斯	喔，拜託！我哪有在背後說別人壞話？
珍	我昨天聽到你在批評寶拉。
邁克斯	那不是我，是賽門。
珍	你少推給賽門，我有聽到是你說的。我受不了你這樣侮辱我的朋友。

邁克斯	喔，是嗎？你又好到哪裡去？你老是用高高在上的口氣對吉米說話。
珍	你亂講什麼啊？我對吉米很好耶。
邁克斯	算了，我不想聽你胡扯了，我要走了。
珍	好啊，隨便你。

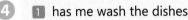

IV Now, Grammar Time!   p. 44

4
1. has me wash the dishes
2. make me work so hard
3. have you tidy the office
4. get me to do things your way
5. I make you stay home
6. I'm tired of always making you share the computer
7. My grandma always lets me do whatever I want at her house
8. I don't know how to get John to apologize to me
9. Will you let me finish speaking, please
10. It's so annoying when you have us finish our reports over the weekend

V Now, Time to Speak!   p. 45

5

Translation   051

莉蒂雅	喬許，你能不能不要一大早就那麼吵，我都快瘋了。
喬許	什麼？我哪有早上吵人？
莉蒂雅	嗯，你每天早上都很吵耶。你很用力關冰箱的門，還有你的腳步聲很大聲。
喬許	好啊，好啊，那你呢？你總是把廚房弄得亂糟糟。
莉蒂雅	你在開什麼玩笑？我什麼時候把廚房弄得亂糟糟了？
喬許	一直啊，你每次用過廚房後就變得很髒。而且我也早就看不慣你霸佔電視。
莉蒂雅	你搞錯了吧，我才沒有霸佔電視，你竟敢指控我霸佔電視？
喬許	好吧，好吧，不要發飆，冷靜一下。
莉蒂雅	好，嘿，我們別把這件事放在心上了，我們不應該吵架的。
喬許	我同意，對不起。
莉蒂雅	我也是。

6   Sample Answers

1. It was Judy, blame someone else, Judy told me to do it
2. do I (ever) take advantage of you, borrow money from me and never pay it back, Don't lose your temper

11

3. clean my room, irresponsible, you accuse me of being irresponsible, help around the house, babysit your brother

4. It's so annoying when you, I never talk behind your back, deny it, insulting me, are always so mean to everyone

Translation

1. 母親｜杰克，你是不是從我皮夾裡拿了錢？
   兒子｜不是我，是茱蒂。
   母親｜我看到是你拿的，不要推給別人。
   兒｜好吧，是我拿的，可是是茱蒂叫我拿的。

2. 伊娃｜我受夠了你每次都利用我！
   丹｜我幾時開始利用你了？
   伊娃｜一直啊，你跟我借錢從來不還的。
   丹｜好啦，好啦，冷靜一下，不要生氣。

3. 女兒｜你為什麼一定要喋喋不休地叫我整理房間？
   父親｜我非這樣不可，因為你太不負責任了。
   女兒｜你怎麼可以說我不負責任？
   父親｜嗯，你從來不幫忙做家裡的事，你也從來不照顧你弟弟。

4. 艾薇｜彼德，你在我背後說我壞話，這樣真的很可惡。
   彼德｜什麼？我沒有在你背後說你壞話啊。
   艾薇｜不要不承認，珍妮都跟我說了。我真的厭倦你這樣詆毀我。你對大家都很惡劣耶。

VI Now, Time to Pronounce! p. 47

8 | 1 always | 2 I | 3 so | 4 my | 5 try | 6 you (054)

Unit 06

I Topic Preview p. 48 (055)

1. I wish I hadn't quit my job. It was a really bad decision.
   You could have been promoted by now.

▸ 真希望我沒有辭職，那真是個錯誤的決定。
   而且你現在可能已經升職了。

2. Do you have any regrets?
   I could have studied harder in school, I guess.

▸ 你有任何遺憾嗎？
   我想我在學校時應該更用功讀書才對。

3. What's your biggest regret?
   I shouldn't have been so mean to my mom when I was a teenager.

▸ 你最遺憾的事情是什麼？
   我青少年時，不該對我媽媽那麼壞。

4. It's a pity you can't speak Spanish, isn't it?
   I should have paid more attention in Spanish class.

▸ 真可惜你不會說西班牙，對吧？
   我上西班牙文課的時候，應該要更專心一點。

5. If you had prepared for the interview, would it have made a difference?
   Yes, if I had prepared for the interview, I think I would have got that job.

   How would your life be different now if you'd married Yumi instead of marrying Claire?
   Well, I would probably be happier, and I'd be living in Japan instead of England.

▸ 如果你有準備面試，結果會不一樣嗎？
   對啊，如果我有準備的話，我應該會被錄取。

   如果你娶的是由美而不是克萊兒的話，人生會有什麼不同？
   嗯，可能會比較快樂吧，而且我就會在日本定居而不是英國。

Sentence Patterns (057) p. 49

- 你有任何遺憾嗎？
  你最遺憾的事是什麼？
- 我真希望我放棄／沒放棄學鋼琴。
- 我在學校時應該更認真讀書。
- 我 16 歲的時候，應該／不應該離開家。
- 你不再跟彼德說話，很可惜吧？
- 我應該跟他保持聯絡的。
- 如果你學的是歷史，人生會有什麼不同嗎？
  如果你學商（而沒輟學），人生會有什麼不同？
  如果你學的是數學呢？
- 如果我學商，我就會從商了。
- 我現在就會當老師了（而不會失業）。
- 我現在就是百萬富翁了。

III Now, Time to Listen! p. 50

1 | b, c (R), d (R), e (R) (058)

1. traveled, would have visited (059)
2. you'd be, if you'd been nicer
3. have paid more attention
4. wish I hadn't turned down

Man	Do you have any regrets, Sally?
Sally	I do have one big regret. I wish I had traveled more when I was younger.
Man	I guess now there's no time, right?
Sally	Exactly. If I'd traveled more, I would have visited so many countries by now. The only country I ever visited was Spain with my family when I was a kid.
Man	Are you close with your family now?
Sally	No, not really.
Man	That's a pity.
Sally	Yes, it is. I shouldn't have been so cruel to my little sister when we were young.
Man	Do you think you'd be good friends now if you'd been nicer?
Sally	Yes, I think so.
Man	What about school? Do you have any regrets about school?
Sally	Um, I used to fall asleep a lot in class. I could have paid more attention, I guess. Oh, and I wish I hadn't turned down Chris Martin when he asked me out. Do you know he's a lawyer now?
Man	If you hadn't turned him down, you could be married to him now.
Sally	I know. I feel so stupid!

男子	莎莉，你有任何遺憾嗎？
莎莉	我有一件很遺憾的事，就是年輕時沒有到處旅遊。
男子	我猜你現在沒時間去旅遊了，是嗎？
莎莉	沒錯，如果以前有多去旅遊，現在應該去過很多國家了。我唯一去過的國家，就是小時候和家人去過的西班牙。
男子	你現在和家人還很親嗎？
莎莉	不怎麼親了。
男子	真可惜。
莎莉	對啊，很可惜。小的時候，我不應該對我妹那麼壞。
男子	如果你當初對她好一點，你們現在會成為好朋友嗎？
莎莉	我覺得會。
男子	那麼學校呢？你對學校有什麼遺憾嗎？
莎莉	嗯，我以前上課時常常睡著，我覺得我應該要專心一點才對。噢，還有克里斯·馬丁追我的時候，我不應該拒絕他的。你知道他現在是律師嗎？
男子	如果你當時沒有拒絕他的話，你現在可能已經嫁給他囉。
莎莉	我知道啊，我覺得自己好蠢喔！

1

W	Are you OK, Joey? You look upset.
Joey	My girlfriend just broke up with me.
W	Oh, no. That's terrible.
Joey	It's all my fault. I should have been more thoughtful.
女子	喬依，你還好嗎？你看起來很難過。
喬依	我女朋友剛跟我分手。
女子	噢，不。那樣真的不好受。
喬依	都是我的錯，我應該更貼心一點的。

2

W	Bonjour, monsieur. Qu'est-ce que vous voulez manger?
Joey	Oh, I'm sorry. Do you speak English? Darn. I wish I'd paid attention in French class.
女子	早安，先生，請問您想吃什麼？
喬依	噢，對不起，請問你會說英文嗎？可惡，我當初上法文課時應該認真一點。

3

W	Do you play any musical instruments, Joey?
Joey	No, I don't.
W	That's a pity. I love a man who can play music.
Joey	I shouldn't have given up learning the piano when I was a kid.
女子	喬依，你會演奏任何樂器嗎？
喬依	我不會。
女子	好可惜喔，我很愛會樂器的男人。
喬依	我小時候學鋼琴真不應該半途而廢。

4

W	Joey, are you still friends with Pete?
Joey	No, not anymore.
W	Oh, that's a shame.
Joey	Yeah, it is. If I hadn't forgotten his birthday, we'd still be friends.
女子	喬依，你和彼德還是朋友嗎？
喬依	不是，我們沒有往來了。
女子	真可惜。
喬依	對啊，如果我沒有忘記他的生日，我們還會是朋友。

5

W	Joey, I need the rent for this month before the end of the week.
Joey	Oh, well, if I hadn't quit my job, I could pay you. But I did. Could you give me a break this one time?
W	OK, but just this once.
女子	喬依，要在這個星期以內給我這個月的房租喔。
喬依	喔，唉，假如我沒有辭職的話，一定會給你，可是我現在沒工作，可不可以寬限我一次？
女子	好吧，但是下不為例喔。

2　**1** b　**2** c　**3** a　**4** c　**5** b　(060)

3
  1 **a.** Daisy   **b.** Mel   **c.** Simon
  2 **a.** Simon   **b.** Daisy   **c.** Mel
  3 **a.** Daisy   **b.** Mel   **c.** Simon
  4 **a.** Mel   **b.** Simon   **c.** Daisy

Script & Translation

Mel

Hi. I'm Mel. I studied law in college. I worked extremely hard, and now I'm a successful lawyer. When I started college, I left home, and I loved living by myself. I also broke up with my high-school boyfriend while I was in college. He was a great guy. I shouldn't have broken up with him. If we hadn't broken up, we'd probably have a family now.

梅兒

嗨，我是梅兒，我大學主修法律，我非常認真念書，現在我已經是一名成功的律師。我進大學的時候就離鄉背井了，我喜歡一個人生活。大學時，我也和高中交的男朋友分手，他人很好，我實在不應該跟他分手的。如果我們沒有分手，現在可能已經共組家庭了。

Simon

Hi. I'm Simon. I lived with my parents while I was at college. I should have moved out because my parents pressured me a lot. They made me study law instead of history. My grades were pretty good. But I could have worked harder, I guess. The thing is, if I'd studied history, I could have become a history teacher instead of a lawyer. That was my dream, but I did meet my wife at college, so it wasn't all bad!

賽門

嗨，我是賽門。我大學的時候和父母一起住，我真應該搬出來的，因為他們給我很大的壓力。他們要我念法律，不讓我念歷史。我的成績很好，但是還可以更用功一點。問題是，如果我念的是歷史，就可以當歷史老師，而不是律師，那才是我的夢想。不過我在大學時認識我太太，所以也不算太糟！

Daisy

Hi. I'm Daisy. I studied law, too. I liked it, but I should have worked harder. My grades were terrible. Then, when I was in my second year, I dropped out of college because I'd got a job in a bank. Now, I really wish I hadn't dropped out. I got fired from my job at the bank last week. If I'd finished college, I'd have been a rich lawyer by now.

黛西

嗨，我是黛西，我也是學法律的。我喜歡法律，但是卻不夠用功，我的成績很差。而且大二的時候，還因為要去銀行上班而休學。我現在很後悔休學。上個星

期，我被銀行裁員。如果當初我有念完大學，我現在就會是一名富有的律師了。

IV Now, Grammar Time! p. 52

4
  2 you had studied,
     I had studied,
     I could/would have passed
  3 she had said yes,
     she had said yes,
     We would be engaged
  4 your parents had been rich,
     my parents had been rich,
     I would have visited more countries

V Now, Time to Speak! p. 53

5

Translation

克莉絲汀	羅伯特，你最大的遺憾是什麼？
羅伯特	嗯，如果我那次考試沒有作弊，就不會被退學了。
克莉絲汀	對啊，真的很遺憾。
羅伯特	我知道。如果我沒有作弊，可能已經是一名醫師了。你呢？你有任何遺憾嗎？
克莉絲汀	有，我不應該偷那支錶的，我覺得我應該要誠實一點。
羅伯特	如果你沒有偷那支錶會怎樣？
克莉絲汀	我就不會被關兩年了。

VI Now, Time to Pronounce! p. 54

7
  1 [j]   **2** [w]   **3** [w]
  4 [j]   **5** [w]

Script

1 really is   **2** new idea   **3** too old
4 dry ice   **5** glue on

8
  1 [wʊd ju]   **2** [ʃʊdəntʃu]
  3 [dɪdʒu]   **4** [dont ju]   **5** [kʊdənt ju]
  6 [mitʃu]   **7** [kʊd ju]   **8** [putʃʊr]

Script

1 would you   **2** shouldn't-you   **3** did-you
4 don't you   **5** couldn't you   **6** meet-you
7 could you   **8** put-your

Unit O7

I Topic Preview p. 56

1
Good friends should always support each other.
I think so, too. And they shouldn't talk behind each other's backs, either.

▸ 好朋友應該永遠互相支持。
我也這樣覺得，而且也不該在背後說彼此的壞話。

2
Who's your best friend?
Jessie is my best friend.
How long have you known her?
About 10 years.
So is she your oldest friend, too?
Yes, that's right!

How well do you know Darren?
Not very well. He's just an acquaintance.
Are you two good friends?
Yes, but we haven't known each other very long.

▸ 你最好的朋友是誰？
我最好的朋友是潔西。
你認識她多久了？
大約十年了。
所以她也是你認識最久的朋友囉？
對，沒錯。

你跟戴倫有多熟？
也沒有很熟，算是認識而已。
你們是好朋友嗎？
對，但是我們沒有認識很久。

3
I like dancing, and so does he. We're such a good match.

I like dogs, but he likes cats. I don't think we're compatible.

▸ 我喜歡跳舞，他也是，我們真是天作之合。
我喜歡狗，他喜歡貓，我覺得我們不適合。

4
What do you think makes a good relationship?
I think a good relationship needs trust and patience.

▸ 你覺得維持良好關係的要訣是什麼？
我覺得一段良好的關係需要信任和耐心。

Sentence Patterns 072 p. 57

- 好朋友應該永遠互相支持。
- 誰是你認識最久的朋友？
  馬克是我認識最久的朋友。
- 你認識他／她多久了？
  我認識他／她大概七年了。
  我從高中就認識他／她了。
- 你們怎麼認識的？
  我們工作認識的。
- 你跟珍妮很熟嗎？
  沒有很熟，我們只是同事。／很熟，她是我室友。
- 我喜歡古典樂，他／她也是。
- 我們很合。
  我們喜好相似。
- 你們兩個是最好的朋友嗎？
  是啊，可是我們沒有認識很久。
  是啊，我們已經認識十年了。
  不是，我們只是認識而已。
- 我喜歡往外跑，但他喜歡待在家，我覺得我們並不合。
- 你覺得維持良好關係的要訣是什麼？
  我覺得一段良好關係需要真誠和感情的投入。
  你必須要誠實和善體人意。

III Now, Time to Listen! p. 58

1

		073
Jane	oldest friend, 11 years	
Sam	best friend, college	
Ollie	acquaintance, Tanya's birthday party, one year	
Tanya	English class, two years	

Script & Translation

Lisa	Who's that, Mark?
Mark	That's Jane. She's my oldest friend.
Lisa	Oh, really? How long have you known her?
Mark	We met on the first day of junior high school. So that's 11 years.
Lisa	Hang on. I thought Sam was your oldest friend.
Mark	No, Sam is my best friend. But I've only known him for about three years.
Lisa	Where did you meet him?
Mark	I met him in college.
Lisa	Oh, I see. Hey, look. Ollie's here.
Mark	Oh, yeah?
Lisa	Are you and Ollie good friends?
Mark	No, not really. We met at Tanya's birthday about a year ago, but we're just acquaintances.

Lisa	Oh, right. Who's Tanya?
Mark	Tanya's my girlfriend.
Lisa	Oh, yes! Sorry. I forgot. How long have you been dating?
Mark	Well, we met two years ago in my English class, and we've been dating since then.

麗莎	馬克，那是誰啊？
馬克	那是珍，是我認識最久的朋友。
麗莎	喔，真的呀？你認識她多久了？
馬克	我們讀國中的第一天就認識了，所以總共 11 年了。
麗莎	等一下，我以為山姆才是你最久的朋友。
馬克	不是，山姆是我最要好的朋友，但是我才認識他大約三年而已。
麗莎	你在哪裡認識他的？
馬克	在大學認識的。
麗莎	喔，了解。嘿，你看，奧利也在這裡。
馬克	喔，是嗎？
麗莎	你和奧利是好朋友嗎？
馬克	不算是，我們是一年前在譚雅的生日認識的，不過僅止於點頭之交而已。
麗莎	喔，這樣啊。譚雅又是誰？
馬克	譚雅是我的女朋友。
麗莎	喔，對！抱歉，我忘記了。你們在一起多久了啊？
馬克	嗯，我們是兩年前在英文課上面認識的，那個時候就在一起了。

②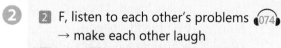
- ② F, listen to each other's problems (074) → make each other laugh
- ③ T　④ F, soccer → video games
- ⑤ T　⑥ F, affection → trust
- ⑦ T　⑧ patience → honesty

Jan	Who's your best friend, Billy?
Billy	Jack is my best friend. We've known each other since high school.
Jan	That's a long time. What do you think makes a good friendship?
Billy	Well, I think good friends should always make each other laugh.
Jan	I think so, too. That's very important. But what about having similar interests?
Billy	Oh, yeah, definitely. That's also important. Jack and I both love video games and rock music.
Jan	Well, that's cool. You seem to enjoy each other's company.
Billy	Yeah, we do. And we share secrets with each other. I think a good friendship needs trust.
Jan	And honesty. You shouldn't keep secrets from your friends.

珍	比利，你最要好的朋友是誰？
比利	傑克是我最要好的朋友，我們從高中的時候就認識了。
珍	好久喔，你覺得維持友誼的秘訣是什麼？
比利	嗯，我覺得好朋友一定要逗對方笑。
珍	我也這樣覺得，這點很重要。那麼你覺得共同的興趣呢？
比利	喔，對，當然要，那也很重要。傑克和我都愛打電動和聽搖滾樂。
珍	喔，好酷，你們好像很喜歡膩在一起。
比利	對啊，而且我們會分享彼此的秘密，我覺得友誼是需要信任的。
珍	還有真誠，你們不應該有秘密。

③ b, c, d, f　(075)
- ① needs affection　② care about (076)
- ③ Understanding　④ You need to, too
- ⑤ on the same wavelength
- ⑥ trust　⑦ compatible

Ashley and Josie are: ___c___

Ashley

Josie is my girlfriend, but we don't have a good relationship. A good relationship needs affection. You should care about each other. You also need to listen to each other's problems. Understanding is really important for a relationship. You need to have similar interests, too. The thing is, Josie and I aren't on the same wavelength. She likes to go out with her friends; I like to stay home and watch movies. Josie doesn't trust me, either. She won't share any of her secrets with me. I just don't think we're very compatible.

艾許利

喬西是我女朋友，但是我們處得不是很好。一段良好的關係需要放感情，不應該漠不關心。雙方也要聆聽彼此的問題，互相諒解才能維持關係。雙方還要有類似的興趣。問題是，喬西和我的觀念不同。她喜歡和朋友出去，我喜歡在家看電影。喬西也不信任我，她有很多秘密不告訴我，我們真的不太適合。

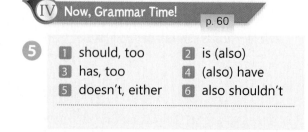

Ⅳ Now, Grammar Time!　p. 60

⑤
- ① should, too　② is (also)
- ③ has, too　④ (also) have
- ⑤ doesn't, either　⑥ also shouldn't

1 She isn't a good roommate, and she is a bad friend, too.

2 Friends should be affectionate with each other, and friends shouldn't upset each other, either.

3 We don't make each other laugh, and we irritate each other all the time, too. / We don't make each other laugh, and we also irritate each other all the time.

4 We are on the same wavelength, and we don't keep secrets from each other, either.

5 He ignores me, and he doesn't respect me, either. / He ignores me, and he also doesn't respect me.

VI Now, Time to Pronounce!
p. 63

9 1 a 2 b 3 a 4 b 5 b 6 a (078)

🎧 Script

1 No! **Fred** is my best friend . . .

2 No! I met Sam at **work** . . .

3 No! He's **very** honest . . .

4 No! A good **marriage** needs trust . . .

5 No! We've known each other for 11 **years** . . .

6 No! She loves **me** . . .

10 1 a 2 b 3 a 4 a 5 a 6 b (080)

🎧 Script

1 **John** is a really nice roommate, too.

2 I've known Sally for **five** years.

3 I think a good friendship needs **respect**, too.

4 Jane isn't very **patient**, either.

5 A good **friend** should support you, too.

6 I met James in a **nightclub**.

Unit 08

I Topic Preview
p. 64 (081)

1 How much do you make each month?
I make $2,000 a month at my job.
Do you have any extra income?
I make an extra $200 a month selling stuff on eBay.

▸ 你每個月賺多少錢？
我的工作一個月賺 2,000 元。
你有其他收入嗎？
我每個月靠 eBay 網拍賺進 200 元。

2 How much do you spend on essentials every month?
I spend $1,000 on rent, $300 on utility bills, and $150 on groceries.
How much do you spend on luxury items?
I spend about $300 on new clothes and maybe $150 on books and DVDs.

▸ 你每個月的必要支出有多少錢？
我花 1,000 元付房租，300 元付水電費，150 元買日常用品。
你花多少錢買奢侈品？
我花大約 300 元買新衣服，還有大約 150 元在書本和 DVD 上面。

3 So you're saving about $200 a month. That's not enough. I should be saving more than that.
How much do you want to be saving?
I want to be saving at least $500 a month.

▸ 所以說你一個月大約存 200 元。
可是還不夠，我應該要存更多。
你想存多少？
我一個月至少想存 500 元。

4 You spend so much on clothes that you don't have enough money to buy groceries!
I promise that I'll spend less money on clothes this month.
How much are you going to budget for groceries this month?
I'm going to budget $200 for groceries, and $100 for new clothes.

▸ 你花太多錢買衣服了，所以才會不夠錢買日用品。
我保證這個月不會花那麼多錢買衣服。
你這個月打算留多少預算買日用品？
我打算花 200 元買日用品，100 元買新衣服。

Sentence Patterns (083) p. 65

• 你每個月賺多少錢？
我的工作每個月賺 2,000 元。

• 你有額外的收入嗎？
我每個月當家教有 200 元的收入。

• 或許你可以利用空閒時間當保母來多賺一點錢。

• 你每個月有多少錢是必要支出？
我花 1,000 元付房租，200 元付水電費，150 元買日常用品。

- 你還有哪些支出？
  我還要付每個月 20 元的健保費。
- 你想存多少錢？
  我希望每個月至少存 500 元。／
  我一個月應該要存 300 元。
- 你真的花太多錢了！
  你應該減少交通費。
- 你花太多錢付健身房會費，才會不夠錢付水電費！
- 我保證這個月不會花太多錢在外出上面。
- 你這個月打算留多少錢做外食的預算？
  我打算留 250 元給外食。

(III) Now, Time to Listen!

p. 66

1　**1** a　**2** a, 300　**3** b　**4** c　(084)

Script & Translation

Linda	OK, Danny. Tell me. How much do you make every month?
Danny	I make $2,200 a month at my job.
Linda	And do you have any extra income?
Danny	I make about $300 a month tutoring.
Linda	OK. Now, what about your outgoings? How much do you spend on essentials?
Danny	Well, rent is $1,200 a month, and utility bills are usually about $200 in total.
Linda	Right. So how much do you usually budget for groceries?
Danny	I usually eat out, so not that much—maybe $100. I usually spend about $300 eating out in a month.
Linda	Wow! So what other expenses do you have?
Danny	Well, there's my cell phone bill. That's $40 a month. My cable and Internet bill is $160 a month. And I'm learning Spanish, too. Spanish class costs around $150 a month.
Linda	All right. How about transportation? Do you spend much money getting to and from work?
Danny	No, I walk to work.
Linda	And how about entertainment?
Danny	Well, I go out twice a week to a club. That costs about $45 each time, so $360 a month.
Linda	And how much do you spend on luxury items, like new clothes, DVDs, that kind of thing.
Danny	I spend maybe $200 a month on DVDs and clothes.
Linda	OK. So let's add this all up.

琳達	好，丹尼，你說說看，你每個月賺多少錢？
丹尼	我每個月靠工作賺 2,200 元。
琳達	你有其他收入嗎？
丹尼	我每個月當家教大概賺 300 元。
琳達	好，那你的支出呢？你的必要花費有多少？
丹尼	嗯，租金一個月 1,200 元，水電費加起來通常是 200 元左右。
琳達	好，那你通常留多少預算買日常用品？
丹尼	我通常都外食，所以不會留很多，可能 100 元吧，我每個月外食通常要花 300 元。
琳達	哇！那你還有哪些支出？
丹尼	嗯，手機費一個月 40 元，有線電視和網路費是一個月 160 元，而且我在學西班牙文，學費一個月大約 150 元。
琳達	好，那交通費呢？你通勤要花很多錢嗎？
丹尼	不用，我都走路上班。
琳達	那麼娛樂費呢？
丹尼	嗯，我一個星期會去兩次夜店，每次大概花 45 元，所以一個月是 360 元。
琳達	那麼你花多少錢在奢侈品上面，像是新衣服、DVD 那些的。
丹尼	我每個月大概花 200 元買 DVD 和新衣服。
琳達	好，那我們把這些加起來。

2
- a Tutoring / Extra income　(085)
- b Rent　c 200　d Cell phone bill
- e 160　f Groceries　g 300
- h Spanish class　i 360
- j Luxury items / DVD and clothes

3　**1** a　**2** a　**3** b　(086)

- **1** overspending　(087)
- **2** spending, on, pay my utility bills
- **3** cut back on
- **4** budget for groceries
- **5** 120, want to be saving
- **6** recycle, spare time

Script & Translation

Linda	Wow! You're really overspending.
Danny	I know. I'm spending so much on clubbing that I can't pay my utility bills.
Linda	Yeah, you need to cut back on clubbing. How about just going once a week?
Danny	Yeah, OK. So that's only $180 a month on clubbing.
Linda	Right. And you need to cut back on eating out. Spend a little more on groceries and eat at home instead.

18

Danny	Good idea. So how much should I budget for groceries?
Linda	I think $200 for groceries and $50 for eating out.
Danny	OK. So then I'd actually be saving $120 a month. I want to be saving more than that, though—$200 if possible.
Linda	Maybe you could recycle in your spare time for some extra money. You could probably make around $100 a month if you really worked hard.
Danny	Oh, what a good idea!
Linda	Great! Then you should be OK from now on!

琳達	哇！你真的花太多錢了。
丹尼	我知道，我花太多錢去夜店，所以才會繳不出水電費。
琳達	對啊，你花在夜店的錢應該減少，一個禮拜去一次就好了，如何？
丹尼	好，可以。那麼一個月就只要花 180 元在夜店。
琳達	對，而且外食的費用也要減少。把費用花在日常用品，還有在家吃飯。
丹尼	也好。那我應該花多少錢買日常用品？
琳達	我想 200 元買日常用品，50 元外食。
丹尼	好吧。這樣子一個月就可以省下 120 元。可是我想要省更多，可能的話要 200 元。
琳達	或許你可以把空閒時間拿來做資源回收賺點外快，勤快一點的話，一個月可能可以賺 100 元左右喔。
丹尼	喔，這是個好方法！
琳達	太好了！那麼從現在起應該就沒問題了！

V Now, Time to Speak! p. 69

5

Translation Sample Answers

A

A	How much do you spend on essentials each month?
B	I spend $1,500 on _rent_ and $200 on _utility bills_.
A	OK. What other expenses _do you have_?
B	Well, there's health insurance, gym membership, and _my cell phone bill_.
A	Do you spend a lot of money on _entertainment_?
B	Yes, quite a lot. I spend about $300 a month on _eating out_ and _clubbing_.
A	And _how much do you save_?
B	I save $500 a month, but I should _be saving $600_.

A	你每個月的必要開銷有多少？
B	我花 1,500 元付房租，200 元繳水電費。
A	好，還有其他支出嗎？
B	嗯，有健保費、健身房會費，還有手機費。
A	你會花很多錢在娛樂上面嗎？
B	會，花滿多的。我每個月花 300 元左右出去吃飯還有去夜店。
A	那你存多少錢？
B	我一個月存 500 元，但是我應該要存 600 元才對。

B

A	Oh, no! I don't think I can pay _my cell phone bill_ this month!
B	That's because _you spend so much on going out_.
A	What can I do?
B	Maybe you could _sell some of your old stuff online_.
A	OK, but what about next month?
B	You should _cut back on eating out and eat at home more often_.

A	噢，不！我這個月繳不出手機費了。
B	還不都是你花太多錢外食。
A	那怎麼辦？
B	或許你可以把一些舊的東西上網賣掉。
A	好吧，可是下個月怎麼辦？
B	你應該要減少外食的支出，多在家吃飯。

7 **1** b **2** a **3** c

VI Now, Time to Pronounce! p. 71

12

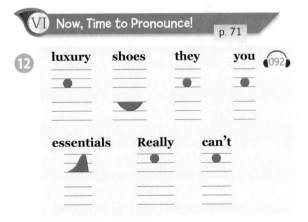

luxury　shoes　they　you 092

essentials　Really　can't

Unit 09

I Topic Preview p. 72 093

1

Wow! You're gorgeous. Can I buy you a drink?

Sure, handsome. Wow! You look so strong. Have you been working out?

Do you believe in love at first sight, or should I walk by again?
That's so cheesy!

▶ 哇！你好漂亮，我可以請你喝飲料嗎？
好啊，帥哥。哇！你好壯喔，你有在健身嗎？

你相信一見鍾情嗎？還是要我再走一次讓你二見鍾情？
拜託，真是爛招！

2 It was really nice talking to you. Let's get together again sometime.
I'd like that. Let me give you my number.

I was wondering if you'd like to go out to dinner with me this Saturday.
Sure, that sounds great. Where are you taking me?
I know a great little Italian restaurant. Can I pick you up at eight?
I'm looking forward to it.

▶ 真的很高興跟你談話，我們改天再約出來吧。
好啊，我留電話給你。

不知道你這個星期六願不願意和我共進晚餐？
好啊，太好了。你要帶我去哪裡吃飯呢？
我知道一家很棒的義大利餐廳，八點去接你好嗎？
好期待喔。

3 I'm quite shy. I'm not the kind of guy who often asks girls out on dates.

I'm a Scorpio, so I'm very passionate. Are you a Pisces? I think we're compatible.

▶ 我很內向，不是那種會常約女生去約會的人。

我是天蠍座，非常熱情。你是雙魚座嗎？我們應該很速配喔。

4 That pickup line is so cheesy!

I just don't think we're compatible.

I prefer guys who are tall, dark, and handsome.

Sorry, you're not my type.

▶ 這樣搭訕很俗耶。

我真的不認為我們合得來。

我比較喜歡高大、黝黑的帥哥。

很抱歉，你不是我喜歡的那一型。

Sentence Patterns 〔095〕 p. 73

Pickup lines 搭訕用語

- 你相信一見鍾情嗎？還是要我再經過一次？
- 你從天堂落入凡間的時候痛不痛？
- 是這裡太熱了，還是你讓我發熱？
- 希望你懂心肺復甦術，因為你美得讓我忘了呼吸。
- 如果我能重新排列英文字母，我一定會把 U（你）和 I（我）排在一起。
- 我是不是認識你？因為你長得好像我下一任女朋友。

Asking someone out 邀某人約會

- 很高興和你說話，我們再約時間聚聚吧。
- 我可以跟你要電話嗎？我改天想約你去玩。
- 我可以哪天約你出去嗎？
- 不知道你這個星期六願不願意和我共進晚餐？
- 你這個星期六有空嗎？我知道一間很棒的雞尾酒吧，我們可以小酌一下。
- 如果你今晚沒事的話，我想約你看電影。

III Now, Time to Listen!
p. 74

1 〔1〕 a 〔2〕 d 〔3〕 b 〔4〕 c 〔096〕

〔1〕 take my breath away, cheesy 〔097〕
〔2〕 take you out, Let me
〔3〕 where, pick me up
〔4〕 look a lot like, lame

Script & Translation

1 M | Hey there, beautiful. I hope you know CPR, because you take my breath away.
W | That's so cheesy.
M | Ha-ha. I know. I'm sorry. Hi, my name's Jake.
W | I'm Tina. You're funny, Jake. Are you an Aquarius?
男 | 嘿，美女，希望你會做心肺復甦術，因為你美得讓我窒息了。
女 | 這種搭訕法好俗喔。
男 | 哈哈，我知道啊，對不起。嗨，我叫杰克。
女 | 我是蒂娜，你很愛開玩笑喔，杰克。你是水瓶座嗎？

2 M | Can I get your number? I'd love to take you out sometime.
W | Yeah, I'd like that. Let me write it down for you.
M | Great. I'll call you.
男 | 我可以跟你要電話嗎？因為我想找一天約你出去。

| 女 | 好啊，可以啊，我寫給你。 |
| 男 | 太棒了，我再打電話給你。 |

3 M | Hi, Jane. this is Tommy. Are you free this Friday? I know a great restaurant where we can have dinner.
   W | Yes, I'm free. What time do you want to pick me up?
   M | How about 7:30?

男	嗨，珍，我是湯米。你這個星期五有空嗎？我知道一家很棒的餐廳，一起吃個晚飯吧。
女	好啊，我有空。你幾點要來接我？
男	7 點半好嗎？

4 M | Excuse me. Do I know you? Because you look a lot like my next girlfriend.
   W | Oh my God. That pickup line is so lame.
   M | So can I get your email address?
   W | Uh, no way.

男	不好意思，我是不是認識你？因為你長得好像我下一任女朋友。
女	噢，我的天啊。這種搭訕的話好爛喔。
男	那麼我可以跟你要 email 嗎？
女	噢，不行。

② 1 a 2 b 3 b 4 b 5 a 6 a 7 a 8 b 9 b 10 b 098

Script & Translation

弗瑞德

嗨，珍娜，我是弗瑞德。我們昨天在公園見過，真的聊得很愉快，不知道你願不願意哪天跟我出去。
如果你這個星期五沒事的話，我想帶你去一家我覺得很棒的餐廳。我們可以吃個晚飯，彼此多認識一些。
我不是那種經常約女孩子的人，所以不好意思，我可能聽起來有點緊張。不論如何，打個電話給我，告訴我你意下如何，好嗎？再見！

IV Now, Grammar Time! p. 76

⑤ 1 which, c 2 who, e 3 where, a 4 who, b 5 which, d

V Now, Time to Speak! p. 78

⑦

Translation 099

男	嘿，你好，我可以請你喝杯飲料嗎？
女	好啊。
男	你是什麼星座？
女	雙魚座。讓我猜猜，你是不是牡羊座？
男	對，沒錯。我們哪天約約吧。
女	不好意思，你不是我喜歡的類型耶。

VI Now, Time to Pronounce! p. 81

⑪ 1 a 2 c 3 d 4 g 102

Script

1 There's a **black**bird sitting on the **green house**.

2 The **red head** is in the **green**house.

3 John is drawing a **black bird** on the **white**board.

4 The **white board** is next to the **red**head.

Unit 10

I Topic Preview p. 82 103

1 When do you have to finish the project by?
   The deadline is 5:00 p.m. Tuesday.
   Do you think you'll meet the deadline?
   Yes, I think so. I'm on schedule.

▸ 你什麼時候要完成這個案子？
星期二下午五點以前要交。
你覺得你趕得出來嗎？
應該可以，我都有照進度進行。

2 Why do you look so worried?
   If I don't finish this by noon, it'll cost the company a lot of money.

   How's the report going? Almost finished?
   No, I'm having some problems with it. It's taking longer than I expected.
   Come on. I need this done by noon. Time is money.

▸ 你為什麼看起來很憂慮？
假如我中午以前沒辦法完成這件事的話，會害公司損失很多錢。

你的報告做得如何？快做完了吧？
還沒，出了點問題，報告比我想像中的費時。
快點唷，今天中午以前要完成，時間就是金錢。

3 How much longer is it going to take you to finish the presentation?
   I need to spend a few more hours working on it. Sorry.

▸ 你還需要多少時間才能完成這份簡報？
我還需要再做幾個小時，對不起。

4 Would it be possible to get an extension on my deadline? I'm really snowed under right now.

OK. How about I give you until Monday?	
That would be great. I should be able to finish it by then.	

> 有沒有可能延期呢？我現在真的忙不過來。
> 好吧，延到星期一可以嗎？
> 太好了，我那時應該做得完。

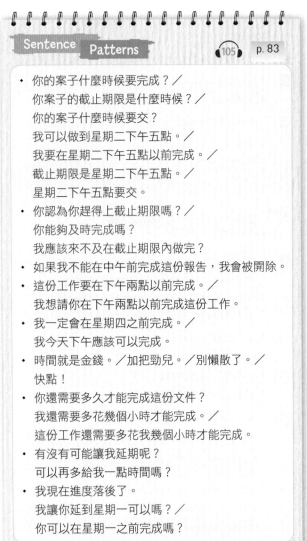

Sentence Patterns (105) p. 83

- 你的案子什麼時候完成？／
  你案子的截止期限是什麼時候？／
  你的案子什麼時候要交？
  我可以做到星期二下午五點。／
  我要在星期二下午五點以前完成。／
  截止期限是星期二下午五點。／
  星期二下午五點要交。
- 你認為你趕得上截止期限嗎？／
  你能夠及時完成嗎？
  我應該來不及在截止期限內做完？
- 如果我不能在中午前完成這份報告，我會被開除。
- 這份工作要在下午兩點以前完成。／
  我想請你在下午兩點以前完成這份工作。
- 我一定會在星期四之前完成。／
  我今天下午應該可以完成。
- 時間就是金錢。／加把勁兒。／別懶散了。／
  快點！
- 你還需要多久才能完成這份文件？
  我還需要多花幾個小時才能完成。／
  這份工作還需要多花我幾個小時才能完成。
- 有沒有可能讓我延期呢？
  可以再多給我一點時間嗎？
- 我現在進度落後了。
  我讓你延到星期一可以嗎？／
  你可以在星期一之前完成嗎？

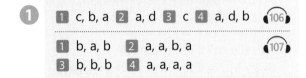

Now, Time to Listen!
p. 84

1

1 c, b, a	2 a, d	3 c	4 a, d, b	(106)

1 b, a, b	2 a, a, b, a	(107)
3 b, b, b	4 a, a, a, a	

Script & Translation

1

M	How much longer is it going to take you to finish the report?
W	Um, maybe another two hours.
M	OK. But remember, if you don't finish by two o' clock, the boss will be really mad.
W	Don't worry. I'll definitely have it done by then. I'm on track.

男	你還需要多久才能完成這份報告？
女	嗯，可能還要兩個小時。
男	好，但是要記得，如果兩點以前沒有完成，老闆會很生氣。
女	別擔心，那時候我一定可以完成，我有照進度在進行。

2

W	When's your project due, Sam?
Sam	It's due by 12 o'clock on Monday, but I'm really behind.
W	How come?
Sam	I'm up to my ears in other work. I just don't have enough time to finish it.
W	OK. I'll talk to the boss. Maybe I can get you an extension.

女	山姆，你的企劃案什麼時候要交？
山姆	星期一 12 點交，可是我進度落後很多。
女	怎麼會呢？
山姆	我其他的工作忙不過來，實在沒時間把這個案子趕完。
女	好吧，我會跟老闆說說，或許可以讓你延期。

3

W	Have you finished the report, John?
John	Not yet. Sorry.
W	How much longer is it going to take?
John	It'll take me another hour or so to finish it, and then I need to spend some time proofreading it.

女	約翰，你做完報告了沒？
約翰	還沒，對不起。
女	還需要多少時間？
約翰	還需要一個小時左右，接著還需要花一點時間校對。

4

W	How's the essay going, Will?
Will	Not so well. I've been sick recently, so I don't think I'll be able to finish it by the deadline.
W	How about I give you until Tuesday to finish it?
Will	Really? That would be great! Thank you, professor!
W	No problem. But if you don't finish it by Tuesday, I'm afraid I'll have to fail you.

女	威爾，你的文章寫得怎麼樣了？
威爾	不是很順利，我最近生病，可能沒辦法在截止期限內完成了。
女	我讓你延到星期二如何？
威爾	真的嗎？那太好了！教授，謝謝您！
女	這沒什麼。不過你星期二如果還是沒寫完，我可能就要把你當掉喔。

2 B (108)

b, c, e, i, j (109)

Mr. Price	How's the paperwork going, Jane?
Jane	Not so good, Mr. Price. I'm a little behind.
Mr. Price	Well, the deadline is this afternoon, so you need to get it done chop-chop!
Jane	Sorry, Mr. Price. I'll try, but I'm finding it hard to concentrate with all the noise outside.
Mr. Price	Jane, you need to stop making excuses and pull your socks up. If you don't finish it by 2:00 p.m., it will cost us a lot of money.
Jane	OK, Mr. Price. I'll definitely have it done by the deadline.
普萊斯先生	珍，你的文件弄得怎麼樣了？
珍	不太好，普萊斯先生，我進度有點落後。
普萊斯先生	嗯，截止期限是今天下午，所以你的動作要快一點了。
珍	對不起，普萊斯先生，我會盡力，可是外面的噪音讓我很難專心。
普萊斯先生	珍，你不能再找藉口了，快點加把勁兒。萬一下午兩點以前沒有做完，我們的財務損失會很大。
珍	好的，普萊斯先生，我一定會在截止期限之前趕完。

3
1. d much longer, going to take you (110)
2. b I've finished, report, spend, time editing
3. e How's, going, When's, due
4. a Would, possible, get, extension
5. c need, done by, Are, on track

1. How much longer is it going to take you to finish? 你還需要多久才能完成？
   It'll probably take me another three hours. 可能還要再三個小時。

2. I've finished the report, but I need to spend some time editing it.
   我已經做完報告了，可是還需要花一點時間校訂。
   Time is money, Tim. Chop-chop!
   時間就金錢，提姆，加把勁兒！

3. How's your essay going? When's it due again?
   你的論文寫得如何？下次是什麼時候要交？

The deadline is tomorrow. I'm really behind.
明天就要交，我落後很多。

4. Would it be possible to get an extension?
   有沒有可能延期呢？
   How about I give you until Monday evening to finish it? 我讓你延到星期一傍晚交如何？

5. I really need it done by this afternoon. Are you on track?
   今天下午一定要做完這工作，你有照進度進行嗎？
   Don't worry. I'll definitely have it done by then. 別擔心，我一定可以在那之前完成。

IV Now, Grammar Time! p. 86

4
1. it, take, to, take (me), proofreading
2. spend, spent, on, pays
3. cost, money, spend, spent / paid, costs / takes, to
4. spend, take, Editing, take

V Now, Time to Speak! p. 87

5

(111)

A 女 你的企劃案什麼時候要交？
   男 我可以做到星期一中午 12 點。
   女 你覺得你來得及嗎？
   男 可以，應該沒問題，我有照進度走。
B 男 愛蜜麗，你的論文寫得怎麼樣？
   女 不是很順利，我現在的進度有點落後。
   男 別忘了我要你在星期一中午 12 點前完成。
   女 好，我到時候一定會趕出來。

6

Mr. Jones	Have you almost finished your _presentation_, Simon?
Simon	Sorry, Mr. Jones. I'm _a little behind_.
Mr. Jones	Well, _the deadline is this afternoon_, so get it done chop-chop!
Simon	Sorry, Mr. Jones. I'll try, but I'm _finding it hard to focus_.
Mr. Jones	Simon, quit _making excuses_. If you don't _finish it by 2:00 p.m._, _I'll find someone else to do it_.
Simon	_Would it be possible for me to_ get an extension?
Mr. Jones	Hmm. How _much longer are you going to take_?
Simon	_It's going to take me another three hours._

Mr. Jones	OK. Have it on my desk by <u>*five o'clock*</u> .
瓊斯先生	賽門，你的簡報快要做完了嗎？
賽門	對不起，瓊斯先生，我有點<u>落後</u>。
瓊斯先生	嗯，<u>截止期限是今天下午</u>，所以動作要快一點！
賽門	對不起，瓊斯先生，我會盡量，可是<u>好難專心</u>。
瓊斯先生	賽門，別再找<u>藉口</u>了。如果你沒在<u>下午兩點以前做出來，我就要找別人做了</u>。
賽門	<u>能不能多給我一點時間</u>？
瓊斯先生	嗯，你還需要多少時間？
賽門	<u>還要三個小時</u>。
瓊斯先生	好吧，<u>五點</u>以前把成品放在我桌上。

Ⅵ Now, Time to Pronounce!
p. 89

⑧  🎧113
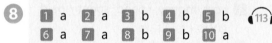

🎧 Script

1 trial	2 employer	3 bow	4 flow
5 great	6 tower	7 greyer	8 try
9 deploy	10 follower		

Unit 11

Ⅰ Topic Preview
p. 90 🎧117

1 Some people have complained about you biting your nails at your desk.
What? I don't bite my nails, do I?
- - - - - - - - - - - - - - - - - - - -
Could you stop cracking your knuckles? It's driving me crazy.
I'm so sorry. I'll try to stop myself in future.

▸ 有人抱怨你在位子上咬指甲。
什麼？我沒有咬指甲啊，我有嗎？
- - - - - - - - - - - - - - - - - - - -
你能不能不要一直折指節？我都快要瘋了。
對不起，我以後會克制的。

2 How can I break this habit?
Maybe you could try replacing your habit with another action.
How did you quit smoking?
I went to see a hypnotist, and he cured me.

▸ 我要怎麼改掉這個習慣？
或許你可以用另一個動作來代替這個習慣。
你是怎麼戒菸的？
我去找催眠師，是他把我治好的。

3 OK. I admit it. I'm addicted to Facebook.
- - - - - - - - - - - - - - - - - - - -
I guess I do sometimes eavesdrop when I'm lonely.

▸ 好吧，我承認，我沈迷於臉書。
- - - - - - - - - - - - - - - - - - - -
我想，我孤單的時候，的確偶爾會偷聽別人說話。

4 If you don't go on Facebook, how do you feel?
I feel really agitated and nervy. I just can't help myself.

▸ 你不上臉書會怎樣？
我會很焦慮不安，我真的沒辦法控制自己。

5 If you don't quit picking your nose, I'm going to have to break up with you.
I'll do my best to stop.

▸ 你再不改掉挖鼻孔的習慣，我就要跟你分手。
我會盡力改的。

Sentence Patterns
🎧119 p. 91

- 很多人都抱怨過你咬指甲的事。／
你能不能不要再折指節了，我聽得很煩耶。／
你那樣翻白眼真的很討人厭耶。
- 我根本不知道我有那樣。／
我沒有滿嘴東西的時候說話吧，我有嗎？
- 我要怎麼改掉這個壞習慣呢？／
你有沒有可以不罵髒話的秘訣？
- 或許你可以／應該用別的事取代你的習慣。
我去找催眠師，他把我治好的。
- 我承認我太迷（看）連續劇了。／
我想，我感到壓力大的時候，的確偶爾會抽菸。
- 你如果不折指節會怎麼樣？
我不折指節就會感到焦慮。
- 你為什麼要咬指甲？
咬指甲能讓我感覺平靜。／我一緊張就會咬指甲。
- 你再不改掉挖鼻孔的習慣，我就要跟你分手。
- 我以後會克制的。／我會努力改的。

Ⅲ Now, Time to Listen!
p. 92

①  🎧120
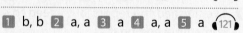 🎧121

🎧 Script & Translation

Dom	Fran, can I talk to you for a second?
Fran	Sure, Dom. What's up?
Dom	Uh, this is a bit awkward, but a lot of our customers have complained about you cracking your knuckles.

Fran	Cracking my knuckles? I don't crack my knuckles, do I?
Dom	Well, apparently you do. And if you don't stop doing it, I'm going to have to replace you, I'm afraid.
Fran	Oh my God! Well, I guess I do sometimes crack my knuckles when I'm stressed. I guess it makes me feel more relaxed.
Dom	Maybe you could try replacing it with something else, like doodling.
Fran	Yeah, OK. Thanks, Dom. I'll do my best to quit.
唐姆	法蘭，可以和你談談嗎？
法蘭	當然可以，唐姆，什麼事？
唐姆	喔，有點難以啟齒，可是我們很多客人抱怨你折指節的事。
法蘭	折指節？我沒有折指節啊，我有嗎？
唐姆	嗯，顯然你有，所以如果你不改掉的話，我恐怕就要把你換掉了。
法蘭	噢，天啊！嗯，我想我一有壓力，的確有時候會折指節，可能那樣能讓我比較放鬆。
唐姆	說不定你可以試著做別的事啊，像是塗鴉。
法蘭	也對，好。唐姆，謝謝，我會努力改的。

② ❶ c ❷ a ❸ d ❹ b ❺ e (122)

Script & Translation

❶	M	OK, I admit it. I do sometimes roll my eyes when I'm annoyed.
	W	Finally! At least you've admitted it now.
	男	好，我承認，我如果感到厭煩，有時的確會翻白眼。
	女	終於！你現在總算承認了。
❷	W	Can you give me any tips on how to stop eavesdropping?
	M	Hmm. Maybe you could try seeing a therapist.
	女	你能不能教我改掉偷聽習慣的方法？
	男	嗯，或許你可以試試看去看治療師。
❸	M	Why do you think you spend so much time on social networks?
	W	I guess going on those sites makes me feel popular.
	男	你覺得你為什麼要花那麼多時間上社群網站？
	女	我覺得上社群網站會讓我覺得受歡迎。
❹	W	If you don't stop drumming your fingers, I'm going to have to stop talking to you.
	M	Is it really that bad? I think you're overreacting.

女	你如果繼續用手指敲桌子，我就不跟你說話了。
男	真有那麼嚴重嗎？我覺得你反應過度了。
❺	M	It's really annoying when you talk with your mouth full like that.
	W	Sorry. I didn't even realize I was doing it.
	男	你滿嘴東西還要說話，真的很討人厭。
	女	對不起，我真的不知道自己會那樣。

③ ❶ Terry ❷ Lisa ❸ Lisa (123)
❹ Tina ❺ Tina ❻ Lisa, Tina

a I'm addicted (124)
b distracted me from
c saw a therapist
d used to talk to herself

Script & Translation

Terry	Lisa, I need your help. I'm addicted to online games, and I don't know how to give them up.
Lisa	OK. Well, maybe you could distract yourself by doing something else, like taking a walk.
Terry	I see. Has that worked for you in the past?
Lisa	Yes, it has. I was addicted to soap operas for a long time, but then I got a pet. Caring for a pet really distracted me from watching soaps.
Terry	Right, I see. But what if it doesn't work?
Lisa	If that doesn't work, you could go and see a therapist. My friend Tina saw a therapist to cure her bad habit. She used to talk to herself nonstop, but now she doesn't do it at all.
泰瑞	麗莎，我需要你的幫助。我迷上了線上遊戲，我不知道該怎麼戒掉。
麗莎	好，嗯，或許你可以做別的事來轉移注意力呀，像是散步。
泰瑞	我懂，你以前試過有用嗎？
麗莎	有用，我以前有好長一段時間迷上連續劇，後來我就養寵物，照顧寵物可以分散我的注意力，就不會那麼想看連續劇了。
泰瑞	說的也是，我懂了。但是萬一沒用怎麼辦？
麗莎	如果沒用的話，你可以去找治療師。我朋友蒂娜就是找治療師矯正她的壞習慣。她以前會不停自言自語，現在完全不會了。

IV Now, Grammar Time!
p. 94

④ ❶ themselves ❷ us ❸ herself
❹ himself ❺ me ❻ myself
❼ you ❽ yourself

V Now, Time to Speak!
p. 95

5

🎧 Translation (125)

Ⓐ
潘	吉姆，這有點難以啟齒，但是有人抱怨你偷聽他們説話。
吉姆	噢，對不起，我無聊的時候的確會偷聽別人説話。
潘	嗯，還好你肯承認。或許你可以做點其他事取代偷聽，例如説塗鴉。
吉姆	對，沒錯，那是好方法。

Ⓑ
愛琳	彼特，你能不能教我一些戒菸的方法？
彼特	好，我問你，你如果不抽菸會有什麼感覺？
愛琳	我如果不抽菸會很焦慮。
彼特	嗯，那你可能要去找催眠師。

7

🎧 Translation (Sample Answers)

A | Could you _please stop picking your nose like that_. It's really _disgusting_ .
B | What? I didn't even know _I was doing it_ .
A | Well, if you don't _quit picking your nose soon_ , I'm going to have to _break up with you_ .
B | OK. Well, what can I do to break the habit?
A | Let me ask you something. Why do you _think you pick your nose_ ?
B | I usually do it _because I'm bored_ .
A | OK. Then maybe you should try replacing _picking your nose with something else_ , like _tapping your leg_ .
B | That's not a bad idea. Thanks. I'll _do my best to quit_ .

A | 你可不可以不要那樣挖鼻孔，很噁心耶。
B | 什麼？我不知道我有那樣做。
A | 嗯，你如果不快點改掉挖鼻孔的習慣，我就要跟你分手。
B | 好，嗯，可是我要怎麼改掉這個習慣？
A | 我問你，你覺得你為什麼會挖鼻孔？
B | 通常是覺得無聊吧。
A | 好，那麼或許你應該改做其他事情，來取代挖鼻孔，例如説拍大腿。
B | 那個方法好像也不錯，謝謝，我會努力改的。

VI Now, Time to Pronounce!
p. 97

10
| ① Jill | ② soap operas | (127) |
| ③ nine | ④ smoking | |

Unit 12

I Topic Preview
p. 98 (128)

1

This is so frustrating! My computer keeps crashing, and I don't know why it's doing that.
Hmm. Maybe it's a virus. Have you run a system scan recently?

Do you know how to get my computer to run faster?
You could perform a disk cleanup. Try deleting your temporary Internet files.

▸ 太令人沮喪了！我的電腦一直當機，我也找不出原因。
嗯，可能中毒了，你最近有沒有掃毒？

你知道要怎麼讓電腦跑快一點嗎？
你可以執行磁碟清理，或試著刪一些網頁暫存檔。

2

What do you mostly use the Internet for?
I use it mostly for reading the news.
Which search engine do you use?
I usually use Google.
Do you download a lot of movies from online stores?
Yes, and music, too.

▸ 你通常上網做什麼？
我多半上網看新聞。
你用哪一個搜尋引擎？
我通常用谷歌。
你會常常從網路商店下載電影嗎？
會，也會下載音樂。

3

This is the newest model. It has an HD camera, 64 gigabytes of memory, and 4G.

▸ 這是最新的機種，內建 HD 畫質相機、64 GB 的記憶體，還有 4G 網路的功能。

4

Stop using your smartphone all the time.
Sorry. I'm just checking the latest soccer results.
That phone has made you really antisocial.

Can you not use your phone while we're eating?
Sorry. I'm just texting my boss.

▸ 你不要一直用你的智慧型手機。
對不起，我只是想查一下最新的足球賽況。
那支手機讓你變得很孤僻耶。

我們吃飯的時候，你不要玩手機好不好？
對不起，我只是想傳簡訊給我老闆。

Sentence Patterns p. 99

- 我的電腦不知道為什麼一直當機。
  可能記憶體不足，你最近有沒有刪除網頁暫存檔？
- 你知道要怎麼讓電腦不要一直自動關機嗎？
  你可以執行系統掃瞄。／試著充電看看。
- 你在用哪一種社群網站？
- 你都上網做什麼？
  我都上網查資料。
- 你下載很多應用程式嗎？
- 你不要一直玩線上遊戲。／
  有了那支手機讓你變得很孤僻耶。
- 你不要在我們說話的時候傳簡訊好嗎？
  對不起，我只是要傳給我朋友。

III Now, Time to Listen! p. 100

1 Jimmy: d Kate: b (131)

Script & Translation

Jimmy	Hey, Kate. Oh, wow! Is that your new smartphone?
Kate	Yeah. It's beautiful, isn't it?
Jimmy	Wow. Has it got 3G?
Kate	Are you kidding me? It's got 4G. This is the newest model.
Jimmy	Nice. Mine's only got 3G. Does yours use Android 4.0?
Kate	No, 4.2. And it's got 16 gigabytes of memory as well.
Jimmy	Only 16? Mine's got 64!
Kate	Oh, right. But I can use a 32-gigabyte memory card in mine.
Jimmy	Oh, well, that's not too bad, then.
Kate	Wait, though. The best bit is the camera. It's a 16-megapixel HD camera.
Jimmy	Wow! I bet that takes great photos! Mine only has eight megapixels, so the photos are sometimes a bit fuzzy.

吉米	嘿，凱特，喔，哇！那是你新買的智慧型手機嗎？
凱特	對啊，很美吧？
吉米	哇，有 3G 嗎？
凱特	開玩笑，是 4G 呢，這支是最新款。
吉米	好棒，我的只有 3G。你的手機是使用安卓 4.0 的系統嗎？
凱特	不是，是 4.2，還有 16 GB 的記憶體。
吉米	只有 16 GB 嗎？我的有 64 GB 耶！
凱特	喔，對啊，可是還可以外接 32 GB 的記憶卡。
吉米	喔，好吧，那也不錯。

| 凱特 | 不過等等，這支手機最棒的是它的相機，是 1600 萬畫素的高畫質相機喔。 |
| 吉米 | 哇賽！拍出來的照片一定很棒！我的只有 800 萬畫素，所以照片有時候會糊糊的。 |

2

1 give me a hand, error message, (132) tried turning it off

2 see your new smartphone, it have 4G, -megapixel HD camera, operating system

3 mostly use, downloading, chatting with my friends, social network, on that

4 just checking Facebook, using your phone, pay more attention

Translation

1	東尼	珍妮，你可不可以幫我一下？
	珍妮	沒問題，東尼，什麼事？
	東尼	我的電腦一直顯示這個錯誤訊息，你知道是什麼問題嗎？
	珍妮	嗯，我也不確定。你有沒有試過關機再重開機？

2	比爾	我可以看你新的智慧型手機嗎？
	珊蒂	好啊，當然可以，在這裡。
	比爾	哇，不錯耶。這支有 4G 嗎？
	珊蒂	有啊，還有1300 萬畫素的高畫質相機。
	比爾	哇！拍出來的照片一定很漂亮。它用的是哪一套作業系統？
	珊蒂	iOS 6。

3	黛比	彼特，你多半都上網做什麼？
	彼特	我多半上網下載電視節目，你呢？
	黛比	我多半上網和朋友聊天。
	彼特	喔，是喔。你用哪一個社群網站？
	黛比	我用 Google Plus，你有上這個網站嗎？
	彼特	沒有，不好意思，我都用臉書。

4	愛麗絲	約翰！約翰！你有沒有在聽我說話？
	約翰	什麼？有啊。不好意思，我只是看一下臉書而已。
	愛麗絲	不要一直用手機好不好，很沒禮貌耶。
	約翰	對不起，我會專心聽你說話。
	愛麗絲	最好是。有了那支手機之後，你都變孤僻了。

3

| 1 b | 2 a | 3 c | (133) |

Problems	2-1-5-3-4	(134)
Internet habits	3-5-1-4-2	
Annoyances	2-4-3-5-1	

Script & Translation

| 1 Lea | Do you download a lot of music, Jimmy? |

Jimmy	No, not really. I mostly use the Internet for downloading movies. You?
Lea	I like to use the Internet to make new friends. I also like to upload my photos, so my friends can see them.
Jimmy	Oh, right. I don't use social networks very often, but I do sometimes chat with people when I'm playing online games.
麗雅	吉米，你下載過很多音樂嗎？
吉米	沒有很多，我多半用網路下載電影。你呢？
麗雅	我喜歡上網交新朋友，我也喜歡上傳照片給朋友看。
吉米	喔，這樣啊。我不常用社群網站，不過有時候會一邊玩線上遊戲，一邊和別人聊天。

2	Lea	Jimmy, do you know how to get my laptop to stop shutting itself down?
	Jimmy	I don't know, Lea. Maybe the battery's low. Have you tried charging it?
	Lea	Yeah, I just charged it yesterday. It should be fine.
	Jimmy	Maybe it's a virus, then. Have you installed an antivirus software?
	Lea	Yes, I have.
	Jimmy	OK then. You should run a system scan.
	麗雅	吉米，你知道怎麼讓筆電不要一直自動關機嗎？
	吉米	我不知道，麗雅。可能電池快沒電了吧，你有沒有充電？
	麗雅	有啊，我昨天才充過，電池應該沒問題呀。
	吉米	那麼說不定中毒了，你有沒有安裝防毒軟體？
	麗雅	有。
	吉米	好，那你應該執行掃毒程式。

3	Lea	What are you doing, Jimmy?
	Jimmy	I'm emailing my boss.
	Lea	But it's 9:00 p.m. We're in a restaurant!
	Jimmy	I know, but this is important.
	Lea	Look, can you not use it right now? It's really rude.
	Jimmy	You're right. I'm sorry. I'll turn it off.
	麗雅	吉米，你在做什麼？
	吉米	我在寫電子郵件給我老闆。

麗雅	可是現在是晚上九點，我們在餐廳裡耶！
吉米	我知道，可是這很重要。
麗雅	喂，你不要現在用好嗎？很沒禮貌耶！
吉米	說的也是，對不起，我現在關掉。

 Now, Grammar Time! p. 103

4 (Sample Answers)

Ⓐ Do you know why my laptop freezes every time I go online?
Do you have any idea what else it could be?
Do you know if the battery is charged?
Can you tell me when you last performed a disk cleanup?
Do you know how to perform a disk cleanup?

Ⓑ Can you tell me what operating system the new model uses?
Do you know if that's good?
Can you tell me if it has an HD camera?
Do you have any idea how much memory it has?
Do you know if I'll be able to use a memory card with that?

 Now, Time to Speak! p. 104

6

 Translation (135)

露西	那是你的新智慧型手機嗎？
丹	對啊，我上個月才買的。
露西	哇，看起來很棒耶！這是什麼型號的？
丹	是三星的 GALAXY S4，有 4G 的功能和 800 萬畫素高畫質相機。
露西	讚！拍攝影片一定也很棒。它用的是哪一套操作系統？安卓 4.1 嗎？
丹	不是，是 4.2！
露西	喔，好。有 64 GB 記憶體嗎？
丹	沒有，只有 16 GB，但是可以外接記憶卡升到 64 GB。
露西	酷。老實說，我下個月也要買新的智慧型手機。
丹	喔，真的嗎？你想買哪一款？
露西	我看上索尼最新出的 Xperia Z Ultra。
丹	我聽過那一支，聽說相機功能很強。
露西	沒錯，雖然只有 800 萬畫素，但畫質非常好。
丹	那支也是安卓 4.2，對吧？
露西	沒錯，也可以外接最大 64 GB 的記憶卡，不過這不是我想買的主因。
丹	不是嗎？
露西	不是，我想買的主因是有設計感，非常纖薄，厚度只有 6.5 公釐。

7

Translation　Sample Answers

1　W　Can you stop using your smartphone while we're having coffee?

　　M　I'm just checking the soccer score.

　　W　It's so annoying.

　　M　I'm sorry.

　　W　Turn your phone off right now!

　女　我們在喝咖啡，你不要玩智慧型手機好嗎？

　男　我只是想查一下足球賽的比數。

　女　很煩耶。

　男　對不起

　女　你現在就關機！

2　M　Can you give me a hand? My computer is running really slowly.

　　W　Have you tried turning it off and on again?

　　M　Yes, I have, but it's still really slow.

　　W　Maybe the memory is full. Have you tried running a disk cleanup?

　　M　No, I haven't.

　　W　OK. Try deleting your temporary Internet files.

　男　請你幫我一個忙好嗎？我的電腦跑得好慢。

　女　你有沒有關機重開看看？

　男　有，我重開過了，可是還是很慢。

　女　可能是記憶體不足，你試過清理磁碟嗎？

　男　沒有。

　女　好，你刪除一些網頁暫存檔看看。

VI Now, Time to Pronounce!　p. 107

9　🎧139

1 Could you **please ask John** to **fix** my comp**u**ter?

2 **What** do you **think** the **pro**blem is?

3 Can you **give** me a **hand** for a **minute**?

4 I would have **helped** you if you'd **asked**.

5 Would you **like** me to **give** you some ad**vice**?

6 **Why** do you **always** have to **text** when we're **eat**ing?

Unit 13

I Topic Preview　p. 108　🎧140

1 I really need to lose a few pounds.

Me, too. The older I get, the harder it is to stay in shape.

My problem is my lifestyle is really unhealthy. I never exercise.

My weakness is fatty foods. And I snack while I'm working.

▸我實在需要減輕幾磅。

我也是，年紀越大，身材也越來越難維持。

我的問題在於生活方式很不健康，我從來不運動。

我的罩門是油膩食品，而且我還邊工作邊吃點心。

2 I want to lose 20 pounds by this time next month.

I want to get rid of my love handles.

My goal is to get a flat stomach.

▸我希望下個月的此時可以減掉 20 磅。

我想要消除腰部的贅肉。

我的目標是瘦小腹。

3 I have to avoid carbohydrates, and I'm only allowed to eat cabbage soup.

That sounds like a fad diet to me.

▸我必須禁吃碳水化合物，而且只能喝高麗菜湯。

聽起來像是極端減肥法。

4 The best way to lose weight is to exercise.

I agree, but eating healthily is just as important.

▸最好的減肥方法就是運動。

我同意，但是吃得健康也很重要。

5 I've been dieting for weeks, but I just can't get rid of my gut.

When I was younger, I could eat anything and not put on weight. Now everything I eat goes straight to my thighs.

I find it really hard not to give in to temptation.

▸我已經節食好幾個禮拜了，但肚子還是消不下去。

我年輕的時候，怎麼吃都不會胖。現在吃的全都胖到大腿去了。

我發現抗拒誘惑真的很難。

Sentence Patterns　🎧142　p. 109

- 我真的需要練一下腹肌。
- 我的壓力越大，就越容易發胖。
- 我的問題在於吃了太多碳水化合物。
- 我無法抗拒冰淇淋。
- 我希望明年的此時可以減掉 100 磅。
- 我想要瘦大腿。／我的目標是練出結實的腹肌。
- 我要避免攝取蛋白質。／
  我一天（只）能吃 1000 大卡。／我不能喝咖啡。
- 最好的減肥方式是少量多餐。

III Now, Time to Listen!

p. 110

1 **1** a, b, d **2** a, c, e **3** a **4** c (143)

Script & Translation

Jane	Marty, I need your advice.
Marty	OK, what's up?
Jane	Well, I need to lose a few pounds, and I was wondering if you had any advice on losing weight.
Marty	Sure. What are your goals?
Jane	I'd really like to lose 10 pounds by this time next month. And I really want to tone up my arms and thighs.
Marty	OK. Well, the best way to do that is to work out for half an hour every day, eat fewer carbohydrates, and stay away from foods with a lot of saturated fat.
Jane	I don't eat many carbohydrates or fatty foods anyway. But exercise? Oh, no! I hate exercise. I'm really lazy.
Marty	Hmm. Well, do you like watching TV?
Jane	Yeah.
Marty	Why don't you exercise while you're watching TV?
Jane	That's a pretty good idea. Thanks, Marty.
珍	馬堤，我需要你的建議。
馬堤	好啊，什麼事？
珍	嗯，我想減個幾磅，不知道你有沒有減肥的好方法。
馬堤	好啊，你的目標是什麼？
珍	我希望下個月此時，我可以減 10 磅，而且我還想練手臂和大腿。
馬堤	好，嗯，最好的方法就是每天運動半小時，減少攝取碳水化合物，遠離富含飽和脂肪的食物。
珍	反正我也不常吃碳水化合物和油膩的食物，但是說到運動，噢，不！我討厭運動，我超懶的。
馬堤	嗯，那你喜歡看電視嗎？
珍	喜歡啊。
馬堤	何不一邊看電視一邊運動呢？
珍	這個方法不錯，謝謝，馬堤。

2 (144)

1 b	❶ pounds (Y)	my gut, goes straight
	❷ flat stomach (N)	
2 c	❶ love handles (N)	is having to exercise
	❷ tone up (N)	
	❸ toned thighs (N)	
3 a	❶ six-pack (N)	carbohydrates, snack
	❷ lose 30 (Y)	
	❸ double chin (Y)	

Script & Translation

1

Sarah	Tell me about your diet, John.
John	Well, I have to avoid carbohydrates and eat half a grapefruit with every meal.
Sarah	How's it going?
John	Pretty well. My goals are to lose 20 pounds and get a flat stomach, and I've already lost 20 pounds.
Sarah	Great! Have you found anything particularly challenging so far?
John	Yeah, I've been dieting for a month now, and I just can't get rid of my gut. The thing is everything I eat goes straight to my belly.
Sarah	Well, keep at it!
莎拉	約翰，你節食的方法是什麼？
約翰	喔，我會避免攝取碳水化合物，還有每餐吃半個葡萄柚。
莎拉	成效如何？
約翰	非常好。我的目標是要減 20 磅，還要練出平坦的小腹。而我已經成功減了 20 磅。
莎拉	好棒喔！那麼目前為止，有沒有哪一部分特別難？
約翰	有啊，我已經節食一個月了，可是肚子還是消不下去，吃什麼都胖到肚子去。
莎拉	嗯，繼續加油喔！

2

John	So, how's your diet going, Sarah?
Sarah	Not too well. My goals are to get rid of my love handles, tone up my arms, and get really toned thighs.
John	So, what's the problem?
Sarah	Well, the worst thing is having to exercise every day.
John	Yeah, I hate exercise, too. What diet are you doing again?
Sarah	I'm doing the one where I'm only allowed to eat red and orange foods, like apples, carrots, tomatoes—that kind of thing.

John	That's a weird diet. Is it working?
Sarah	No. So far I haven't achieved any of my goals.
約翰	莎拉，你減肥減得如何？
莎拉	不是很成功，我的目標是消掉腰部的贅肉、把手臂練結實，還有大腿也要很結實。
約翰	那麼問題出在哪裡？
莎拉	嗯，最痛苦的是要每天運動。
約翰	沒錯，我也討厭運動。你的減肥方法是什麼？
莎拉	我現在採用的減肥法，是只能吃紅色和橘色的食物，像是蘋果、胡蘿蔔、番茄之類的。
約翰	好奇怪的減肥法，有用嗎？
莎拉	沒用，到現在半個目標都沒達成。

3

Sarah	Oh, hi, Barney. Wow, you don't look well. Are you OK?
Barney	I'm fine, I'm fine. It's just the diet I'm on.
Sarah	Oh, what diet's that?
Barney	Well, I have to eat lots of proteins, and I'm only allowed 800 calories a day.
Sarah	That sounds like a fad diet to me. Have you achieved any of your goals?
Barney	You tell me. My goals are to get a six-pack, lose 30 pounds, and get rid of my double chin.
Sarah	Wow, well, you don't have a double chin anymore, and you look a lot thinner.
Barney	That's right! I've lost 40 pounds! I still don't have my six-pack, though.
Sarah	Well, that's OK. Keep at it. Are you finding anything difficult?
Barney	Yeah, I find it really hard not to eat carbohydrates. And I do sometimes snack while I'm watching TV.
莎拉	喔，嗨，巴尼。哇，你的臉色不太好，你沒事吧？
巴尼	我沒事，我沒事，只是在減肥而已。
莎拉	喔，什麼減肥法？
巴尼	嗯，就是攝取大量蛋白質，但是一天只能吃 800 卡路里。
莎拉	我覺得這樣太極端了，你有達到目標嗎？
巴尼	你說呢？我的目標是要練出六塊肌、減 30 磅，還要消除雙下巴。

莎拉	哇，嗯，你沒有雙下巴了，看起來也瘦了許多。
巴尼	這就對啦！我已經減了 40 磅！可是還沒練出六塊肌。
莎拉	嗯，沒關係啦，繼續努力。有沒有特別困難的部分？
巴尼	有啊，我發現不吃碳水化合物真的很難，而且我看電視免不了會吃點零嘴。

3   c   (145)

(146)
1. eat → exercise
2. problem → weakness
3. after I work → while I'm working
4. laziness → temptation
5. get fat → put on weight
6. overweight → in shape

Script & Translation

Matt	Hey, Joan. Have you watched the workout video I gave you?
Joan	Hey, Matt. Yeah, I've watched it. But it's weird; the more I exercise, the more weight I put on!
Matt	What? That's crazy! What's your diet like?
Joan	OK, I admit it's not very healthy. My weakness is junk food, you see? And I like to eat chocolate while I'm working out.
Matt	Oh my God, Joan! No wonder you're not losing weight. You have to control yourself.
Joan	But it's hard, Matt. I find it really hard not to give in to temptation.
Matt	You have to try harder, Joan.
Joan	I know, I know. The thing is, when I was a kid, I could eat anything and never put on weight.
Matt	Well, as we get older, it gets harder and harder to stay in shape. And you have to eat the right food. Eating the right food is just as important as exercising.
麥特	嘿，瓊恩，你有沒有看我給你的健身影片？
瓊恩	嘿，麥特，有啊，我有看。可是好奇怪，我越做越胖耶！
麥特	什麼？太誇張了！你都吃些什麼？
瓊恩	好啦，我承認我吃得很不健康。你知道嗎？我的罩門就是垃圾食物啊，而且我喜歡一邊運動一邊吃巧克力。
麥特	噢，天啊，瓊恩！難怪你會胖，你要克制一點啦。
瓊恩	可是很難耶，麥特。我發現要抗拒誘惑真的好難。

麥特	你要更努力，瓊恩。
瓊恩	我知道，我知道。問題是，以前我小的時候，怎麼吃都吃不胖。
麥特	嗯，隨著年紀增長，會越來越難維持身材。你一定要吃得對，正確飲食和運動一樣重要。

IV Now, Grammar Time!
p. 112

 4 Sample Answers

- a While I'm driving.
- b As I (we) get older, I (we) get fatter.
- c When I was in college.
- d While my husband is sleeping.
- e As I exercise, I burn calories.
- f I was eating cake while watching an exercise video.
- g No, I was thin when I was a child.
- h As my diet improves, I'll feel more energetic.

V Now, Time to Speak!
p. 113

5

Translation　Sample Answers

A | Let me tell you about this new diet I'm on.
B | OK. What's it called?
A | It's called the grapefruit diet .
B | And what does it involve?
A | Well, I have to avoid carbohydrates , and eat a grapefruit with every meal . I also have to eat lots of fats and proteins .
B | Hmm. I don't know. It sounds like a fad diet to me.
A | OK, well, what do you think is the best way to lose weight?
B | Eating fewer calories and exercising regularly . But exercising regularly is more important than eating fewer calories .
A | Oh, but I hate exercising !

A | 我想跟你說我現在施行的新減肥法。
B | 好，什麼減肥法？
A | 叫做葡萄柚減肥法。
B | 方法是什麼？
A | 嗯，要避免攝取碳水化合物，每餐吃一顆葡萄柚，還要多攝取脂肪和蛋白質。
B | 嗯，我不知道，可是聽起來太極端了。
A | 對啊，嗯，那你認為最好的減肥法是什麼？
B | 減少卡路里的攝取量，加上規律地運動。但是規律地運動比減少卡路里還重要。
A | 噢，可是我討厭運動！

VI Now, Time to Pronounce!
p. 115

 10
149

Tim	going	OK	problems
goals	healthily	exercising	goals
at it	Jenny	quit	give up
workout videos	you		video

Translation

珍妮	嗨，提姆，你節食進行得如何？
提姆	還可以，但是我遇到一些問題。
珍妮	喔，你遇到無法達成目標的問題是嗎？
提姆	對啊，我吃得很健康，也有運動，可是只達成了一項目標。
珍妮	嗯，繼續努力。
提姆	我不知道，珍妮，我覺得我應該放棄。
珍妮	不要放棄，我給你一片我在看的健身影片。
提姆	你覺得有用嗎？
珍妮	有用。我靠著這個影片，一個月瘦了 20 磅。

Unit 14

I Topic Preview
p. 116　150

1 | I don't know what to do after I graduate. I don't have any money to go traveling, so what should I do?
Let's look at your options. Since you don't have any money, you could either get a job or continue your studies.

▸ 我不知道畢業後要做什麼，我也沒錢去旅行，我該做什麼呢？
我們來看看你有哪些選擇。既然你沒錢，不是找工作就是繼續升學。

2 | Should I study for a master's degree, or should I take a gap year? I just can't decide.
- -
I'm torn between studying English and studying math. Which one should I do?

▸ 我應該去讀碩士班還是放自己一年假呢？我無法決定。
- -
我無法抉擇主修英文或數學，到底該選哪一個呢？

3 | On the one hand, getting a car would be expensive. On the other, it would give me a lot of freedom.
- -
Getting a tattoo is not only painful but also for life. But then again, tattoos are really cool.

▸ 一方面，買車很花錢；另一方面，開車比較自由。

刺青不僅會痛，而且是一輩子的。但是話說回來，
刺青真的很酷。

4
Have you made your decision?
Yes, I have. I've decided to run for election.
Why did you make that decision?
Because I think it'll be a good experience.

▸ 你做好決定了嗎？
是的，我決定要參選。
你為何做此決定？
我認為這是一個很好的經驗。

5
If you were me, what would you do in my situation?
If I were you, I would do neither.

▸ 如果你是我，面對這種情況，你會怎麼做？
如果我是你，我兩者都不會做。

Sentence Patterns
 152 p. 117

- 我們來看一下你有哪些選擇。／
  我們來縮小選擇範圍。
- 既然你沒錢，你應該／可以……／
  由於你已經會說法文，……可能比較好。
- 你應該／可以主修現代語文或歷史。
- 我應該去讀碩士班，或是休假一年呢？／
  我在讀碩士班和休假一年之間猶豫不決。
- 我們來衡量一下優缺點。
- 一方面，你可以獲得寶貴的人生經驗；另一方面，
  卻是很大的開銷。
- 讀碩士班不僅辛苦，也很耗時。
- 但是話又說回來，你的履歷會比較漂亮。
- 如果你是我，你會怎麼做？
  如果我是你，我會接受這份工作。
- 你決定了嗎？
  決定了，我要讀碩士班。
  為什麼？
  因為我覺得讀碩士班可以開創更多職場機會。
  因為可以藉此機會獲得人生經驗。

III Now, Time to Listen!
p. 118

1   b   a   d   c 153

Script & Translation

1 W | Have you made your decision yet?
   M | Well, I've been weighing up the pros and cons. On the one hand, it'd be good to start making some money. But on the other hand, I'd like to do

some traveling before I settle down, you know?
女 | 你做好決定了沒？
男 | 嗯，我還在衡量優缺點。一方面，能開始賺點錢是好事；但是另一方面，我又想在定下來之前四處旅行。

2 W | OK. Let's weight up the pros and cons.
   M | All right. Pros: not only would it be a good way to get to work, but it'd also make me popular with the ladies. On the other hand, I admit, it could be dangerous.
女 | 好，我們來衡量一下好處與壞處。
男 | 好。好處是，這樣要上班比較方便，在女孩子面前也比較吃香。壞處是，我承認是有點危險。

3 M | If you were me, what would you do?
   W | I'd do it. I think it'd be a good way of meeting new people. And not only that, it'd be fun, too. You might even meet your future wife!
男 | 換做是你的話，你會怎麼辦？
女 | 我會去。我覺得這是認識新朋友的好機會，不只如此，還很好玩，說不定你甚至會遇到未來的老婆呢！

4 W | Have you decided what to do?
   M | Yes, I'm going to do it!
   W | Why did you decide on that?
   M | Because it'll be a once-in-a-lifetime experience! If I don't do it, I'll regret it forever.
女 | 你決定要怎麼樣了嗎？
男 | 我決定就這麼做！
女 | 你為什麼做這樣的決定？
男 | 因為這是千載難逢的經驗！如果我不去做，會後悔一輩子的。

2 A 1 art 2 love art   154
      3 opportunities 4 open up lots of
      5 enjoy it as much as

   B 1 Run for 2 president
      3 great on, résumé 4 work
      5 experience 6 responsibility

Script & Translation

A Michael | Heidi, I'm torn between majoring in art and majoring in business. Which one should I choose?
   Heidi | OK. Let's weigh up the pros and cons of each one.
   Michael | All right. First, studying art.

Heidi	Well, on the one hand, you really love art. On the other hand, you'd have fewer career opportunities. However, if you majored in business, you wouldn't enjoy it as much as art, but it'd open up lots of career opportunities.
Michael	Hmm . . . Thanks. I'll give it some thought.

麥可	海蒂，我正在抉擇要主修藝術還是商科，我該選哪一科呢？
海蒂	好吧，我們來分析兩者的優缺點。
麥可	好，從藝術開始。
海蒂	嗯，一方面，你熱愛藝術，可是另一方面，工作機會比較少；不過如果主修商科的話，可能沒有藝術來得有趣，可是工作機會很多。
麥可	嗯，謝了，我會再考慮一下。

B

Michael	But what about you? Have you made up your mind about running for student president?
Heidi	Um, no, not yet. I've been weighing up the pros and cons.
Michael	Oh, yeah? What are they?
Heidi	Well, becoming student president is not only a lot of work but also a lot of responsibility. On the other hand, it would look great on my résumé, and it would be a great experience. What would you do?
Michael	Me? Well, I'm quite lazy, so I probably wouldn't run. But I think you would be a great president.

麥可	那你呢？你決定要選學生會長了嗎？
海蒂	嗯，還沒。我還在衡量其中的好壞。
麥可	哦，是嗎？怎麼說？
海蒂	嗯，若當上學生會長，不僅事務繁多，責任也很重。不過從另一面來看，會為我的履歷加分，也是一次很好的經驗。你會怎麼做？
麥可	我？嗯，我比較懶，所以我可能不會參選吧。但是我覺得你會是一位非常稱職的會長。

3 **1** b **2** a **3** a **4** b **5** a **6** b, a 🎧155

1 look at, options 🎧156
2 should go either, or
3 were me, would
4 not only give, but also
5 torn between starting
6 on the other hand
7 Seeing as, might be better
8 miss out on, once-in-a-lifetime

Joe	I just asked Sarah out, and she said yes! But I don't know where to go on a date.
Sunny	OK. Well, let's look at your options. Since Sarah loves art, I think you should go either to an art exhibition or to an art-house movie.
Joe	If you were me, which one would you choose?
Sunny	Well, personally, I would go to the exhibition. It'd not only give you something to talk about but also give you a chance to impress her.
Joe	Impress her?
Sunny	Yeah, with your art knowledge.
Joe	Hmm, yeah. But the thing is, I don't really know anything about paintings. I think I'll take her to see an art-house movie instead.
Sunny	OK. It's your decision. Oh, I actually wanted to talk to you about something, too. My professor just asked me if I wanted to do a master's degree, but I didn't know what to tell him.
Joe	Oh, really? I thought you wanted to do one.
Sunny	Well, I do, but I'm torn between starting one this year and taking a gap year.
Joe	If I were you, I'd take a gap year. That way you could travel and gain some interesting life experience.
Sunny	I know. But on the other hand, it would be really expensive, and I don't have much money.
Joe	Seeing as money is a problem, it might be better to do the master's degree right away.
Sunny	Yeah, maybe you're right. But then again, it would be sad to miss out on a once-in-a-lifetime experience. It's such a hard decision!

喬	我剛才約莎拉出來，她說好耶！但是我不知道要去哪裡約會。
桑妮	好，嗯，我們想想有哪些選擇。莎拉喜歡藝術，我覺得你們可以去看美術展或藝術片。
喬	如果是你的話，會選哪一個？
桑妮	嗯，我個人會去美術展，這樣比較有話聊，你也可以趁機大顯身手讓她對你留下好印象。
喬	大顯身手？
桑妮	對啊，發揮你的藝術知識。
喬	喔，也對。可是問題是，我對繪畫一無所知耶。我看我還是帶她去看藝術片好了。

桑妮	好吧，由你決定囉。喔，其實我也有一件事想跟你說。我的教授問我要不要讀碩士班，我不知道該如何回覆他。
喬	喔，真的嗎？你不是一直想讀碩士嗎？
桑妮	是啊，可是我很猶豫該在今年就開始讀碩士，或者先放自己一年假。
喬	如果我是你，我會先放一年假，這樣就可以到處旅遊一下，獲得一些有趣的人生經驗。
桑妮	我知道，可是這也很花錢，我沒有那麼多錢。
喬	如果考慮到錢的問題，那還是先讀碩士班好了。
桑妮	對啊，或許你是對的。但是話又說回來，如果錯失了一生一次的經驗也很可惜。真是難以抉擇！

IV Now, Grammar Time! p. 120

4
- a not only a good salary but also opportunities for promotion
- b either rent a DVD or play video games
- c Not only are, painful, but, also unprofessional
- d neither confirm nor deny
- e Either, run for student president, or, run for welfare officer
- f neither go to Africa nor go to Australia / go to neither Africa nor Australia

V Now, Time to Speak! p. 121

5

Translation 157

巴尼	我不知道畢業後要做什麼。
蘿蘋	我們看看你有哪些選擇，你可以找工作、休假一年，或者讀碩士班。
巴尼	嗯，我還不想找工作，但是又猶豫要休假還是讀碩士。
蘿蘋	好吧，那我們來分析一下優缺點。
巴尼	好。一方面，休假一年比較花錢，但是另一方面，又是獲得人生經驗的大好機會。
蘿蘋	沒錯。讀碩士班會很累，但是話說回來，會讓履歷大為加分。好吧，你有決定了嗎？
巴尼	是的，我決定要休假一年，我想，這種經驗一生也就這麼一次而已。

VI Now, Time to Pronounce! p. 122

8
| 1 5 | 2 7 | 3 1 | 4 4 | 159 |
| 5 6 | 6 2 | 7 3 | | |

Script
1 ski　2 slip　3 swing　4 sphinx
5 spoil　6 smell　7 stay

9
1 [bl]	2 [gl]	3 [mj]	
4 [pj]	5 [kw]	6 [tw]	
7 [fr]	8 [ʃr]	9 [nj]	10 [θr]

Script
1 black　2 glow　3 mule　4 pure　5 quite
6 twelve　7 from　8 shriek　9 new　10 thread

Unit 15

I Topic Preview p. 124 164

1　Tell me a little bit about your education.
I attended Athena University, where I majored in graphic design.
And what about your work experience.
I've worked for my current company for three years.

▶ 談談你的學歷。
我就讀於雅典娜大學，主修平面設計。
你的工作經驗呢？
我在現在的公司服務了三年。

2　Why do you want to work for this company?
I feel like I'm ready for a new challenge.

▶ 你為何想在這間公司上班？
我想要追求新的挑戰。

3　Do you manage your time well?
Yes, I'm very organized.
What are some of your strengths?
My biggest strength is probably my communication skills.

▶ 你善於規劃時間嗎？
是的，我很會規劃時間。
你有哪些強項？
我最大的強項大概是我的溝通能力。

4　What kind of salary are you looking for?
I'm expecting something between $30,000 and $40,000.
Would traveling be a problem?
No, I'd be prepared to travel.

▶ 你期望的薪水是多少？
我期望的薪水在 30,000 到 40,000 之間。
如果要出差可以嗎？
可以，我可以出差。

5 | Where do you see yourself in five years?
In five years, I'd like to be a senior manager.

▸ 你對五年後的自己有什麼期許？
五年後，我想成為一名資深經理。

Sentence Patterns
🎧166 p. 125

- 談談你所受的教育。
  我曾就讀牛津劍橋大學，主修英文。
- 談談你的工作經歷。
  我畢業後曾任職於兩間不同的公司。
- 你為何想來這間公司工作？／
  你為何想應徵這個職位？
  我認為這份工作有助於我的職業發展。
- 我為什麼要雇用你？
  你為何認為你適任這份工作？
  我的領導才能將成為貴公司的一大資產。
- 你能夠負起責任嗎？／你有解決問題的能力嗎？／
  你注重細節嗎？
  我能夠負起責任。／我有解決問題的優秀能力。／
  我非常注重細節。
- 你有哪些強項／弱項？
  我最大的強項是我有領導他人的能力。
  我最大的強項是我的溝通能力。
- 你期望的薪資範圍是多少？
  我希望能有 40,000 到 50,000 之間的薪水。
- 你可以出差嗎？／你可以加班嗎？
  我會隨時準備好出差。／我正好喜歡出差。／
  加班對我來說不是問題。
- 你期待五年後有什麼發展？你的長程目標是什麼？
  我想要成為部門主管。

III Now, Time to Listen!
p. 126

1 False, Chicago → New York 🎧167
2 True 3 False, a tour guide, ~~a reporter,~~ and a translator
4 True 5 False, a new challenge → to develop his career

Script & Translation

Mrs. Peters	OK, Michael. Tell me a little bit about yourself and your education.
Michael	Well, I grew up in Chicago, but then I moved to New York for college.
Mrs. Peters	And you attended . . .
Michael	Cornell University, where I majored in modern languages.

Mrs. Peters	OK, great. Tell me a little about your work experience. According to your résumé you've had two jobs since you graduated?
Michael	Yes. After I graduated, I worked for two years as a tour guide. And right now I'm working as a translator. I've done that for about three years.
Mrs. Peters	And why do you want to work for this company?
Michael	I feel like this company would give me the chance to develop my career.

彼德斯女士	好，麥可。談一下你自己和你的學歷。
麥可	嗯，我在芝加哥長大，後來搬去紐約念大學。
彼德斯女士	你就讀於…
麥可	康乃爾大學，主修現代語言。
彼德斯女士	好，太好了。談談你的工作經歷，你的履歷上寫你畢業之後從事過兩份工作。
麥可	是的，我畢業之後，曾經擔任導遊兩年，目前的工作是翻譯，我做翻譯大約三年了。
彼德斯女士	那麼你為什麼想來我們公司上班？
麥可	我覺得貴公司能夠讓我的職業生涯有所發展。

2 a, c, e 🎧168
   a, c, f, h, i 🎧169

Script & Translation

Mrs. Peters	What makes you think you're suited to this job?
Michael	Well, I think my communication skills will be a real asset to this company. I also really enjoy a challenge.
Mrs. Peters	And do you work well as part of a team?
Michael	Yes, certainly. I love working with other people.
Mrs. Peters	What's your biggest weakness, do you think?
Michael	Hmm. I think my biggest weakness is my time-management skills.
Mrs. Peters	Oh, yes? In what way?
Michael	Well, I sometimes focus too much on one thing, and then don't have enough time to finish the rest of my work. I'm doing my best to improve, though.

彼德斯女士	你為何認為自己適任這份工作？
麥可	嗯，我認為我的溝通能力會是貴公司的一大資產，我也勇於接受挑戰。
彼德斯女士	你適合參與團隊工作嗎？
麥可	當然可以，我熱愛與他人合作。
彼德斯女士	你認為你最大的弱點是什麼？
麥可	嗯，我想我最大的弱點是時間規劃的能力。
彼德斯女士	喔，是嗎？在哪些方面？
麥可	嗯，我時候我會過於專注某一件事，導致耽擱了其他工作。但是我會盡我最大的努力改善這個問題。

3 ⓐ 1　ⓑ 5　ⓒ 3　ⓓ 2　ⓔ 4　🎧170

🎧171
- ⓐ years' time → years
- ⓑ short → long
  CEO → managing director
- ⓒ salary → pay range
- ⓓ Do → Would, like → be willing
- ⓔ sounds → suits me
- ⓕ long hours → overtime

Script & Translation

Mrs. Peters	Let me ask you, where do you see yourself in five years?
Michael	Well, I'd like to be a department head in five years.
Mrs. Peters	And your long-term goals?
Michael	Well, in the long term, my goal is to become a managing director.
Mrs. Peters	I see. So what kind of pay range are you looking for?
Michael	Well, the ad said between $30,000 and $35,000. I think that's fair.
Mrs. Peters	And would you be willing to travel?
Michael	Oh, yes, traveling suits me just fine.
Mrs. Peters	And what about working overtime?
Michael	Um, I wouldn't be prepared to work overtime too often, but sometimes would be OK.

彼德斯女士	我問你，你期待自己五年後有什麼樣的發展？
麥可	嗯，我希望五年後升到部門主管。
彼德斯女士	你的長程目標呢？
麥可	嗯，長遠來看，希望能夠做到董事總經理的職位。
彼德斯女士	了解。那麼你期望的薪資範圍是多少？
麥可	喔，您的徵人廣告上面說薪資是30,000到35,000之間，我覺得那樣還不錯。
彼德斯女士	你願意出差嗎？
麥可	喔，沒問題，我喜歡出差。
彼德斯女士	會排斥加班嗎？

| 麥可 | 嗯，我不希望常常加班，但是偶爾加班是沒問題的。 |

IV Now, Grammar Time! p. 128

5 ⓵ on　⓶ over　⓷ about　⓸ with　⓹ for　⓺ to　⓻ against　⓼ at

V Now, Time to Speak! p. 130

7

Translation Sample Answers

ⓐ

M	Where do you see yourself in two years?
W	In two years, I'd like to be a team leader.
M	What are your long-term goals?
W	I'd like to start my own business.
M	What kind of salary are you looking for?
W	I'm looking for between $30,000 and $40,000 a year.
M	And would you be willing to work overtime?
W	Yes, I would.

男	你怎麼看待自己兩年後的發展？
女	兩年後，我希望能成為小組長。
男	你的長程目標是什麼？
女	我想要創業。
男	你期望的薪資是多少？
女	我希望年薪能有 30,000 到 40,000 元。
男	你願意加班嗎？
女	願意。

ⓑ

W	So what kind of pay range are you looking for?
M	Somewhere between $20,000 and $25,000.
W	And would you be willing to work weekends?
M	Hmm, I'd prefer not to.
W	OK. So where do you see yourself in five years?
M	In five years I'd like to be a senior manager.
W	And in 10 years?
M	In 10 years I'd like to be the CEO.

女	你期望的薪資範圍是多少？
男	20,000 到 25,000 之間。
女	你週末也可以上班嗎？
男	嗯，我希望不要。
女	好，那麼你對自己五年後有什麼展望？
男	我希望五年後能當上資深經理。
女	十年後呢？
男	我希望十年後能成為執行長。

9
1 (John) thinks (up new ideas) 174
all the (time).
2 Do you (pick things up quickly)?
3 (Don't) give (up yet).
4 (Jane) dropped (out) of (college) after
a (year).

Unit 16

I Topic Preview　p. 132　175

1
We live in a small house, so maybe a small
dog or a cat would be best.
But I'm allergic to cats, and I don't like dogs.
How about a fish, then?
Hmm, that's not a bad idea.

▸ 我們的房子小，所以可能養小型貓狗比較好。
可是我對貓過敏，又不喜歡狗。
那不然養魚呢？
嗯，這個主意不錯。

2
Tell me about this dog.
He's a three-year-old male Labrador.
Has he been neutered?
Yes, he's already been neutered.
Why is he up for adoption?
He was abandoned by his owner.
What's his personality like?
He's very energetic and he loves people.

▸ 說說你這隻狗的事。
他三歲，是公的拉布拉多。
他結紮了嗎？
對，他已經結紮了。
他為什麼會被送養？
他被主人棄養了。
他的個性怎麼樣？
他很活潑好動，也很親人。

3
How often should we feed him?
You should feed him twice a day.
What brand of food would you
recommend?
I'd recommend Happy Pup Dog Food.

▸ 我們要多久餵他一次？
你們應該一天餵他兩次。
你推薦什麼牌子的飼料？
我推薦「快樂幼犬飼料」。

4
When should we get him neutered?
You can get him neutered when he's six
months old.
Is there anything else we should do?
You need to get him vaccinated annually.

▸ 我們什麼時候要帶他去結紮？
你們可以等他六個月大的時候，帶他去結紮。
還有其他應該做的事嗎？
你們每年都要帶他去打預防針。

Sentence Patterns　177　p. 133

• 我先生想養狗，可是養狗很麻煩。
那麼養貓呢？貓比較不用顧。
• 如果你養魚，要餵魚、換水……
• 我們不是很勤奮，所以養魚可能比較好。
• 你說一下這隻狗的事。
他五歲，是公的貴賓狗。
• 他結紮了嗎？
• 他／她為什麼會被送養？
• 他／她的個性怎麼樣？
他／她跟小孩子十分玩得來，也很愛給人抱。
• 我們多久要遛他一次？
你們一天要遛他兩次。
• 你推薦哪一牌的飼料？
我推薦「凱特小貓飼料」。
• 什麼時候應該帶他／她去打預防針？
等他／她六週大的時候，就可以帶去打預防針。

III Now, Time to Listen!　p. 134

1
1 c　2 c　3 b, a　178

Script & Translation

James	Fran, I was thinking. Maybe it's time we get a pet. What do you think?
Fran	Yeah, OK. What pet should we get?
James	How about a dog?
Fran	Ugh, no. Dogs are too much work. You have to walk them every day, and they make a mess everywhere.
James	I guess you're right. What about a cat then? You don't have to walk a cat, and they're usually very clean.
Fran	Yeah, cats are nice. I wouldn't mind getting a cat. But wait a second. Aren't you allergic to cats?
James	Oh, yeah! How could I forget?
Fran	Oh! I know. Let's get a rabbit! They're so cute and cuddly!
James	Sure, that's a great idea!

詹姆斯	法蘭，我在想，也許我們該養隻寵物了，你覺得呢？
法蘭	對，好啊。我們應該養什麼寵物？
詹姆斯	養狗如何？
法蘭	啊，不要，養狗太麻煩了。你要每天遛狗，而且他們還會到處搗亂。
詹姆斯	你說的對，還是說養貓？不用遛貓，而且他們通常都很乾淨。
法蘭	對啊，貓是不錯，我不介意養貓。但是等一下，你不是對貓過敏嗎？
詹姆斯	喔，對！我怎麼忘了？
法蘭	喔！我知道了，我們養兔子吧！他們可愛又好抱。
詹姆斯	可以啊，好主意！

2

a Tom, M, 3 years, shy, loving, yes, abandoned (179)

b F, 3 months, no, yes, have enough room

c Max, 10, bad-tempered, no, died

Script & Translation

a

Tina	So, who's this little guy?
Manager	This is Tom. He's a three-year-old male Birman.
Tina	Oh, he's so cute!
Manager	Yeah, he's quite shy but very loving when you get to know him.
Tina	Has he been neutered?
Manager	Yes, he has. And he's been vaccinated, too.
Tina	Why is he up for adoption?
Manager	He was abandoned by his owner.
Tina	Oh, that's terrible.

蒂娜	那，這小傢伙叫什麼名字？
負責人	他叫湯姆，今年三歲，是公的巴曼貓。
蒂娜	喔，他好可愛。
負責人	對啊，他很害羞，可是你們熟了之後，他會很親人。
蒂娜	他結紮了嗎？
負責人	他結紮了，也打過預防針。
蒂娜	他為什麼會被送養？
負責人	他是被主人棄養的。
蒂娜	喔，好可惡喔。

b

Tina	Wow, this cat is beautiful! Hi there, sweetie! Is it a boy or a girl?
Manager	This is Sally. She's a three-month-old female ragdoll.
Tina	She's so beautiful!

Manager	Yes, she is. Sally's mom gave birth to seven kittens, and the owner just didn't have enough room for them, so they all came here.
Tina	Has she been spayed yet?
Manager	No, not yet. We like to wait until they're at least six months old before we spay them. But she has been vaccinated.
Tina	She looks very playful. Is she very energetic?
Manager	She does like to play, but she's also very gentle, so she won't go too crazy when you play with her.

蒂娜	哇，這隻貓好漂亮！嗨，你好，小甜心！牠是男生還是女生？
負責人	她叫莎莉，三月大，是母的布偶貓。
蒂娜	她好漂亮！
負責人	對啊，莎莉的媽媽一次生了七隻小貓，她的主人沒有足夠的空間可以養他們，所以全都送來這裡。
蒂娜	她結紮了嗎？
負責人	還沒，我們想等她至少六個月大，再帶去結紮。但是她打過預防針了。
蒂娜	她好像很愛玩，她很好動對不對？
負責人	她的確很愛玩，可是她很溫馴，如果你跟她玩，她也不會玩太瘋。

c

Tina	Hello there, big guy! Wow! You're bad-tempered! What's his story?
Manager	This is Max. He's a 10-year-old male mixed breed. His owner died, so he came here.
Tina	Poor guy. I bet he misses his owner.
Manager	Yes, he's a very loyal cat.
Tina	And he's been neutered and vaccinated?
Manager	He's been neutered, but he hasn't been vaccinated this year. So if you decide to adopt him, you'll need to get him vaccinated as soon as possible.

蒂娜	嗨，你好呀，大個子！哇！你脾氣不太好喔！他的背景是什麼？
負責人	他叫麥克斯，是十歲公的混種貓。因為主人過世，所以以被送來這裡。
蒂娜	可憐的孩子，我相信他一定很想念他的主人。

負責人	是啊,他是一隻非常忠心的貓。
蒂娜	他結紮和打預防針了嗎?
負責人	他結紮過了,但是今年還沒打預防針。所以如果你要認養他,要盡快帶他去打預防針。

3 female, ragdoll, mixed / (180)
less than six months old,
loving, playful but not too crazy, Sally

Tina	I'm going to the cat shelter this afternoon to adopt a cat. I'm so excited!
Friend	What kind of cat are you looking for?
Tina	Well, I'd like a really loving cat, and one that's playful but not too crazy.
Friend	Would you prefer a male or female cat?
Tina	I think female, definitely, and I'd like a kitten, too—less than six months old.
Friend	Any particular breed you'd prefer?
Tina	Hmm. I quite like mixed breeds actually, but I also really love ragdoll cats.
蒂娜	我今天下午要去貓咪收容所認養一隻貓,我好興奮喔!
朋友	你想養哪一種貓?
蒂娜	嗯,我要養一隻很親人的貓,要很愛玩但是又不會玩得太瘋的。
朋友	你比較想養公的還是母的?
蒂娜	我一定是想養母的呀,而且我想要小貓,不到六個月大的。
朋友	你傾向養哪一個品種呢?
蒂娜	嗯,其實我還滿喜歡混種的貓,可是我也好愛布偶貓。

4
a change their water, (181)
change it once every,
brand of fish food, I'd recommend
b get him neutered, often should I walk,
be enough, golden retriever,
twice a day would be
c thinking of getting, loyal and lots, is
too small, get a small dog, Yorkshire
terrier, too high maintenance
d is allergic to, make really good,
pretty low maintenance,
all you have to do, feed them

Translation

A	女	我多久要換一次水?
	男	你每兩天要換一次水。
	女	你推薦哪一牌的魚飼料?
	男	我推薦金牌魚飼料。
B	男	我什麼時候可以讓他結紮?
	獸醫	六個月大之後都可以。

40

	男	好,那多久要遛狗一次?一天一次夠嗎?
	獸醫	嗯,像他這麼大隻的黃金獵犬,一天遛兩次會比較好。
C	男	我們考慮要養寵物,可是不知道該養哪一種。
	女	養狗如何?他們很忠心又很好玩。
	男	我知道,可是我們家太小了。
	女	你可以養小型犬,例如約克夏。
	男	約翰不喜歡小型犬,他說他們不好照顧。
D	男	我想養貓,可是我太太對貓過敏。
	女	太可惜了,貓是很好的寵物。
	男	我知道,貓不怎麼需要顧,而且也很親人。
	女	不然養倉鼠?倉鼠很可愛,而且你只要餵他們,還有清理籠子就好了。
	男	好主意。

IV Now, Grammar Time!
p. 136

5
1 scared of   **2** good with
3 responsible for   **4** allergic to
5 grateful for   **6** tired of
7 fond of   **8** similar to

6
1 I need to take my cat to get neutered, but I haven't got around to it yet.
2 My puppy always goes to the bathroom on the carpet. I hope he'll grow out of it soon.
3 My cat Minx is quite short-tempered, so she doesn't get along with other cats very well.
4 We'd better take Pickle to the vet. I think she's come down with something.
5 I think it's important for owners and their pets to look out for each other.

VI Now, Time to Pronounce!
p. 139

9

Translation (182)

金姆	我覺得貓這種動物很酷。
雷米	我恨貓!我覺得他們的脾氣真的很差。
金姆	可是另一方面,狗又挺麻煩的。
雷米	這你就大錯特錯了,養狗是最佳選擇!

10

Translation (183)

威爾瑪	你為什麼不養狗?
布萊恩	不行。(我們房子太小,而且約翰會過敏。)
威爾瑪	真可惜,我們養了三隻狗。(兩隻拉布拉多和一隻貴賓狗。)
布萊恩	真好,但是我想一定很麻煩吧——(要遛狗那些的)。